Overlooking
Camp

'Hiding-Place'
Cistern

Southern
Bastion

...tern
...ace

Bathing
Pool

The Ram Tower

Ramp

Encircling Wall

Roman Camp

MASADA IN 73 A.D. A FEW
DAYS BEFORE THE ROMAN
ASSAULT.

THE VOICES OF MASADA

DAVID KOSSOFF

THE VOICES OF MASADA

Drawings and Maps
by the Author

VALLENTINE, MITCHELL · LONDON

First published in Great Britain in 1973 by
VALLENTINE, MITCHELL & CO. LTD
67 Great Russell Street,
London WC1B 3BT

Copyright © 1973 by David Kossoff

ISBN 0 853 03144 4

Printed in Great Britain
by W & J Mackay Limited, Chatham

Contents

A note on the illustrations
The illustrations which accompany the story
are based on the remarkable finds made by
Yigael Yadin during his two-year excavation
of the Masada mountain-top. The bird's-eye
view of Masada the day before the Romans
went in is, like the story itself, part imagination and part fact.   D.K.

Prologue

It is strange how a story germinating in the mind often attaches to itself a title. The 'voices' of Masada murmured in my mind long before I put pen to paper. The voices were not loud, they did not shout, made no insistent demand. Not at first. And at the beginning not all the voices were there. They grew in number.

If this voices-in-the-head, Joan of Arc business bothers you, consider then a note pad by a telephone. Voices call, and you make a note. If the calls have to do with the same thing, the notes will take on a shape, a pattern. Later, even long after, the notes will recall the thing—and the voices will be heard again in the mind. Thus it was with the voices of Masada, in a way. But no telephone; no pad. A thing here, a thing there. Let me tell you.

In 1963 Professor Yigael Yadin, one of Israel's leading archaeologists, announced that he was to fulfil a lifelong ambition by excavating the entire plateau on top of a small mountain on the western shore of the Dead Sea called Masada.

The English Sunday newspaper *The Observer*, which supported the venture, told of the professor's plans and also gave a brief history of the mountain, telling of how, on Masada, in AD 73, nearly a thousand Jewish freedom fighters were encircled and besieged by a Roman force ten times their number. It told how the Jews, known as Zealots because of their single-minded zeal for God, chose, when all was lost, to take their own lives rather than submit to Roman slavery. The article told us also that the event had been recorded by the historian Flavius Josephus some years later.

It was recorded by no one else. Certainly not by the Romans, for whom it was a costly face-saving operation—the end of the Roman-Jewish 'War' having been celebrated in Rome some three years before! The war which had ended with the razing of Jerusalem and the destruction of its magnificent Temple. Masada was a mopping-up operation. It was dealt with and the Romans went away. It was not written down, except by Josephus, their historian.

Flavius Josephus, born Joseph ben Matthias of priestly Jewish family, who became a turncoat, a traitor and a Roman. The happening at Masada was recorded by Josephus at second hand, with typical embellishments, but with a rare absence of the self-glorifying pen which cheapens much of his writing. It was described fairly briefly, occupying no more than two pages of his four-volume *Jewish War*; but the happening, even in the turgid translation by Whiston which for many years was the only one, shone like a jewel.

But who reads Josephus? you might ask. I asked the same. Few; but oddly, people seem to *know* about Masada. 'A famous last stand', 'A mass-suicide to cheat the enemy', 'An act of courage of some kind'.

An act of courage. Some nineteen hundred years ago. Recorded briefly by a not too reliable historian and available in a difficult translation.

Yet when the *Observer* article appeared, inviting volunteers to help with the dig, to pay their own way to Israel, to work for nothing and live under canvas in a notoriously uncomfortable desert area, the response was staggering. From all over the world they came, knowing of the nineteen-hundred-year-old act of courage and determined to share in its resurrection. They toiled in the burning sun and slept through ice-cold nights. They used shovels and scalpels, brooms and tiny paint brushes. They moved hundreds of tons and delicately sorted fragments weighing ounces. Yadin, bald uncle to them all, recognized a miracle in his hands and held it firmly, with love. It took two years, and Yadin wrote down the whole thing, brilliantly, leaving nothing out.

It was enough. The telephone pad was nearly full. Josephus was now read again in the splendid translation by Williamson. Another voice spoke: The Dead Sea Scrolls, found thirty miles north of Masada on the same shore, seemed to have the same fierce zeal as my fighters who had given the Romans such a rough time.

The research began to take shape; the absorbing time of books-leading-to-other-books, the pinning up of maps and pictures. What was to be our ninth trip to Israel (for we love that tiny indomitable country, that land of Zealots) was postponed for a while. I wasn't ready; and the book was to be begun in Jerusalem.

The research brought forth a stage for the drama as incredible as its players. Masada, a flat-topped mountain fortified by Herod the Great nearly a hundred years before the last stand of the Zealots. But no rough fort in a wilderness; a place of palaces and citadels, where a comfort-loving despot could feel at home. Yadin uncovered it all: great food storehouses, steambaths, swimming pools, villas, an astonishing water storage system. All in an arid desert.

It took time, the gathering of facts, but when at last, on a July dawn, I stood upon Masada, everything was familiar. Only the *dimension* had been missing. Now the reading and maps and pictures took on reality, full size. At that moment, as the sky lightened, the same sky that had looked down nineteen hundred years ago, the voices became louder, and insistent.

'..seven only survived Masada. A woman related to Eleazar, in intelligence and education superior to most, an older woman, and five children'–

Josephus,   *The Jewish War*

BOOK ONE

1 The Promise

Storage Jars with owner's names

I

Well, it is over. Our 'palace in the sky', as Eleazar used to call it, is now down to earth. Certainly our palace at times seemed to be more of heaven than of earth, supported as much by the fervour and joyous bravery of the Zealots as by the great mountain it stood upon.

It is over. Masada is done. Once more the whole country is under the heel of the Romans. Less than three years since Jerusalem, my beloved Jerusalem, was ground into dust by that same heel. Jerusalem, beautiful beyond words, made into a blood-soaked wasteland, and the heart of the city, the Great Temple, built to last a thousand years, torn out and scattered like chaff.

Masada is done. For the rest of my life—and I will live long, for I have a story to write—I will remember the silence. Masada, which gave me so many memories, such joy, so many songs and shouts and sounds to stay in the mind, greeted the Romans, in the morning, with silence. So tidily they lay, my friends. Only the blood, so much blood, told that they lay in death, not in the sleep they needed so much. So tidily, so lovingly, with their arms round each other, they lay. Even the Final Ten, even the Last One, had fallen or lain near to his own. How well Eleazar had known us, how many times he had made us more than we thought we were, had taught us bravery and dignity and strength like his own—and had made these qualities grow in *us*, become *our* own. And so it was at the last.

How alive we were! How keyed up, how exhilarated, how

ready to fight to the last drop of blood. And we were strong. No siege-starvelings were we, no dwellers in caves of fear. We lived in a palace and we fought like kings! We knew about fighting to live—and winning. Yet Eleazar was right. 'Burn only your belongings,' he said, 'but leave the food stores and the water and the oil and wine. Leave the vegetable gardens and the fruit trees. Let the Romans see that we died among plenty, as free men, and thus remained free.'

Keyed up, full of life and strength, we listened. At first unwillingly, almost with disbelief, then with fear, and then—for this was our Eleazar speaking—with trust and faith.

And so the Romans, shouting and clanking, were met, in the morning, with silence. The crackling of flames, not loud, upon the rise, from the palace, and our own footsteps, the seven of us, as we walked towards them; but otherwise, silence. Even in this thing, the leaving of the seven, Eleazar had judged perfectly, had seen more clearly than the rest of us.

'Not you, my cousin,' he said, 'not you, my Ruth. And not the old woman, for we have no sword to pierce the leather hide of that one, she will live for ever, that one. And not the five orphans. They must have their chance, and the old woman and you will see to it. And you, my Ruth, will write down our story. Not only of Masada, but of Caesarea and Jotapata and Gamala and Gerasa and of our beloved Jerusalem. Much you saw yourself; of that which you did not see you will find witnesses. Your father, my uncle, was guided by God to give you the education and learning you have and guided by God also to choose the right daughter to give it to!'

He laughed to cheer me but I could not join him. I was near to tears, and of confused emotions. For I knew both that he was right and that I did not want to go on living when Masada was dead. When Eleazar was dead.

'The Romans will in no way harm you,' he went on, 'their shock will be too great, and because they admire resolution and bravery they will know what we have done. And their anger—for we have given them a terrible time—will disappear.

Choose the moment of your appearance carefully. Speak only to the officer in charge, if possible to Silva himself.' He smiled. 'Our Roman "conqueror" will not expect to meet a woman of beauty and dignity with eyes the blue-green of the Dead Sea below us and with the grace and form of one of their own statues. He will not expect to hear a voice, warm and expressive, possessing many languages, or to meet the mind of a Solomon. A mind as broad and smooth and beautiful as the brow that contains it.'

He had words, my Eleazar.

It was all as he had foreseen. We were in no way molested. The children were treated gently and with the humour and kindness that all soldiers have. The old woman, my beloved Sarah, won over by this—and always at home among fighters—was soon a favourite. Her humour was pure barrack-room, of the streets, fast and without respect. She gave orders. 'Make a toy!' she would say to a sergeant-armourer, 'The war is over. There are children to keep happy. Your swords are sharp, make a toy! Carve a doll! The child is sad, it has seen terrible things. Get busy, you great ox, make a toy!' And the soldiers would laugh, and get busy, and make toys.

In those first few days down in Silva's camp, which had looked so small from the top of the mountain and yet was so large, I do not know what I would have done without Sarah. I have never been a weeping woman and have sometimes envied those who can find relief in tears. I was the eldest of six, and when my mother died the youngest was barely four years old. The most beautiful of us all, he, David, had taken from my mother in his birth all her strength and health. When she died it was an end long expected. A book quietly closed, a curtain drawn softly.

My father and I sat facing each other. His eyes were quiet and dry, as were my own. I was nearly thirteen. 'We do not weep,' he said, 'you and I. We consider, and weigh things up, and get on with it. No man could be prouder of his first-born than I am of you. No son could be more in accord with my mind than you, my daughter. With no one am I more at ease. You are a distillation of all that is best in me and all that was best—and most beautiful—in your mother, may her dear soul rest in peace. For nearly four years you have been mother to your brothers and sisters, without complaint. You have put aside your books and a little of your childhood too, I think. I cannot give you back your childhood, but to your beloved books you shall most certainly return.'

I had sat quietly, without reply. His expression changed a little. A sort of compassion, a sort of puzzlement. 'We do not weep, you and I. Yet tears have their place; they do not show weakness, they do not belong only to women. Great David wept, Moses also. Jacob wept, and Abraham. God himself wept—and weeps still for us.' He opened his arms and I went to him and sat on his knee, my head into his shoulder, loving, as always, the smell of him. 'It is all right to weep, Ruth. No one will know. I won't say a word. And who knows, perhaps if you weep, I will. If God shows you how, maybe He will show me.'

I could not. Full of tears, none came. And so it has always been. Hours I spent down in the Roman camp looking up at Masada, now just a mountain again, with no sign of life. And indeed there was no life up there. No Jewish life. A graveyard, with every single body known to me. Surely enough for tears? But none came.

I was left alone. The soldiers and their officers were curious, but stayed away. I had no fear of them—despite very full knowledge of the atrocities committed by the Roman army all over my defeated and blood-soaked country. But equally I knew, because for ten years I had lived among soldiers, that armies are composed of ordinary men living under circumstances and pressures which are not ordinary. Here was no need for atrocity, for bestiality. Some children and two women: sole survivors. The war over, Masada conquered, a thousand bodies to be disposed of. Bodies in rows, in groups, in families.

We feared no violence, my Sarah and I. She, because she

7

feared nothing at any time—and was a match for most men anyway—and I, because I have a certain quietude, a stillness, upon which bluster shatters and savagery grows cool.

This again from my father, when I left my books to become a Zealot. 'Your beauty has a certain dignity, my Ruth, the intellect shows through a little. This can disturb a man, for most men are frightened by brains in a woman. Among enemies the fright may turn into violence, revenge for unsuccessful encounters in the past.'

'What then should I do?'

'Be still. Of level gaze. Examine the man with quiet eyes. Consider him, listen to his words, and answer without emotion. Leave pause between statement and answer. Show no fear, only a mild academic interest. Examine the specimen, unimpressed but polite.'

My father, bless his sweet memory, was inventing no technique for me. He was showing me what I, by habit, always did. Indeed it is no wonder to me that I never married. Who could live with such a quiet-gazer, such a without-emotion examiner?

So I was safe among my captors. Woman-hungry officers of Roman manners and Italianate good looks became polite and considerate. Found for me writing materials, and a table and chair. Built me an awning, were courtly, and told me of their families.

2 Silva

The 'Judea is Conquered' coin struck by the Romans in 70 A.D.

When all was done upon the mountain, when everyone was dead and the Romans came in through the gap in the wall, we waited, as Eleazar had told us to. We waited, hidden, and heard more than we saw. Indeed it was too dark to see, just after dawn, the Masada dawn that is unlike anywhere else.

We heard the Romans, as we heard everything else, with absolute clarity. It had always been of wonder to me how clearly we could hear the sounds of the siege camps far below. Every sound carried. It was of use to us, we became expert at recognizing changes in activity, preparations for assault, special drills, commands. When the great attack ramp was half-built, and looked as solid and strong as our mountain, Silva, General Flavius Silva himself, spoke to us from the ramp, and he had no need to shout. We heard every word. He spoke correctly and formally, telling us to surrender, to give up all resistance, that we were now alone, that the whole country was now subdued, that we could not but be beaten and destroyed. It was a strong voice, unemotional, the voice of power, the voice of Rome. No sound but the voice, and we heard every word. Eleazar gave a soft order and one of the slingmen wrapped a rockball in oil-soaked rags, put a flame to it and sent it arching into the blue sky to land, in a shower of sparks at Silva's feet. We heard its flames and we heard its defiant thud.

And on that calm mid-April morning, when all was over, as

the sky lightened, we heard every sound also. The soldiers came up the ramp fast, carrying ladders and platforms to bridge the gap between their great ram tower and our broken wall. We heard them call to others about the flames, the smoke, the fires everywhere. Then more soldiers, and more. Then a silence, except for the roar of the flames. Then, as if by order, a great shout to bring us out to fight. The shout died away and, as though to emphasize the non-reply to the shout, the flames momentarily lost their roar. We could hear the puzzlement.

Then we heard, for the first time, Roman feet on our plateau. Quick trained feet, to this direction and that, to see and report back. Then more feet, and a forming up. There was no inch by inch search. They seemed to know. Silva told me later that the silence of death, or emptiness, is different from the silence of ambush or concealment.

'One develops an instinct. All the senses are involved. Even touch, for the very air has a feel. You learn to see what is there, and what is missing. Fear has a smell, as does victory. What you hear is important—and what you do not. I was taught to listen to the *noise* of a camp, not to the words.'

'Did your instinct tell you what you would find on Masada?'

'No. The fire was a hint but I allowed for it. We ourselves had set your wooden repair wall alight and the wind made it a furnace. We retired, knowing that the next morning would see the end of the matter. You would not be able to build another such wall by morning.'

'How was the fire a hint?'

'It burnt too long. And seemed to move south. From below we had no way of knowing that the move south was not the wall but the palace. Your friends chose a handsome crematorium.'

This was pure Silva. A flatly delivered remark, of calm perception.

'As I told you, I did not go up with the men that morning. Not at first. My officers are men of considerable experience but there is nothing in regulations that would have prepared them for what they found. Which is why they sent for me.'

'Were *you* prepared?'

'Forewarned—by their messenger. But not prepared. Neither was I prepared when *you* appeared.'

Oh, wise Eleazar. Indeed, beloved friend, our Roman was not prepared. But I go too fast. This with Silva was later, down on the plain, after the dinner, before I met old Reuben.

Let us not go fast. For on that calm mid-April morning the events had a tempo that was not fast; the events had to do with the dead, who go slow.

So we waited, Sarah and I, listening to the sounds: of running feet, of flames, of puzzled shouts. We waited until our ears told us that 'The General' had arrived. 'Silva,' we heard, 'Send for Silva, get the General!' We waited, and when we were sure we joined hands with the children and walked out into the morning sunlight.

The youngest child began to whimper and Sarah swung him up on to one muscular arm without losing step. The palace was alight from end to end. Our hiding place, the great water cistern, was over two hundred yards away, to the south, and the palace was a sight to break the heart. We walked on.

We were near the small palace, about half-way, before we were noticed. A young soldier, little more than a youth, saw us and shouted to a large crowd of officers and men who, with their backs to us, were watching the blaze.

We walked on, and as we approached the men parted and watched, silent, as we passed between them. Then the officers made a path and we stood before Silva. He waited for me to speak and listened until he had heard enough. Then he rapped commands and the men, well trained, jumped into action. They brought loose earth and sand and water and broke down walls and doors and soon the fire was under control.

Silva, who had not spoken again to me after his orders to the men, and had moved away a little, to stand alone, in thought, now came back.

'The old woman will look after the children,' he said. 'You

will come with me. If you have told me the truth, the sight will not surprise you. If you have lied—' He stopped. He knew it was no lie. Beyond belief, incredible, not in regulations; but he knew, with his instinct of many senses, that it was no lie.

We had been standing near the small bathing pool, not far from the terrace outside the throne room. We walked along the eastern face of the palace and round to the front, to the great archway. To our right was the charred gap in the rampart wall and beyond it, the top of the armoured ram tower, nearly a hundred feet high, its base on the colossal ramp, out of our sight.

I paused a moment, and Silva stopped also. He was pale, contained, with a sort of anger in him.

'Waste,' he said, following my look. 'Waste. Of effort, of men. Not ours only. Yours also. Your God, whose rule alone you will accept, who made all men, so you believe. Seemingly, if they are Jews, he made them mad also in their devotion to him. Rome rules the world, in justice and good sense. With more sense than gods, who know nothing of rule. But for your madmen only *their* God must rule. So we witness yet another vast gesture. Another heroic last stand. On top of a mountain in the middle of a desert. We alone shall see it. And forget it. Waste. For nothing. Soon this place will be what it was before, a Roman garrison, and your friends will be forgotten.'

They will not, my General, they will not.

We went through the arch and into the inner court. Silva went ahead but one of the fire-fighters stopped him and pointed to the left, to the service and staff buildings, which were built round a large courtyard, open to the sky. The place.

So tidily they lay, my friends, so lovingly, with their arms about each other. Open to the sky, uncharred, unmarked by fire. No crematorium, Silva, no charnel-house. Eleazar knew well what he did. No pyre. A frame, a setting for his friends, wherein the jewel of their bravery gleamed like the sun, open to the sky.

Silva stood silent. Near him, officers. Soon more. Then soldiers, with dirty faces from their fire-quenching. Feet crunched over debris; from all around, the crackle of flames and the thump of falling roof timbers. But no voices, no speech. Silva, bare-headed, looked round at a tall officer, helmeted, and the man loosened his chin strap and took off the helmet. Others followed, till all were like Silva. All stern, frowning to control the face, lest tears should come. Ordinary men, in circumstances not ordinary. Yet much of the scene before them was ordinary. Small children, many with a favourite toy; young mothers, some with a babe at breast; youths and girls, bare-foot and slim, near the adults they would never become.

Silva moved first. He looked at me, perhaps observing my dry cheeks, and made a gesture that meant all would be taken care of, and another that meant I should leave with him. We went back to Sarah and the children. Silva left us and soon officers came and we were helped across the ladders and on to the ramp. We walked down without looking back.

3 The Camp

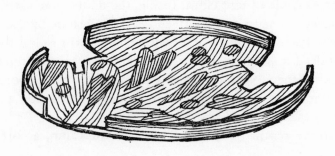

A Nabatean bowl.

3

At the bottom of the ramp we were taken across to what
we knew to be the siege wall. We had watched it take
shape, with wonder, for it completely encircled Masada and
seemed to have been built in a very short time. It was the first
part of the siege work done by Silva and our first intimation
that Masada was to be taken *at all costs*, for it seemed that men
by the thousand were brought in to build it. 'Slave-labourers,'
Eleazar told us, 'prisoners-of-war, people of Israel, Jews. Jews
of Jerusalem, of Tiberias, of Caesarea, of Galilee. Jewish slaves
are walling us in.'

From above, the builders had looked like flies and the wall a
thing of inches, to step over. But on the plain the wall took
dimension and was frightening. It was twice as high as a man
and at least six feet thick. Sarah walked beside me, looking
grim, a child on either side, the little one still on her arm.

The troopers led us along the wall a little way and then
through a gateway into a large compound attached to the wall.
It was an army camp, with an ordered, tidy look. There were
rows of what looked like small houses built of rough stone
with roofs made of tent cloth. Inside, the floors were earthen,
hard packed. The tent-roofs given height and slope by the use
of poles. Each dwelling had a bench or platform round three
of its sides for sleeping or sitting on, and was big enough for
eight or ten men. Near to each row of dwellings was a cooking
place, with here and there men working, who looked at us
curiously as we walked past.

When we reached the central area of the camp, a sort of

parade ground, our troopers gave us over to an older man of higher rank and he and two other officers stood in front of us, silently. There was no hostility. I sensed that he knew our story.

He murmured a word or two to his companions and I spoke to him in the same street Greek. His head came round sharply.

'We are all tired,' I said, 'and the children are hungry also. If you would deal with us quickly we promise to give no trouble of any kind. I speak for my friend as well, who is more warlike than I.'

He smiled. 'Forgive me,' he said. 'My orders are to take you to the General's camp without delay. It is about a half mile. There you will have food and drink and shelter.'

He walked with me, taking, with great naturalness, the hand of Deborah, our seven-year-old. I warmed to him. Sensitive to my fatigue and silence, he talked easily, expecting no reply. He told me that he had served on many fronts, as an engineer. His name was Lucius and he had great admiration for Silva.

'Only Silva would have built the ramp,' he said. 'The design and construction of siege-machines, of catapults, of rock-throwers and battering-rams, and the earth mounds and hillocks upon which they stand or move, has been my job since leaving military academy. But that ramp is no earth mound, no hillock. Certainly it is largely of earth, tens of thousands of tons, but it is a structure; it has wood and stone—and blood—for many died in its making. Silva needed a hill to capture a mountain. He told us where it was to be and when he wanted it finished. Eight camps also he ordered, and a wall right round the mountain. If I may say so, madam, you and your friends gave a great deal of hard work to a great many people.'

I kept silent. From a step behind, Sarah: 'It wasn't wasted. The hill captured the mountain.'

We walked through a gateway in the camp wall and across open ground, the siege wall to our right. Ahead of us, about two hundred yards away, was another camp, bigger than the one we had just left. As we approached, sentries saluted, and we passed between them. Again the surprise at the dimension and solidity of the walls and gateways, so minuscule from above.

'Silva's camp,' said Lucius. 'The largest, and truly the camp of a Commander-in-Chief.' The sun was now high and I felt hot and soiled; his cheerful normality began to grate upon me. But my irritation passed in a moment. This was no obtuse man. This cheerfulness was rule-book; regulation. The best way, the proven method with the vanquished helpless. For conquerors used to victory there was no doubt a prescribed courtesy. And in its use, Lucius showed sensitivity.

I looked at Sarah, and she gave me her grim smile, with raised eyebrows. As so many times before she showed me with one look that she knew my thoughts, had been having those same thoughts herself—to the same conclusion.

'. . . for studying the omens in the stars or in the flight of birds.' Lucius was pointing to a raised platform. He moved his pointing finger a little and I gave my attention, to match his courtesy.

'There, the altars, for prayer and sacrifice parades. Beyond that, where the men get their pay, and further to the left, the market—where they can spend it!'

We walked on, seeing, as in the smaller camp, many rows of the tent-houses in the form of side turnings leading from wider roads which were perfectly straight and went right across the camp from one wall-gate to another. North-south, east-west. Where they crossed, in the centre, there was a wide, open space.

'Parade square,' said Lucius.

As we walked on, across the square, Lucius pointed ahead, at larger, more important buildings: 'Officers' mess; head-quarters; command post; armoury.' As we passed a raised platform: 'For ceremonial parades; where the General stands when he has something to say. Not often used. No great speech-maker, the General.' We stopped outside the command post and Sarah and the children came nearer. He smiled at me, our eyes level. I am tall for a woman. 'Madam, we are at your destination. Have no fear. We have no fight with women and children.'

Sarah's face was like stone, her eyes ice-cold. She held out her hand and Deborah went from Lucius to her without a word. 'It may be, engineer,' she said clearly, in her own Galilee-tinged Greek, in tone to match her eyes, 'it may be that engineers do *not* fight women and children. Maybe your duties are just to provide the means for *others* to do so. For let me tell you, engineer, that a lot of women and children *are* dead.' She made a little gesture with her chin, to each side, to the children. 'These five are orphans, whose mothers and brothers and sisters were killed by Romans who have no fight with women and children.'

Lucius said, 'A great many Romans are dead too, Madam. Follow me, please.' He turned and went in.

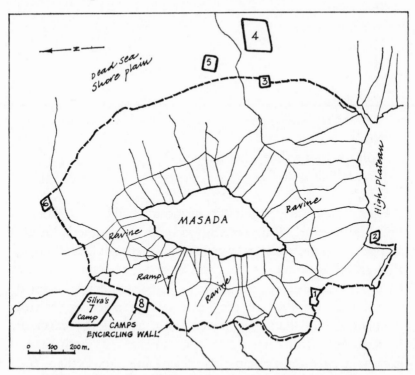

Map of Masada showing the 8 Roman Camps and the encircling wall

Inside it was cool, with a feeling of emptiness and efficiency. We were told to sit down on a long bench which we did thankfully. Simon, nearly six and for half his life on the top of a mountain, lay along the bench with his dark curly head in my lap. Simon of Jerusalem, born in war, with the broad brow his father must have had, or his mother. We knew neither. Simon we found in one of the sewers we used for communication. A filthy three-year-old scrap, with no fear in him at all. He knew his name and where he lived. There was nothing there. Flames and smoke. On Masada he'd had many mothers and fathers, until this day's dawn, with its own flames and smoke. He lay still, his eyes on mine.

'Are we prisoners of war, Ruth?'
'Yes.'
'Will we be tortured?'
'For what reason?'
'For our secrets.'
'Do you know any?'
'No.' He seemed sad at this. Then:
'Will they give us food soon?'
'Yes, positively.'
'Will we try to escape?'
'No.'
'Will we wait to see what happens?'
'Yes. Is that wise?'
'Yes.'

On my other side, Judith, whose mother had been my friend. For Judith, nearly fourteen and with all her mother's beauty and gentleness of spirit, all was now finished. All life, all hope, all desire to continue. Masada was finished; and the last resistance; and the Revolt; and Joseph. Joseph with whom she'd shared the very beat of the heart, every secret, every free moment. Older than their years, both, as was the effect of Masada. But with each other, the same age as each other. Eleazar my cousin, perhaps here was a mistake. Perhaps too big a gesture, this of the families. 'Whole families, with no exceptions.' It was clear, understood, accepted, even by the doubters and the timorous, for desperation has its own logic. 'The orphans are to live and have their chance,' you said. Poor Judith, who wanted only the chance to join Joseph's family, to join in their death. But she lived, an orphan to be given a chance, and Joseph, fortunate enough to have parents, was dead, his chance gone. It will take time, Eleazar, this of Judith. For this was a child living, who wanted to be high on a mountain, dead. It will take time.

She sat close to me, her shoulder against mine with weight enough to tell her sadness. She looked down at Simon's curls and I was grateful that Joseph's hair had been lighter, and straight. She put her fingers lightly on the curls.

Simon: 'How long to the food?'

'Soon now.'

'And then we will see what happens.'

'Yes.'

'What if it's nasty?'

'What, the food?'

'No, what happens.'

'We will discuss it.'

'Will the food be Jewish food?'

'Possibly.'

I looked along the bench at Sarah, still with the little one on her arm. She was waiting for my look, had listened with a glint of amusement to Simon, the hungry Zealot. Between us, also with their eyes on mine, the twins Deborah and David, Div and Dov. Our ten-year-old comedians, whose gaiety in the last days had been more than food and drink to the thousand. Also of Jerusalem were they, orphaned when the second wall came down. Children of the market, the alleys. Twins indeed they were, with their wide, rather flat faces and the bright black eyes and the snub noses. Short, strongly made, quick. But now still, serious, eyes on mine.

I was aware of a subtle change in my relationship with my fellow survivors. I was to be made Leader as well as Historian, like it or not. Perhaps Sarah's glint of humour was partly an awareness of this. They were waiting for me to assume command. As though also aware of the moment, the little one, Sami, unburied his face from Sarah's shoulder and added his gaze to the others.

'We will do as we are told.' I said. 'We will eat when we are given food and I will insist that we remain together. I think the engineer was telling the truth when he said we have nothing to fear. We must try to think only of what is to come, not what is gone.' The girl's shoulder was too still against mine, too sad. 'Judith will be head of family, and must be obeyed.' The shoulder stiffened, she sat straight, and turned, listening.

Hard put to find more words of command I was spared the necessity, for our engineer was back, with unimpaired good humour. Regulations, no doubt. Rule-book.

'We had to move some men around.' he said. 'The seven of you would look rather strange all alone in the prisoner compound we have ready and it would not be correct [ah, rule-book] to put you in the labourer camps—although many who live in them are Jews. You will live here for the time being, in the General's camp. In a soldiers' hut. It is big enough to take you all. We will go there now.'

The 'hut' was one of the tent-roofed houses at the end of a long row of identical houses. It had been emptied. On the bench that went round three sides, and which served also as a bed, there were three piles of army blankets. They were clean and more than enough. The children looked lost.

Sarah: 'All blankets to be shaken out and folded lengthways and laid on the bed-ledge. No creases. Everybody working. Judith in charge. Ruth and I are just outside.'

Outside, Lucius said, 'This part of the camp is comprised mainly of older men. Old campaigners. To that side, senior officers. There will be no trouble. Your food will be the same as the men, the cooks will make extra. Some food will be brought presently. The main cooking is later in the day. I do not know this camp as well as my own but you will find plenty

to interest the children. It is a busy place—and soon busier—
for our work in this area is now done and there will be movings-
on and changes. You may wander at will, but not outside the
walls.'

He left us. 'Our work in this area is now done', hung in the
air.

Sarah surveyed our tent-house. 'I am accustomed to better,'
she said, 'and have lived in worse. I must get used to living at
ground level.' She stuck her head inside the flap and started
one of the Zealot songs in her strong, oddly musical voice.
After a moment the children's voices joined in. She came back,
wiping an eye. The singing in the tent was clear, pure, moving.

And so we settled in, and more quickly than I would have
thought possible our new life down on the plain became
routine. The battle over, the siege completed, Masada conquered, the camp had a feeling of garrison, of barracks, of
peaceful soldiering. The discipline and orderly method for
every task was impressive. We woke to trumpets, and to the
smell of cooking food: for the legionary was a well-cared-for
soldier and the cooks rose before the trumpeters. We were in
no way 'locked up' or restricted.

When we awoke from our first night down in the camp (and
how well we had slept, how exhausted we were, how glad to
be all together, on our blanketed shelf, with our smallest ones
snuggled close, safe and warm) Sarah went with the children
to explore, cautiously, the nearby roads of walled tents. I
stayed behind and sat looking up at my mountain, wondering
at my own feeling of detachment, as though all I had seen was
in my imagination only. It worried me. When Sarah returned
I told her. She looked up at the mountain, then down at me.

'From here you see a mountain with a flat top. Too high and
too far away to make out detail. It's unfamiliar. You were up
there nearly three years, but you have only seen it once before
from below, when we came from Jerusalem—and you saw it
from the other side. From down here the only familiar things

you can see clearly are the ramp and that cursed tower—and they are Roman, not Jewish. Come, you've looked enough. Let the children tell you of all the wonders they've seen on their first morning.'

'Yes. Let them come. It's pleasant here.'

'No. You go to them, and we will face the other way, *away* from the mountain.'

Our family, with Judith, its head, were back in the cool of the hut, lively with after-outing chatter. Even Judith, who had wept in the night like a new widow, had light in her eye—and our smallest, Sami, on her lap.

I sat, and was told of soldiers going about their routine after-breakfast chores, with minimum clothing and maximum barrack language, suddenly finding a young and fascinated audience in the charge of an elderly woman with a certain amusement in her eye.

'Got very confused, some of them,' said Sarah.

Div and Dov told of an armourer who'd promised to give them each a belt. Simon had found a small green bird in a cage just inside a hut. He and baby Sami, soon within the tent, round-eyed, had been nearly knocked flat by the lumbering entrance of the bird's owner, an enormous trooper with a huge grey beard, who'd thought he was seeing things, that the sun had got him. Roaring out of the hut to tell others, another surprise. A short, strongly-made elderly woman, with three more children! Lucky trooper, lucky soldiers, to be surprised by an *un*armed Sarah. Many of your fellows, over the years, had not had such good fortune. My lady of the little knife, leader of men.

The children chattered on, interrupting each other and repeating themselves. Sarah sat quietly, listening, confirming a detail when asked, taking no sides. Indefatigable, made of iron, she seemed tired. I watched her, seeing every now and then a change of expression unrelated to what was being said, a tiny frown, an inward look in the eyes. I thought her unaware of my scrutiny but as I looked again her eyes were waiting. A serious, steady look, and my mind went back.

4 Sarah

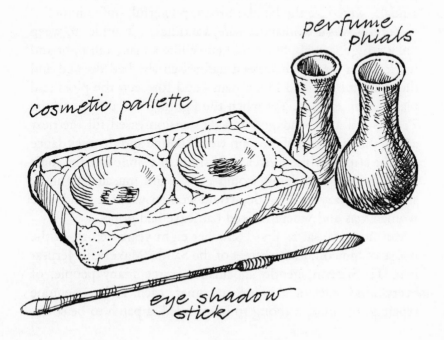

perfume phials

cosmetic pallette

eye shadow stick

4

Sarah sat as she had when first I saw her, her hands loose in her lap, her body relaxed but not slumped. Her shoulders, wide and strong for a woman, well back and supporting the high-held head that was so much a part of her outlook and spirit. The hands that lay so still were square, blunt-tipped, like those of an artisan, a craftsman, brown, strong, male. The square firm jaw was rather masculine too, as were the thick grey hair, cut short, and the eyebrows. The feet, in rough sandals, were like the hands: broad, powerful, unfeminine.

Yet this was a woman, A wife, a mother, a shoulder to weep on, a refuge, a rock. She could curse like a man, and fight and work like a man. When need had arisen she had dressed and thought and planned like a man—and foreseen the plots and plans of other men. Yet when the fighting was done, and the Zealots fed and bandaged and the tension eased till the next affray, the grim line of the chin would soften and the eyes dance and the strong white teeth would show in a smile like the sun's warmth itself and Sarah would glow—and muscled fighters, still a little dizzy from battle, would wonder who the handsome woman was and where the old battleaxe had gone.

But now she sat as first I saw her eight years before, in the house of Simeon, in the Street of the Sandal Makers, in Jerusalem. To Simeon, gentle shoemaker, came many people, of every kind, each a genuine customer, each with a genuine repair to be done, a thong to be mended, a patch to be sewn.

Also they brought news, intelligence of the Romans, messages of the resistance groups elsewhere. Commands were passed over the counter at Simeon's, plans perfected, schemes completed. To Simeon's would come those with tidings as well as those who wanted them. Those looking for lost ones would 'take a shoe to Simeon', and lost ones would go looking for their own.

Also fighters would come. To the upstairs room. To be bandaged, or hidden, or to report, or to rest. For that time, eight years before, was the time of Procurator Florus. Gessius Florus, who followed Albinus, and made that gory-handed tyrant seem an angel by comparison. If Albinus made dry the tinder of revolt by the heat of his repression, then Florus it was who set the flame to it—and laughed when the blood flowed. Laughed and pillaged, and tortured and killed. From Emperor Nero came Florus. A mad Nero, soon to die in screaming lunacy, among flames. Florus was our Nero, and bettered his Emperor in cruelty and corruption of every kind.

So fighters there were at Simeon's, with every day need for more, for the war was unavoidable, the yoke too heavy, the load too great.

Twice a week I 'took a shoe to Simeon', for at that time my job was intelligence, and from Simeon and others in the city like him the Zealots gathered much information—and were expert at making clear pictures and practical plans. Two years before Sarah appeared, I had gone for the first time to Simeon, my mind made up, a pair of house sandals, as instructed, in my hand.

Simeon: 'Fine workmanship. And carefully looked after. Or not much worn.'

'True. I have little use for leisure slippers. These are not times of leisure.'

'I must agree.' Waiting.

The slippers put on the counter toe to toe, as instructed. The words, as instructed.

'Had I married, my mother-in-law's name would be Naomi.'

'Then you must be Ruth.'

'Daughter of Joel.'

'You are expected. Go out of the shop, round to the back and into the gate two doors along. Go upstairs and come back two houses. All the upper rooms are connected. This part of the market is a rabbit warren.'

More of this later. Soon I was a Zealot with clearly defined duties and considerable discipline.

Yes, twice a week I took a shoe, and as once I was sent 'round and up the back two houses' so were others. And as once I had been carefully questioned in the upper room so now I questioned others. I was good at the work. My father had seen well my detached and unimpressed nature, and people meeting it became truthful—and truth was essential in the selection of a Zealot.

It was the day before Sabbath that I met Sarah, in the afternoon. Florus had been procurator nearly thirteen terrible months and every day had seen some new terror or outrage. He was the very King of Crime, the insatiable spider in the middle of a vast web of extortion and violence. Every kind of excess and sin was permitted, openly, as long as payment was made to Florus for the privilege. New and inhuman taxes were invented and graft and corruption had spread across the land like a plague.

But it was not of Florus that Sarah spoke, but of Cumanus, procurator of Israel fifteen years before and successor of the foolish Tiberius Alexander, who—despite his part-Jewish blood—had caused such trouble.

In the upper room she had sat, good Sarah, hands in lap, steady-eyed.

'I am of the market,' she said. 'The fruit market between Fortress Antonia and the second wall. I have had a stall in the same part for many years. I am known by many. My name is Sarah. The shoemaker downstairs knows me also. We are much the same age, he perhaps a bit older. I am fifty-five.'

She looked less, although the face showed signs of much

care. The complexion was ruddy, healthy. The voice and posture had the same sort of vigour.

'We know of you through Simeon,' I said.

'Good. Then he will have told you I want to join your War Party.' A quick grin. 'I would a Zealot be, like the song. And my grandson also.'

'A grandson? We have no note of your grandson.'

She leaned a little forward. 'No note, eh? What note *do* you have? Any? I'm not surprised. No great talker, old Sarah; people have their own troubles, they don't need to know of mine.'

'We need to know a little, I'm afraid.'

'Why?' Blunt, sharp.

'Because it says here you want to fight. To be with a fighting unit. To be trained to use weapons. A bit unusual for a grandmother of fifty-five, would you not agree?'

The head went back in a delighted roar of a laugh. She wiped her eye.

'I like you, young woman. What's your name?'

'Ruth.'

'How old are *you*?'

'Twenty-eight.'

'Too old for my grandson. Pity.'

'How do you know I'm not married?'

'I know more than about fruit, lovey. You're not married. You're a loner—and a scholar too. Am I right?'

'Go on.'

'Books show in the face, you know. Like drink. Everything shows in the face. Even in your beautiful face, lovey. The books and the wanting both to join in and to be left alone. Puts a fellow off a bit, don't you find?'

Her candour was that of a child, impossible to resist.

'It does rather. I'm not married. . . . But I'm supposed to ask *you* questions.'

Another laugh. 'Carry on, lovey, or shall I save you the trouble and just talk? It's not a long story, and in no way out of the ordinary. Jerusalem is full of people like me, who've lost part of their family in the various troubles. Our Romans, bless 'em, make plenty of trouble.'

'Which part of your family did you lose?'

'Husband, son, and daughter-in-law. Same day.' The smile had gone. Her eyes held mine. A little pause. Her twinkle came back.

'Not yesterday, lovey, fifteen years ago. In the Passover Temple Riot. I wasn't there. I was looking after the baby. My first grandchild. My only one, as it's worked out. My husband had gone with my son and his wife to the Temple to see the afternoon sacrifices—she'd never seen them. She was from the North and after they married they made their home on the coast, just south of Joppa. Nice girl. Same age as my son near enough. Married at nineteen—and dead at twenty-two. Because Cumanus, our procurator, lost his head and brought infantry-men in to control crowds he'd allowed to be insulted into frenzy. A panic started and people rushed for the gates and got trampled on and crushed to death. Hundreds were killed. Some of the younger men started to fight and were cut down by the Romans. I didn't know a thing. I'd just finished laying the table for our Passover supper. It looked lovely. The baby'd been as good as gold. When I got the news I didn't believe it. Funny, y'know, how the mind works. When it finally sank in and I'd rushed like a mad woman to queue up and identify my lot, my first thought was: who's going to eat all that food? For I believe in plenty.

'Forty-one my husband was when he was killed. Very pleasant man. A joiner, on his own. So was my son. People were kind, but you don't sit around, you know, you get on with it. I was an only child and my husband was of poor family way up in Galilee. You get on with it. The baby helped. I had a good reason for everything, see. The baby. I didn't rush. I had a good think. Then I sold my husband's tools to a handcart maker, and took a handcart and some money as payment. With the money I filled the cart with fruit and I was in business. Fine outdoor life. The baby loved it. He's a fine boy, my grandson—and bright. Seth, his name is. We've talked it over and we'd like to do our share in getting rid of the Romans. The country is going to explode soon and nothing can stop it. Enough is enough. This bastard Florus will be the one to touch it off. The market says so, and the market's never wrong. Any questions, lovey?'

fruit & egg-basket motif in floor mosaic

It was sharp, the query, with a funny face to give it humour.
'Er—how old is Seth?'

'Seventeen. Old for his years and strong as a horse. He *is* a
horse! He pulls the cart all day long! He sells from the cart, all
over, and I have a stall.' The funny face again. 'Self-contained
news-gathering and courier service we are.' Again now the
steady eyes.

We talked on, and every minute that passed bound me to her
more. It is too easy to say that I'd found the mother I'd lost at
twelve. I remembered my mother well enough to know how
completely different she was from Sarah, in every way. Neither
was it that Sarah was by her very nature a mother. This also is
too simple. With Sarah I could laugh out loud. Not even with
my beloved father could I do that. I do not lack humour but am
a smiler only. Reserved, too serious, too locked. But Sarah was
like a gusty wind, and buffeted me out of my usual ways. With
her I became a different Ruth. This gusty wind, believe me,
was no violent insensitive hurricane. Indeed not, for when,
weeks after our first meeting, at supper with her and Seth, I
laughed out loud, free, for the first time, she said comfortably,
'*That's* better, my dove, that's better.'

Seth was tall, broad in the shoulder and muscular. He was
darker-skinned than his grandmother and bore little resemblance to her. His eyes were deep-set in a broad brow. His jaw
line was a different shape from Sarah's but showed the same
resolution. His disposition was quieter than hers, but he had the
same warmth and humour. He was as she'd said, older than his
years—in some ways. In others, an uncertain, fatherless,
seventeen-year-old.

At that time the word fatherless was much in my mind, for it
was not necessary to sell fruit in the market to know the way
the wind was blowing—and my father had been observing the
currents and eddies of history all his life. When, at twenty-six,
I had joined the Zealots, it had only confirmed his own con-
clusions. He made no objection to my decision and listened
carefully to my reasons. He nodded, seeing more than I'd said.

A man of peace, he was brought nearer to the growing heat of revolt by my involvement—and grew sadder.

About half a year after Sarah appeared he spoke to me, in his 'formal' way, to cover emotion. We sat in the shade, in the garden.

'You are twenty-eight, my Ruth,' he said, 'and your wisdom matches your beauty. Therefore I take the liberty of offering a long-pondered and sorrowful thought for your gentle consideration.'

I said nothing. 'Your sister Rebekah is long married, and far away in Cyrene. My gentle son Saul is where he wants to be, a priestly scribe in the Temple, a goodly achievement for a twenty-three-year-old, and Sharon will soon be both nineteen and married on the same day—and off to Cyprus, which shows wisdom in her husband. Which leaves Rose, who cares only for her brother David, who so needs her care.' This was the great double sadness, that the beautiful child whose birth had finished my mother's life had remained a child. At seventeen, with the same beauty, a child.

'So consider, my Ruth, if this sad country is the best place for an unwarlike widower of bookish ways and his two youngest children, the one a nurse to the other.'

'I have considered. It is not. Where will you go?'

They went to Armenia, to a cousin of my father, who had a large house. It was best, and sensible. But when they were gone, I, who for years had needed them so little, had been so independent of them, was lost.

Sarah took me over in typical fashion. 'Buy a handcart!' she said. 'You don't need that great house at all. You've hardly used it, except to sleep in, for years. Move in with us. No shrines, my lovey, no wandering through empty rooms. Move in with us! Bring only your books. We are going to need that house soon. Fighting men get hurt.'

Indeed they did, but that came later.

5 Dinner with Silva

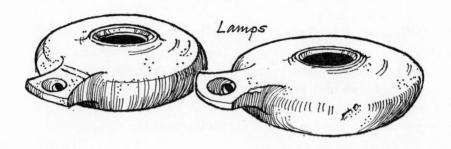

Lamps

5

We had lived down on the plain, in Silva's camp, for nearly three weeks before I told Sarah of my resolve to keep my promise to Eleazar and write down the story of Masada. I am not sure quite why I held back. I had no doubt in my mind that I would do as Eleazar had asked. It was after all the request of a brave man just before death. Even lesser men are obeyed in such circumstances. It may have been that I was daunted by the size of the task; not sure how to start—or where. But the time came to tell Sarah, and—as many times before—to tell a worry or problem to Sarah was to have the worry removed, the problem solved.

She had not been lazy, my Sarah. She and the children were known to the whole camp, and had become a diversion, a group of welcome visitors, a unique and remarkable group of war prisoners. Only one soldier, a half-drunk decurion, had been unpleasant. He had made as if to lay hands on Judith, and Sarah had had the point of his own shortsword to his throat with one powerful wristflick too fast to see. The soldier's companions had roared with glee and the story went round the camp like wind.

'I meant it to, lovey,' said Sarah calmly, later. 'After all,' with a wicked glint, 'we are two defenceless women, with young children.' She visited the soldier next day, drank and laughed with him, and he became her slave. She roped him in, found a job for him. 'He's got no more fighting to do, he might just as well help keep the children interested.'

'Keeping the children interested' was her sole activity, and her reasons were uncomplicated. The children were to enjoy today, look forward to tomorrow; they were *not* to think of yesterday, of the mountain, 'not for a while.'

She was tireless. Anyone in the camp whose work or duties held some interest for the children found that he was expected to lecture, demonstrate, explain in detail, even teach! Her fame grew. 'Zealot Sarah' was known everywhere. Her quick wit and blunt humour were irresistible.

I did not often go with her and the children. A day or two after we came down from the mountain, a huge reaction overcame me, and a lassitude I could not shake off. I was not ill, but tired, sleepy, leaden-limbed. Sarah understood, was brisk, made it a virtue almost.

'Good thing! Stay out of sight. You're a bit too good-looking to go walking round an army camp, for all your serious face and your great sad eyes. I don't need you with me, I'll come to no harm, I'm an ugly old market woman! And another thing. If you stay home the children have got someone to tell it all to when they get back. Good!'

Sometimes Judith would stay with me, a quiet sensitive companion, and I made her talk, so that her dead Joseph became alive again, became a slim lively boy, not a dead soldier hero.

And the days went by. Sarah, scrounger extraordinary, organized stools, plates, forks, pillows for our heads, towels and soap, a piece of mirror. Sandals were repaired, a brush and comb arrived.

The day I decided to tell Sarah about my promise to Eleazar she herself had news to tell, but first she listened to me. I told her in our 'quiet time', as she called it, after the children had settled down for the night and we would sit outside in the cool dark air with a small lamp between us. She listened carefully. A pause, then gently:

'You told me of the promise on the night you wouldn't remember.' She went on, not waiting for reply. 'Yes. It should be done. I will help. I'm better with people than you are, my dove. Everybody talks to Sarah. I'll find people for you. Truthful people, with good memories. Then you can ask them questions in that same calm way you did when you were a recruiting officer.' She chuckled in the gloom and was serious then, for a moment. 'Yes. It must be written down. It must not be forgotten, this of the mountain, of Masada. And it can be, for our thousand died long after the tens of thousands, long after the war was lost. Who cares, my Ruth, who cares? We will find the people—we will go everywhere!'

'If we are allowed. We are prisoners.'

Now her news. 'We may not be for long. Tomorrow we are to have our evening meal with the General.'

'With Silva?' I had not seen him since the morning of the fires on the mountain-top. It was a surprise. 'I thought he was gone from the camp.'

'Perhaps he did go, and has come back.'

'Tell me.'

'Well, as the children told you, today they had a drawing lesson in the officers' mess. One of Silva's staff is an official war artist—and of some reputation, I'm told. Certainly he draws well—and yesterday did not mind at all when the children watched him for a while. I'm sure he would have offered to give them an afternoon even if I hadn't suggested it. A nice man—and a born teacher. I told him so.'

'Did that please him?'

'Of course. Well, whilst the children were busy Silva came in. He seemed a bit surprised.'

'A children's drawing class in the officers' mess of a desert siege camp. Understandable.'

'I suppose so. But he was very pleasant. Asked after you and said he'd heard that we were making ourselves at home in his camp and would you and I eat with him tomorrow night. I said yes.'

'What gave you the impression we wouldn't be here much longer?'

'The artist officer told me that Silva and his staff are moving on and that the camps are to be cleared. The mountain is to be a Roman garrison and a lot of the labourers and work-prisoners are to be allowed to go home. It's all finished now, as he put it.'

We were both silent for a moment. I think we both felt as though a phase was ending, a new one beginning.

The next morning, just after we'd eaten the good breakfast that we shared with our soldier neighbours, we had a visitor. A woman, attended by a young legionary. She was dark, of rather full figure and nearly my own height. She was perhaps a little older than myself, about thirty-eight or nine, with a smiling, vigorous way. She was expensively dressed in colourful clothes, had a jewelled comb in her hair and rings which caught the sun. She was at ease, and returned Sarah's hard gaze with good humour. I sensed she was curious about me.

'I am sent,' she said, in a low-pitched attractive voice, 'by the children's art master, who did not know he was any such thing till yesterday.' Sarah chuckled. 'My name is Claudia.' To Sarah: 'You I know to be Zealot Sarah. So you,' she went on, turning to me, 'must be Ruth.' Her smile was easy to return. 'The art master, who is called Antony, has sent me to ask if I can in any way assist you in the matter of this evening's dinner party.'

'Assist us?'

'Good Antony likes me to be "decorative", as he calls it, at all times and indulges me with a large wardrobe and many bits and pieces. Looking decorative is really all I have to do.'

Sarah: 'Do you mean that you are here to help us look a little more decorative? For the General? We *owe* him something?'

I put my hand on her muscular arm. 'It is very good of you,' I said. 'We both know it is meant well, but we are in mourning. It would not be proper to be too—er—colourful. If—'

Sarah: 'Tell the General we will wash our hands and faces and comb our hair. We—'

39

'If you have loose garments of sober colour with sleeves it would be much appreciated.'

Sarah: 'If you are really hard up for something to do—'

'We do not really need jewellery, the luxury will be in wearing something else after so long—'

Sarah: '—you can come and look after the children this evening whilst *we* are eating with the General!'

Claudia threw back her head and her laugh was rich and free. Her teeth were even and white. After a moment Sarah, unaccustomed to such a reaction to her 'hard' note, added her own bark of a laugh. I was pleased.

'I will send my maid, who will be good company for your own young beauty there,' Claudia said, looking at Judith, who had come with the other children to see who was laughing. 'She will bring the clothes at lunchtime for you to select, and later will come to make them fit. She is very clever, not much older than that one—and is Jewish and comes from Jericho.'

Soon she was gone and I avoided Sarah's eye for a while and ignored her mutterings. She took the children off but was back promptly at lunchtime, which was unusual—for she and the children were generally invited to stay and eat in other parts of the camp, not returning till late afternoon. But I said nothing.

We ate, and then Judith took the others to watch the daily sword drill—which was thrilling and frightening in its toe-to-toe reality.

The little maid sent by Claudia came heavy-laden, with over-garments, undershifts, shawls, headcovers, soft sandals and—in a cedarwood box—cosmetics and perfume. The colours of the clothes were muted, and the materials soft to the touch, and sweet-smelling.

Sarah put one square hand on the heap of clothes and felt the smoothness. I waited.

'Too good for a market woman.'

'Nothing is too good for you.'

A pause. 'Dinner parties with generals!'

'It is correct, for you are a general also.'

A keen look. 'Do *you* want to go?'

'You said we would. Both of us.'

'What about all this finery?'

I risked it. 'I have worn these clothes for about a month. I sleep in them, I have no others. They are dirty and they smell. I see no betrayal to the blessed memory of my friends in wanting to feel clean again.'

My eyes began to smart. Sarah said: 'One of the cooks in the officers' mess has a very big copper basin. He will lend it to me and later on we will wash all over, hair as well. Thus we will not dirty the fresh clothes.'

We made it a grand bath night for all, with relays of hot water from two nearby cooking fires and lookouts posted at tent flaps and squealings and sighs of bliss and deep snugglings into towels. Then decorously, behind a hung blanket, Sarah scrubbed herself, and I followed.

We dressed and showed ourselves to the children, who responded in the most gratifying way. Then the little maid, having tended her mistress, came with pins and clips to put the finishing touches to the folds of our garments and to our newly washed hair.

We were called for and escorted across the darkened camp by the young legionary who had accompanied Claudia earlier. He told us we were going to Silva's quarters, which lay back from the main parade square inside their own wall. He left us at the gate and we were taken to the entrance of the low stone-built house by a guard. Claudia greeted us and took genuine pleasure in how nice we both looked. She herself looked magnificent, her piled hair glittering with jewels, her low-cut draped gown superb. It was astonishing to see her, after the walk through regimented rows of army tents, the atmosphere of a desert battle station everywhere. I said so, partly to offset a grimness emanating from Sarah.

Claudia smiled. 'It is mainly for Antony, whom I like to please,' she said lightly. 'But also for the General, for this is to be his farewell party. Not that good Silva likes this kind of thing. He prefers your type, Ruth. Ah well, you can't please them all. I need rather a lot of icing and sparkle, you don't. If I had your kind of looks, I would also leave well alone. Come, let us join the others.'

We walked through into a central courtyard with the low walls of the house on all four sides. There were large lamps and low tables and comfortable chairs, and plants in stone urns. Claudia's use of the word party had prepared me, with a certain shrinking, for a large and noisy crowd, but only five people waited, including a woman. One of the men was Lucius, the officer who had brought us from the camp at the foot of the ramp to Silva's camp. After a moment I realized that the man nearest to Lucius was Silva, whom I had seen at close quarters only once before, on the mountain, on the morning. He had been in uniform then, armoured, armed. Cold-eyed he had been, with tense jaw and bitter mouth.

Now he stood smiling, at ease, dressed in a house-toga of white wool, his feet in sandals. His hair was dressed more loosely than in the field, and was plentiful, with much silver in it. He took a step forward but paused, for Claudia, who obviously enjoyed being hostess, was gaily dealing with the introductions. Her Antony was a tall fair man in his middle forties who made good jokes about Sarah's 'discovery' of him as a teacher of drawing. 'My students' chaperone' he called her, 'my class disciplinarian'.

The woman was about fifty-five, with a rather patrician profile and a certain stiffness of manner. Her husband, the fourth man, was a visiting legate from the South, whose name was Linias. He resembled his wife, and had the same manner, but humour showed through also, and was warming. Both were courteous, and treated Sarah with a certain deference, which puzzled me a little. Claudia, behind her hand, explained.

'It pleases Silva to tell Linias that Sarah is a captured Leader of Zealots, not a woman prisoner in charge of orphans.'

'Does Silva need to impress Linias?'

'Not for a moment. No, Silva has a strange kind of humour

and greatly enjoys the comedies of manners.'

We sat awhile and male servants brought chilled wine and
passed olives and almonds. The talk was a little constrained at
first, over-polite, but guided by Claudia and 'high-ranking'
Sarah soon loosened and became more friendly. Silva said
little, but listened to each speaker with full attention. A little
way from us, on the same paved area, was a round table set for
eight. It was inviting, for now, relaxed, I felt hungry, and
appetizing smells were in the air.

Sarah, more direct, lifted her head and sniffed, and Silva
chuckled.

'Come,' he said, 'the food is telling us it is ready—and I'm
hungry. Our guests, I am sure, will not mind if we go to table.'
He rose and gave a sinewy hand to Sarah, who was on her feet
in a moment. Claudia seated us and I found myself to Silva's
right with Sarah to his left. 'Flanked by Zealots,' he said. 'It's
not the first time.'

Antony, on my other side, laughed as he helped Beatrice, his
neighbour, into her chair. Next to her, opposite Silva, Lucius
joined the laugh. It was not sycophantic, the laughter. Silva had
a dryness which gave good value to wit.

To Sarah's left sat Linias, well satisfied with the arrangement,
for on his left sat Claudia, who had the kind of natural manner
which made men feel attractive and special.

The food appeared without delay. Silva made it clear that
eating should take precedence over conversation and even
Claudia attended to her plate with little chatter. Sweetmeats of
a surprising delicacy were brought, and fruit. Various kinds of
nuts appeared, in silver dishes, and dates stuffed with sugary
fondant.

We stayed at table. The chairs were comfortable and it seemed
Silva's habit to do so. The talk went back and forth, avoiding
all reference of war and conquest—and of the mountain,
hidden from us by the house and the night.

Sarah it was, not unexpectedly, who changed the tone,
deepened the subject. Turning to Silva, she took the moment

to say to him bluntly, 'I hear you are leaving the camp. When may we?' It was said softly, to be heard only by him and me, for I had turned on her first word.

Silva looked first at her and then at me, his expression quizzical.

'Soon. It is being arranged.' As Sarah drew breath to reply, his tone hardened slightly. 'Have patience. You are suffering no hardship as I understand.' Sarah grinned wickedly and his own eye glinted in appreciation of her.

'. . . he is more Roman than we are!' sang Claudia from the other side of the table, and the others laughed.

'Who is?' asked Silva.

'The good Flavius Josephus, friend of our beloved Vespasian. 'Tis said the Emperor takes no action without first consulting his soothsayer. Even Titus, his son, does not have his ear so firmly as good Josephus.'

Silva said, 'Claudia, you are the most beautiful gossip I know.' He did not sound very amused.

'Oh come, darling, it's true! Vespasian is a nice simple soldier who makes a nice simple emperor. He has about as much political sense as his cupbearer, and anyone with subtlety, who can read the signs, he respects. And Josephus has made an art of knowing which way to jump!' She was a little drunk.

'We will talk of other things,' said Silva. 'It would seem tactless to talk of ex-enemies in the present company.'

Sarah, who rather enjoyed a spot of discord, added a little mischief. 'Oh, *we* don't mind, do we Ruth? After all how often do we hear of Vespasian, to whom we gave such trouble, or of Titus, who is not the man his father was in the field.'

I shot her a warning look but noticed that Silva's smile was back, though perhaps a little tauter. She went on.

'*We* don't mind hearing about ex-enemies, and we think that you are very tactful in everything, General. It's a lesson. I don't remember ever treating an ex-enemy the way we've been treated. Mind you, we have never *won* a war. A battle or two, never a war.'

The silence was complete. Claudia had a tear on her cheek.

'To be honest,' said Sarah, 'I'm a little out of touch with how people are treating people in this country of mine. For three years I've been up a mountain. I know how Romans treated Jews and Jews treated Romans *before* I went up.'

'It is well known to me also,' said Silva levelly. 'The war is over, my Zealot. Have another fig.' It was said coldly, without kindness. Sarah was going against his wish to close the subject, against the rule-book, and his disapproval was positive and steely.

Lucius said, with gentle tact, 'Good Flavius Josephus, I am told, is more historian than soothsayer. A recorder of events, an archivist. And respected in such circles, I hear.'

Claudia, recovered: 'Oh, he is *able*. And far better educated than most men I know. But most men I know [a jewelled hand to both Linias and Lucius, a mouthed kiss to Antony] are *nicer*.' The laughter came back to the table. Sarah, no fool, joined in.

'Who is this recorder, this ex-enemy, this soothsayer? Flavius Josephus? Sounds like a Roman. What, are you fighting among yourselves now?' She laughed, much enjoying her own joke. The table, relieved, joined her. Not Silva.

'Indeed, you have been out of touch up on your mountain,' he said. 'Flavius Josephus is no Roman. And positively ex-enemy.' He sipped wine. 'Ex-Jew too, I'm told.'

Claudia: 'Silva darling, you are the handsomest gossip I know!' This time Silva joined the laugh. Sarah and I did not. She waited a little, her chin forward.

'Josephus?'

Silva sat back in his chair, his head turned to her. I looked past his cheek into her eyes fixed on his. His voice was light, amused.

'Joseph, actually, my Zealot.' Sarah began to go pale. 'General Joseph ben Matthias.'

Sarah: 'Of Jotapata?'

Silva: 'Of Jotapata.' He turned to look at me with cool eyes for a moment. Silva, of the strange humour, was enjoying himself. He turned back to Sarah, whose white face and thunderous brow had stilled the table. I was trembling, for this 'of Jotapata' was to Sarah spark to tinder. In starving Jerusalem she would stiffen the faint-hearted and restore the flagging with her: 'For Jotapata we fight—to revenge treachery! To undo the work of a traitor!' A clarion call with tears of rage and sorrow in it. Of Joseph, son of Matthias, general, my Sarah had opinions. But not to prompt dinner-party talk.

She had not moved. Her effort at control was heroic, and successful, because she found humour in my expression, worried and concerned. And also because, as she told me later, 'I don't give *any* satisfaction to Romans, good dinner or not!'

She put her hands in her lap, looked round the table. At Claudia, who sat wide-eyed and uncertain, she smiled, with liking.

'General Joseph ben Matthias, now known as Flavius Josephus, eh? I *am* out of touch. I have never actually met him, I have only seen him from a distance. Not near enough to touch, to lay hands on, as you might say. Ruth and he are the same age. He seems young to be a writer of history, a—what did you call it—an archivist? Mind you, he would know a lot, having served on both sides!' To Silva, with a comic politeness:

'I am right I suppose, it is of *our* recent—er—troubles he is writing?'

'Of the Revolt, the War, yes.' Silva was bored now with the way the talk had gone. He turned to me.

'It will be necessary for you, at some time in the near future, to relate to Josephus in some detail what you know of the recent "troubles", as our honoured guest puts it. We Romans set great store by official records, logs, day-books, histories. And the larger, the more expensive the campaign, the more detailed the record. Your mountain was *very* expensive. The emperor will want many words—and pictures—to know why. Good Antony here, who paints so beautifully, is really only a recorder of scenes for a history book.'

Claudia: 'Don't be unkind, Silva. Poor Antony is sensitive, an artist, easily hurt.'

Antony, next to me, laughed, and put his hand tragically to his brow.

'There!' said Claudia, and came round the table taking his head to her bosom. 'There, there. *Nasty* Silva!' It was full of charm, of laughter. Our mountain was to be painted and written about, was suddenly a party joke, a divertissement.

Silva: 'Josephus, I am assured, is uniquely suitable for the task of writing the history of the past few years. He will go everywhere.'

Sarah said grimly: 'Let him go well guarded.' Then a smile began, a special full-of-mischief face that always heralded an outrageous remark. She turned her face full-beam on Silva. '*Our* side has a historian too, also uniquely suitable for the task—and better looking than yours!'

'Who?' asked Silva, impaled.

'Ruth!' With a big dramatic gesture to me—and a wicked wink, too. The table was interested, curious, with overlapping questions.

'So,' said Sarah, to Silva, 'we have to have an agreement, an arrangement. We are quite happy to give details to Josephus about our "recent happening" if he will give us a little detail on one or two of his own happenings, not so recent.'

'Agreed. When?'

'Not yet. And not here. We will not forget any of our details. We have work to do, people to find, places to visit. He will understand, being in the same line of work. We will not leave the country or go into hiding. He will find us without difficulty.'

'Agreed.' Silva turned fully in his chair to face me. 'Is all this true?'

'Yes. The intent is true—and the way of it is clear in the mind. It is not yet begun.'

'When did you decide? It is a big work.'

'It is a promise.'

'Nevertheless, big work for a woman.'

From Sarah: '*Two* women. And we will not lack friends. Your ex-enemy might not be so lucky in that respect.'

Silva spoke over his shoulder. 'Claudia, you have my permission to leave the table, and to take your Zealot friend with you. I would have a few words with our fair historian. We will join you all in a moment.' His smile was real but it was an order and the others rose and moved across to the other chairs without delay, without remark. He waited until they were seated and talking, and turned again to me.

'The moving out will begin in about ten days. This is the command camp and will be the last to go. There are eight camps.'

'I know. Must we wait till the last also?'

'Have you anywhere to go?'

'We want to leave here.' I sounded more vehement than I'd intended, unmannered. He made no sign. 'I mean we want to go from where the mountain is—the children are young—the nights are bad—'

With firm tact: 'And you are eager to begin the work, to keep the promise? I understand.' He spoke on, his eyes away, aware of my stress. 'Very well. It is a matter of re-arranging a sequence only. It will be done. You will leave as soon as is practical. Discontent and temper will have to be mollified— not the children's but the troopers', for the sequence of disbandment is known, and change of any kind is very disturbing to the common soldier. "Rights" often seem more important to him than food. Sometimes it is necessary to remove the food to restore the sense of values.' A thin smile. 'Please do not concern yourself. Ours is a very disciplined army. We do as we are told. All of us.'

He sat quiet a moment, indrawn, in thought not to be shared.

'Your mountain represented an unfinished task. In Rome there are triumphal arches and carved plaques and streets named to commemorate the successful putting down of what is

called The Judean Revolt. The treasures of Jerusalem have
been in Rome for three years. The arches and other monuments
nearly as long. We were perhaps a little quick with the monuments.' His voice was in no way derisory. It was detached in
tone, cool, academic. He went on.

'As I said before, we are great historians and recorders. It is
part of our culture, our way of life. I have a certain respect for
those who practise the writing of events. I have met and
spoken to many.' He looked into my eyes to show candour—
and there was but one meaning in his next words. 'If you wish,
in the next day or two, we can meet and speak together also.
It amuses me to think I may figure in a *Jewish* history of this
mountain.'

'It would be of great value, for such work is new to me. It
will perhaps show me where to begin. Thank you.'

'Good. Tomorrow. Mid-morning. I will send a man. Come,
let us join the others.'

As we sat I felt tired and rather sleepy and I was pleased when
Sarah, not long after, made a joke and rose to her feet, saying
that the ex-enemies had now to go home to their children.

Lucius said he would walk back with us and we were
glad of his company. As we lowered our voices near the
tent, aware of sleeping children, so did he, and it was en-
dearing.

When he left us, we stayed outside for a moment and I
related to Sarah the little conversation I'd had with Silva. She
listened carefully, well pleased with the positive promise of our
release, and very thoughtful when I told of Silva's offer to
'contribute' to the story.

'God's hand is in it,' she said at last, with conviction. 'I saw
only Jewish voices in witness. The other side is also important.
I did not see it.'

'Nor I.'

A deep chuckle. 'I shouldn't tell Silva that he is an instrument of God, he may not appreciate it. Myself, lovey, I think
he is Satan's brother. Come, to bed.'

Silva and I spoke together three times. We met in the middle of the morning, three days running, each time for about one hour. We sat in the courtyard where we had eaten that night. An awning gave shade. At the end of each session an old man brought cool drinks made of fruit juice.

Silva's manner on all three occasions was punctilious, absolutely correct, almost unfriendly. But he taught me much, which may have been his plan. 'To experience, to have taken part, is to recall subjectively—and not necessarily with accuracy. To be detached is the first essential in a recorder. The emotions should not be involved. Passion should be directed only toward exactitude, detail—and economy.'

He would sit facing me but often with head turned in profile. His face was bony, hard-looking, clean-shaven. The eyes were deep-sunken, the brows sparse, with a stern frown-line above an imperious nose. The mouth was thin, down-turned, unforgiving. The whole face was transformed when he smiled, which was rarely. It was a mocking, rather cynical smile, but warmth was there too, impossible to suppress. I was left with the feeling that Silva spent a lot of time suppressing warmth.

His mind was ordered, as was his way with words. The first morning we spoke of Roman colonization, of how the vast empire grew, of the way that conquest gets easier. 'The most potent weapon is fear, or a reputation for invincibility. People must feel they can never win, should never resist.' He developed this theme and I sat, calm-faced, loving my tiny country that had made such wreckage of such theories. After a time, talking to a too-quiet historian, he stopped. I tried to show nothing in my face, but he caught my thought and flushed.

'Fanatical belief in miracle-working deities, or in revolutionary ideals, can make the work harder, can delay completion of course, but the end-result is the same. As history shows—and will show—many times.'

I said nothing—and did not smile either. He gave me a searching look, and was sharp.

'We will speak now, if you wish, of the procurator, or province-governor, system.'

Poor stern Silva, you were not the first to underestimate my stiff-necked people, who upset theories—and disturb empires.

But I learned from Silva. 'Ask me that again,' he would say. 'In different words, to *make* me think back, to *prod* my mind, to *force* accurate recollection.'

Or: 'Now ask me in a way to corroborate detail you already have, to fill in gaps, to complete the picture.'

Or: 'Do not suffer self-indulgent monologue. Learn to interrupt, to guide the flow, or bring it back to the main channel.'

On the third and last morning he told me of his orders to conquer Masada—'with an absolutely free hand, using if necessary every Roman soldier in the whole of Palestine'. He spoke of the vast labour force pressed into service, without right of refusal. 'Standard practice in the case of a resistant population. Once resistance is overcome their status is that of slave—and they're lucky to be left alive. Standard practice. The Roman way.' Statements of this kind were made without heat, the eyes cold, observant.

We spoke lastly of background: the backcloth, the setting for event, the seed, often ignored or unnoticed, from which mighty happenings spring. He dwelt on this subject at length, making me wait for his reason for doing so. He rounded off his opinion tidily, as was his way, by showing how it was necessary, when recording present events, to relate them to the past.

'Which brings me,' said Silva with one of his rare, unexpected smiles, 'to Reuben, whom I give to you as a sort of parting gift.'

'Reuben?'

'The old man who will soon bring us the last fruit drink we shall share, for this is our final meeting. I go north tomorrow.' He paused a moment. I said nothing. 'Reuben is a house servant. He looks after my clothes and sees that my food is as I like it. He was found for me by the labour-force master. He

comes, I think, from Galilee. We do not speak often, for it is
not my habit to encourage familiarity in servants, but I have
conversed enough with him to know that he has not only a
remarkable memory but also considerable learning and breadth
of mind.' Another smile. 'It is of course possible that *he* has
avoided discourse with *me*. It is understandable. I am not only
Roman but woefully uneducated. You may have him today,
for the whole afternoon. He is quite willing. I told him about
you this morning.'

'I am grateful. Why are you doing this?'

'To please myself. I told you the other evening that I have
high regard for accurate records. It pleases me to help achieve
this in your case. Ah, our last drink approaches.'

As the old man came nearer, Silva got to his feet and waited.
He made no move to assist with an obviously heavy tray held
in frail, shaky hands; he wished merely to make the intro-
duction formally, standing up. The tray safe on the low table,
Silva spoke.

'Reuben, this is Ruth, of Masada, of whom I told you.'

The old man's eyes seemed less old than his body, which was
bent and thin. They were pale, under deep brows. Reuben
held his head slightly tilted, but not in a deaf person's
way; more to suggest a gentle weighing-up, an appraisal.
A little nod followed the appraisal. The eyes went back to
Silva's.

'Ruth will return after the midday meal and you may talk
together here,' said Silva, with no sharpness. 'You will have
no duties and you will not be disturbed.'

Reuben gave his little nod to Silva—of whom he was
obviously quite unafraid—and then again to me, with a little
smile. And went softly away.

Silva and I sipped our fruit juice silently. He remained
standing as if to make clear that the sitting down was over, the
talks finished. I felt no regret—or any other emotion. I felt
drained, dry-eyed, tired. It was to continue for a long time,
this deadness. I think now, but am not sure, that Silva's blunt

sharpness with me over the three days was an attempt to relight a spark, to bring life back. I am not sure.

We said very little else. Our farewell was brief. I never saw him again.

vine leaf mosaic

6 Reuben

Measure Jugs

6

When I got back to our tent-house Sarah was waiting. Judith had taken the children to see the goats. I told her all about my morning, and about Reuben, who was to take up my afternoon. She listened, as always, with care.

'A strange one, that Silva. According to some of the men, very fair but very cruel. Quite ruthless. Hard as rock. No one will ever know *that* one's thoughts, lovey, so don't *you* try.'

'I promise.'

She busied herself with preparations for the children's return and meal. I helped, using the time to tidy my mind and prepare questions for Reuben in the way that Silva had taught me.

In the event, all I had to do was listen—and make notes—for the old man's mind was as orderly as the shape of his words.

Upon arrival at Silva's house I was taken immediately to the courtyard. The sun was high and it was extremely warm but the area below the awning was cool, and restful. Reuben was waiting, sitting in Silva's chair rather primly, with hands on knees and space between the chairback and his body.

He did not get up but gave the little nod and waited till I had seated myself.

'A tiring walk for you at this time of day.' The voice was silvery, with a slight quaver, educated.

'Not really. It is not far and I was eager to come.'

'I have arranged for cool drinks to be brought, and some sweetmeats I concocted myself.' His assumption of the position of host along with the host's chair was natural, and very charming. 'They will come right away.' And they did.

We used the drink and confections (which were delicious) to ease our way into acquaintance. He nibbled only, and sipped. His form was very spare, and his head was small, delicate, the skin fine and lined. His hair was pure white, and seemingly had no weight, for it floated rather than lay close. His forehead was high and had visible veins in the temple hollows. His cheek-bones were prominent, and the nose bony. The chin was hidden in a beard as white and gentle as his hair. His hands and feet were long, stringy, old. He wore a grey robe, rope-belted, which left his forearms and lower legs bare. His sandals were worn, dried-up.

The niceties completed, he sat silently, gathering thoughts, his eyes distant.

'I met Eleazar of Masada only once,' he mused, and the odd title diluted the pain of hearing the name. It was meant to, I think. 'And it is of his family I shall speak.' It was on my tongue to tell him that I was of that family, that I was cousin to Eleazar, but I did not, and became wiser by the omission.

'I am, as far as I can calculate, some seventy years old,' said Reuben, with raised eyebrows, as if in surprise, 'and of late, I must admit, I seem to recall better the things of my childhood than those of last week.

'I am of Galilee, of a long-living family, and there have been scribes and priests in our line for many generations. I have been both, arriving at no position of eminence in either calling. It is in my nature to be a looker-on, a spectator. We have our place, we who are a little detached.' A sharp glance from very alert grey eyes. 'You would understand, I think.'

'Yes.'

'How famous your Eleazar and your friends of the mountain were. The word zealot will, I'm sure, go into our language. I hope so; they gave it an honourable meaning.' He paused, his eyes unfocused, thinking. 'Yet nothing is new; nothing happens except in relation to what has gone before. Your

Eleazar's uncle, Menahem, who was my second cousin and born in the same year as me, took Masada from the Romans some seven years ago, seizing its store of arms to equip the men who were with him and his followers in Jerusalem. It was a courageous and much-talked-of venture.'

'And timely. We were very short of arms in Jerusalem—of any kind.'

'Yes. Audacious, and typical of Menahem. Yet he was repeating, perhaps without knowing it, an action taken by his own father over seventy-five years ago—five years before Menahem and I were born.'

'The taking of Sepphoris?'

'The taking of Sepphoris. By Judah the Galilean, father of Menahem. Great Herod had died that year and there was much confusion. My own father, a peaceable man, was drawn into the "No Ruler but God" movement started by Judah and found himself emptying the armoury of Sepphoris in exactly the way that Judah's third son, Menahem, armed his men from the arsenal of Masada. It was one of the few adventures of my rather timid father's life and he was proud of it. When I was a child I heard the story many times, and thought my father rather a hero. Masada and Sepphoris. An interesting repetition of history, would you not agree?'

'In the matter of the raiding of the arsenals, yes.'

He was gentle with me. 'I meant only in so far as the armouries were concerned. The revolt was soon suppressed, with great cruelty, by Varus of Syria, and the people of Sepphoris were made slaves. Masada held out for seven years—and avoided slavery.'

'And avoided slavery.'

He gave his attention to an insect on his forearm; and then to a nearby flower in a stone urn. It was tactful and relaxed.

'Judah the Galilean was not enslaved,' he continued mildly, 'nor my father. They escaped, and others also. To Damascus. A wise move. Many Jews in Damascus, many friends. It was in Damascus some ten years later, when I was five, that we heard about the new troubles. Bigger troubles. A bad year, that one, here in Israel. Archelaus, son of Great Herod and king after him, was taken off his throne by Rome and sent away. He was not mourned—indeed it was the people who asked Rome to get rid of him. A bad king, who did great harm and inflicted terrible cruelties.'

'Had Archelaus ruled over all that his father had ruled?'

'No. Over half. The rest was divided between his brothers, Antipas and Philip. Herod knew that his sons were not like him.'

'Didn't Rome have a say in the division?'

'Rome had a say in everything, but kept away. Archelaus made it necessary for them to come nearer; to come among us. A bad year.'

'Was Judah with you in Damascus during those ten years?'

'No. Apparently he and his followers went to the monastery at Qumran—or so my father believed. Certainly Judah would have had no freedom under Archelaus. He had no use for kings, even good ones. "No Ruler but God" is no new idea, good Ruth. 'Tis said that Hezekiah, Judah's father, began it.'

'Is it certain that Judah was with the community of Qumran?'

'It is logical to think so. His followers and the Essene order of Qumran were not so different in their way of life—or in their closeness to God. They *needed* no ruler but God. They obeyed God's every rule and commandment with absolute devotion.'

'Were not the Essenes of seventy years ago a closed, pacifist order? Men of peace? Men who had taken refuge in the wilderness?'

'Not quite. To live in the wilderness, for whatever reason, requires great fortitude, great discipline. As to their being pacifist, I'm constantly surprised that this idea persists. It is not *against* God to fight for what is right; for what is God's will. And who was more likely to take up arms for God the King, the only King, than the Essenes of old, hardened desert-dwellers. Your late, brave friends had the same blood in their veins.'

We were both silent for a moment. Reuben gave me a slightly concerned look, for fear he had made me sad, but was reassured. A tearless one, me.

'Archelaus went away,' he continued, 'and Rome sent us a new kind of ruler, called a "procurator". We would be allowed our tetrarchs, our part-kings, our puppet-princes, but over them would be a man of Rome, a procurator. And so Coponius came to us with orders to count us and classify us for taxation and other purposes. We were to be reminded that our country was a very small and unimportant piece of a mighty empire, whose head was no king but an emperor! An emperor declared divine by priests trained to make such declaration.

'So Coponius came to count us and take tribute and tax from us, and soon Judah appeared also, his words making even more sense. "To pay the tribute," he said, "to pay the tax was to acknowledge heathen rule when our duty was to God alone." He raised a revolt, with many followers. But we were shown that procurators were not just tribute-gatherers and head-counters. The revolt was crushed with the utmost savagery. Hundreds were killed—Judah too—and many crucified. The Romans have always had a great belief in crucifixion as a corrective for disloyal thoughts in subject peoples.

'Judah was killed and his body displayed, with others of his party, as a warning. We were to be left in no doubt that small pieces of great empires did as they were told, without disturbance or argument. Judah left three sons: Menahem, who was my age, five, and Jacob and Simon, who were older. Their mother and mine were cousins. After Judah was killed they all came to live in Damascus. At first with us, and then after a little while in their own house not far away.

'We went back to Galilee when I was nearly twenty. Not to Sepphoris, but to Capernaum, where my father had some family. At Capernaum was a college connected with the Great

Temple in Jerusalem, where scribes for holy books were trained. I was scholarly and had a bent in that direction.

'Coponius had gone and the procurator who succeeded him also. Gratus was now our procurator. In Rome the divine Emperor Augustus had died in a most mortal way and the divine Tiberius reigned.'

'Did Menahem's family go back to Galilee with you?'

'No. They had gone earlier, to Bether, just below Jerusalem. He and his brothers were absolutely united in the matter of continuing the work their father had begun.'

'Did you keep in touch with Menahem and his brothers?'

'Yes. But we did not meet often until I finished my studies and went to live in Jerusalem. That was when I was twenty-five, and it was the year that Gratus went home and Pontius Pilate came to us as procurator. Antipas was tetrarch of Galilee and Caiaphas High Priest in the Temple. I had much to do with Caiaphas. I was part of the archives department of the Temple and Caiaphas took a great interest in our work. He was a little overshadowed by his father-in-law Annas, who was the real power behind the throne—and everybody knew it. In the same way, Lady Herodias was the power behind Antipas. He was a fair ruler, Antipas, and in some respects strong, but his wife Herodias made of him a weakling and a fool. I met Herodias a number of times. A frightening woman.'

He was silent for a few moments as though considering which path to follow in his memory. I asked no question.

Ivory & bone objects

'Pilate was a bad man,' he said at last, softly. 'A man of great arrogance—and great power. He cared nothing for the feelings or thoughts of the people he was sent to rule. Yet he was basically a coward. A refined, Rome-educated bully. I did not approve of him.'

I could not resist it. 'Was he aware of your disapproval?'

The gentlest smile. 'No, good Ruth. A scribe does not, in his thirties, tell a Roman governor of his disapproval. One observes, and waits.'

'For what?'

'For justice, for the moment of overreaching—and the fall. Pilate lasted ten years and left Judea in disgrace. Recalled. A bad man. He used great force to rule, great cruelty. The scourge and the cross. If Archelaus pointed the way to revolution, so did Pilate. During his time a hunger grew in the people for a deliverer, a Messiah. There was a return to simple baptism, to simpler speech in prayer. Some fine preachers emerged, not from the Temple, but from the people. Fishermen, carpenters, tax-gatherers . . . more than thirty years ago . . . were you born?'

'No.'

'Pilate left and then Marcellus came. Soon, in Rome, the divine and immortal Tiberius was helped to a rather unheavenly end by the divine Caligula, who reigned in his place. Talk to Lucius, Ruth, about that period. He was at court and it will interest you—and have some bearing.'

'I will. Was the town of Tiberias on the Sea of Galilee named after Tiberius?'

'Yes. Built by Antipas in his honour. Antipas admired all things Roman, and loved building as much as Great Herod, his father. The building of Tiberias did him little good. Tiberius was dead soon after. Then a lot of lies were told to the new emperor, Caligula, about Antipas, and he and his Herodias found themselves in great trouble.'

'Who told the lies about Antipas?'

'His own brother-in-law, Agrippa, brother of Herodias, and

like her a person of great ambition. But a remarkable man, Agrippa. Lucius knew him well.'

He went quiet again. Again sorting the mind.

'Caligula, friend of Agrippa, who reigned only four years, also added fuel to the fire that was to burn our country. He was mad, I think. Not at first; being an emperor made him mad. He issued edicts and announced plans that proved it. One of his plans would have brought to our poor little country destruction and carnage. You may say that it *has* come. True, but it could have come thirty years ago.'

'What was the plan?'

'To erect a statue of himself, as Jupiter, in the Temple in Jerusalem. In the Holy of Holies. Lucius knows more of this than I.'

'I will talk to him.'

'Good. It is of Rome, and Rome belongs in your book. It was in Rome, after Caligula, that Agrippa found himself cast in a strange role. A kingmaker. Again Lucius; a good story.'

He seemed now rather weary. I asked him if he would like to stop, to rest, for we had covered much ground. He assured me that he was perfectly well able to continue, and we did, but it would be of value, good reader, if we return to Reuben's words after we hear Lucius, to whom I spoke that same day in the officers' mess, not far from Silva's house.

7 Lucius

western Palace
floor mosaic

7

'I was about eighteen when I first met Agrippa,' said Lucius, 'but I'd heard a lot about him. He had been educated in Rome and stayed on, supported by his mother. He seemed to be known to everyone. He was a courtier. He had been a great friend of Drusus, Emperor Tiberius' younger son, right up until Drusus died. Soon after his friend's death, Agrippa went home, for his mother had died also and his allowance stopped: he left a great many unpaid bills. His credit, even as grandson of Herod the Great, was not endless, and at home he nearly starved. Then his uncle Antipas, married to his sister Herodias, kindly gave him a job in government—and told everyone how kind he'd been! Rather silly that, for Agrippa was a very proud man. He was by nature a bestower of favours, not a receiver. He put up with it as long as he could (he had four young children) and then resigned and went back to Rome—which was when I first met him. A good-looking man, about forty-five or six.

'I had just begun at court as a junior equerry and my main work seemed to be the collection of gossip. Agrippa, once he had settled in, started to make friends among important people. He became very friendly with Emperor Tiberius, and a great pal of Gaius, grandson of the emperor's brother. Gaius was then just a private citizen, but rich and popular. When he became emperor after Tiberius he called himself Caligula, and changed, a sort of madness overcoming him; but at that point he was just one of the court, with no great influence. Certainly not enough influence to save his friend Agrippa from half a year in prison.'

'Why was he in prison?'

'An error in tact. He made a most lavish dinner party for Gaius and the drink flowed. At one point Agrippa sat Gaius in a great carved chair and knelt in front of him, offering up a prayer that Tiberius might soon die so that he, Agrippa, might have the joy of seeing Gaius lord of the world. The emperor got to hear of it and was furious—and threw Agrippa into a dungeon. No trial—and no apologies accepted. He could be very rough, the old man. In fact he did soon die, helped on his way by Gaius, some said.

'Gaius was proclaimed emperor, changed his name to Caligula, and Agrippa was released. There is a legend attached to Agrippa's stay in prison, if you are interested.'

'I am interested in everything. Reuben said that "all has a bearing". I think so too. Please tell me.'

'It is called the Legend of the Owls. One day, when Agrippa was in the exercise yard of the prison, standing under the only tree and feeling very depressed and shut away from the life he loved, a large owl suddenly alighted on the branch right over his head. In daylight. He was superstitious, and terrified by the huge staring eyes looking down into his own. He could not move. Then the owl flew away. A fellow prisoner from Germany, with some reputation as a soothsayer, told him that the owl was a sign of good luck, and that he would soon be as free as the owl. "But," said the German, "be warned also; if an owl rests above your head again in daylight, you will die, in five days".'

'Did it come to pass?'

'May I continue the story of Caligula?'

'Yes. Forgive me.'

'Caligula freed Agrippa and made him tetrarch of the lands in the north of Israel in place of Philip, Agrippa's uncle, who had just died. Agrippa didn't rush to sit on his new throne. He stayed on in Rome for over a year. When he did finally go home he found that his sister Herodias was very put out indeed by his becoming equal to—if not better than—her husband Antipas, also a tetrarch. She was bitterly jealous and couldn't rest—or let poor Antipas rest either. So she nagged and nagged until he agreed to go with her to Rome to ask Caligula for a kingdom, at least. Agrippa was told of the trip and made his own plans—and a more experienced intriguer you couldn't find. When Antipas got to Rome a fully prepared case of treason and disloyalty was waiting for him and he and the good Herodias were banished. His lands were added to those of Agrippa who, now that he had so much, decided to be a king and not a tetrarch. Caligula made no objection. Nothing was too good for his old friend. Why should he *not* be a king? After all, he, Caligula, was a *god*, as everyone knew.'

'Reuben spoke of a statue of Caligula as a god, as Jupiter.'

'Yes. Some Greeks in Alexandria broke into a synagogue and erected an altar to the God-Emperor Caligula. The Jews threw it out—and Caligula took it very personally. His divinity was in doubt. He should have left well alone. We had had trouble in the past with how touchy the Jews were about their "one and only God". He should have crucified a few and handed out a few big fines and forgotten it. Instead, he decided to replace their one and only God with himself, as Jupiter, in marble and gold, twice life size, to be placed in the Temple in Jerusalem, in the Holy of Holies, the sanctum sanctorum.

'I was much involved, and remember it well because it was my first trip abroad. Caligula ordered me to go to Syria and tell Petronius, who had recently been appointed legate there, what he had decided to do and to make all arrangements for setting the statue in place. No expense to be spared.

'I was given seals and letters of authority to show the matter was of the utmost urgency and the fastest possible route was worked out for me. I felt most important. I was only twenty-one and it was a long journey, nearly two months usually; we did it in about six weeks. Petronius was up in the north, in

Antioch, settling in and getting the feel of his new job and the country. I knew the content of the despatch but not the details, which made Petronius go pale—and me too. Caligula's orders were that the statue was to be taken to Jerusalem and erected. There was to be no discussion with anyone. If the Jews objected in any way, the orders were to kill at will and enslave the rest. "Kill and enslave" was not an order unknown in military matters; our empire was not made without such measures, but to use it upon people at peace, already occupied, and for such a reason, was lunacy.

'But Petronius was a professional soldier and he gathered his forces. Eventually we marched south with no less than three full legions and a very large auxiliary army of Syrians. By the time we left, the whole country knew what was to happen and the Jews were in turmoil. Many were in absolute despair. Others just did not believe it—until they saw the statue, which was not hidden. It was huge, in marble, glittering with gold and silver and precious stones. It was mounted upright on its own carriage and marched at the head of the column, with trumpets and drums in front and behind. Flanking were officers on matched white horses, each carrying standards of Imperial Rome in gold and showing the head of Caligula—these also to be placed in the Temple. All as laid down in the orders brought by Equerry Lucius to Legate Petronius.

'We went through absolutely silent villages, though we knew them to be Jewish. Silent except for weeping and the wail of prayers. It made the men jumpy. Below Tyre we took a more inland route, passing west of Gischala, and then went towards the coast again, to Ptolemais.

'Outside the city, on the plains, were the Jews, in their thousands. I was curious to see how Petronius, whom I'd come both to like and respect, would cope, for his orders were very clear indeed, giving him the absolute power of the emperor. No discussion, the orders said.

'He halted the column and asked for the leaders and spokesmen of the Jews, who spoke with a certain dignity. Petronius listened with great patience and without expression, or comment. Then made up his mind to be firm and clear. "Not a discussion," he told me, "that's against orders. A clear statement."

'He spoke of the great might of Rome, of the great power of the emperor, who ruled half the world. He pointed out that *all* the subject races had statues of Caesar among their own gods; that for the Jews alone to object was not only unreasonable but was tantamount to rebellion and deliberate insult, carrying awful penalties, which he would be quite happy to describe.

'The Jews' Elders were not much dismayed by this and went into some detail about their ancient Law and customs. "Our Lord God", they said, "does not permit graven images of *any* kind to be placed *any*where in our land, let alone in his Holy Temple, built to his glory." They went on at some length, and finished by saying that they had no choice but to obey their Lord God.

'Then Petronius, who looked very strained, asked them if they wanted to fight mighty Rome and great Caesar over such a matter. To go to war.

'They were silent, and then the Elders made a path and a very old man came forward, obviously their most venerable and respected Rabbi or Leader or such. He was supported on each side by younger men, with great care.

'"We pray and offer sacrifice for Rome and its people every day," he said, "twice a day. And for great Caesar also. But if Caesar wishes to set up an image in the middle of our lives, in the Temple of Jerusalem, then *he* must make sacrifice, of a whole people; for we are prepared to perish here with our wives and children before this shall happen—as are our brethren in the other parts of this land, with *their* children." His voice was silvery and very clear. That was all he said, not another word. I shall never forget it.

'There was absolute quiet. Then Petronius told them that he would make no decision for a day or two, and we withdrew.

'During the next few days he called meeting after meeting, big public ones, with hundreds present, and small private ones with their leading citizens and men of most influence. He was patient and careful. He tried everything: persuasion, advice, a soft voice and the "Roman" tone. He detailed the risks, the terrible anger of Caligula, his own difficult position.

'Nothing he said had any effect at all. Poor Petronius. He hardly slept for days. We shared a large apartment, and on about the eighth morning he came into my bedroom. He looked awful. "We are going back to Antioch," he said. "I come of farming stock and this land should have been sown weeks ago. The people pray and fast and wait but they don't work their land. We can have both carnage *and* famine. You will go back to Caligula at once, with all speed, and tell him what has gone on here. Tell him that unless he wants to destroy both the people and their rich crops he must allow them their ancient Law and forget the statue."'

'How did the emperor react when you told him everything?'

'Like a madman. He smashed things and frothed at the mouth. He hurled a boy slave so violently against a pillar that his skull was cracked like an egg. Then he kicked the child's body till he tripped over it and fell, and lay screaming like a stuck pig. I was afraid to move, like everyone else. We stood and waited for our god-emperor to get up. When he did, he was calm and in a rage even more dangerous. He told me to take a letter back to Petronius, right away, to say that the statue was to be erected as ordered and that he, Petronius, must expect death as punishment for delaying the execution of that order.

'I left within the hour. And as good weather and fair winds had blessed and hastened my first voyage, so great storms and hurricanes bedevilled my second. More than three months it took me to return to Antioch, and every day at sea was a misery, for I was as distressed in mind as I was in body.

'At last the endless journey was over, and as we docked Petronius came aboard and straight to my cabin. We faced each other and I was truly sick at heart.

'He listened to me without speaking and I gave him the letter. He broke the heavy seals, unrolled it and read it slowly.

Then he tore it across and threw it down. He began to laugh
and for a moment I thought his reason, his mind, had gone.
But it was a real laugh, and he put his hands on my shoulders.
"Forgive me, Lucius," he said, "but it was too good a moment
not to enjoy. Caligula is dead. He was assassinated only a few
days after you left. The messengers bringing me news of his
death took a different sea route from you, had a much calmer
voyage and arrived nearly a month ago!" Then he started to
laugh again and so did I, and we laughed till we cried.'

In recalling the moment Lucius laughed anew, freely, but
soon ceased, for I could not join in. I am poor company for a
laughing man. To cover the slight awkwardness I said: 'Thank
you for this of Petronius and Caligula. What of Agrippa and the
Legend of the Owls?'

He chuckled. 'No. Too soon. A gap to be filled in first. After
the mad Caligula, who came next, my historian?'

'Claudius.'

'Correct. Claudius, of the halting speech and the shy ways
and the pale face. Claudius, so silent when a child that people
thought him backward. Nephew of Tiberius, uncle to Caligula.'

'Reuben said that in the matter of the Emperor Claudius,
Agrippa was involved. Reuben used the word "kingmaker"
and said you knew the story.'

'Indeed I do, but not first hand. From my father, who was
of the Senate and told the story well, and with a certain malice,
which was his way. I was not there. Will you accept the story
of the *son* of an eyewitness?'

'Willingly. You could not have been there. You were here in
Israel, with Petronius, laughing. And before that, for three
months at sea.'

'Correct, my historian! You are a careful listener.'

'Thank you. Who assassinated Caligula?'

'It is difficult to say. He had many enemies and treated with
contempt the "old" families, the aristocracy, the patricians.
Many thought that the patricians had arranged the killing.
Certainly their behaviour following the killing had a certain

ready-for-the-moment feel about it. In the Senate there was immediate tension between the patricians and the military junta, the generals of the praetorian guard. Almost before Caligula was cold the generals were searching for the next emperor, and in his own apartment, where he lived secluded and out of sight, they found Claudius. He was the one, the perfect puppet—and indeed the only choice—*and* next in line! They were a powerful group, the praetorian guard, and they issued a proclamation and rushed Claudius out of the city to a huge army camp. Poor Claudius, who loved a quiet life, found himself surrounded by arms and power and shouting men.

'The Senate remained calm. A motion was tabled which ordered the remaining military to guard the city and, in view of the mad savagery of the late Caligula, to take all necessary action to prevent his uncle, Claudius, of the same blood, taking over the throne. Then they passed resolutions to restore the Rule by Aristocrats, the patrician way, as in the old days.

'At this point, enter Agrippa, on a visit to Rome. Although in my opinion I think he was looking after his interests. He knew the ways of Rome very well; better than many Romans. Also, he had a marvellous political subtlety. Anyway, there he suddenly was, in the Senate, in the middle. The obvious go-between. First he listened carefully to the patricians and then he went, invited, to the generals, and listened as carefully. Back and forth he trotted, with Rome teetering on the edge of civil war. Claudius could not handle the situation, but Agrippa could, and did. There was no violence at all. At his instigation the Senate were invited to the generals' camp and made welcome, and right away a great thanksgiving service was held to thank God for his timely intervention—and for making Claudius emperor. When the service was over, to thank Agrippa for his timely aid, Claudius gave him all the lands in Israel that had been Great Herod's, and more.

'Agrippa went home right away, feeling rather an emperor himself. But he soon found that the mixture of moderate Claudius and powerful patricians made a very strong Rome.'

Lucius was silent for a moment, looking thoughtfully at me. He spoke then, with a certain tact.

'From that strong Rome came a sharp order some time later which, if disobeyed by Agrippa, would have made this conversation unlikely.'

I made no answer.

'Agrippa, with his now huge income from his much enlarged kingdom, spent freely, to the public good. Now a great king, he became kingly, with a mild manner and a careful observance of his religion. He put up many fine buildings and began to construct a wall around Jerusalem which, if completed, would have been impregnable—or so it was said.' He paused. 'Marcus of Syria wrote and told Claudius about the wall and the sharp order came from Rome to stop the work at once. Which Agrippa did. . . .'

There was nothing to say. The unfinished great wall of Agrippa was a fact of life. It was known to me.

'Soon after, Agrippa died,' said Lucius—and then, to lighten it, 'Time for the Owl Legend! Are you ready? How much do you recall?'

'That a German soothsayer told Agrippa that as one owl once brought a great change in his life, so the appearance of another would end it.'

'Well done. It ended in Caesarea, in the fifty-fourth year of his life. He was in his prime. He was popular, and deservedly so. He ruled fairly and showed good sense at all times. He had four children and was proud of them. Claudius trusted him so much that for three years Israel had had no procurators. If Agrippa still had the vast ambitions and vanities of old he kept them firmly in check.

'Until Caesarea. Agrippa had organized a great Festival of Games in honour of Claudius, to whom he owed so much. Every important person from far and near was there, the Greeks and Syrians and Romans far outnumbering the Jews.'

'Were *you* there? Or is this still your father's story?'

'No. I was there as a junior consul representing Rome. I was, with other important persons, in Agrippa's own royal box on the west side of the arena. I saw everything.'

'Please go on.'

'It was mid-morning on the second day of the games and we were waiting for Agrippa to arrive and start the first event. He made a marvellous entrance. Into the arena in a huge chariot behind eight white horses. He was in the most splendid robes I've ever seen, all made of Damascus cloth, a fabric which was almost entirely pure silver. Head to toe, everything: shoes, gloves, the tall head-dress, everything. Superb jewels. The chariot circled the arena, which was in shade, and stopped by the curved staircase which led up to the royal box. As Agrippa came up the stairs he came into full sunlight. He glowed and shone in the most astonishing way. Cheering broke out; wild applause. Then the Greeks and Syrians began the "flattery shouting" that they've made into a sort of poetic art. Caligula had some of them at court. Sickening.

'"You are a god!" they sang. "Before this we thought you a man, a great king, but mortal; a man. Now we see thee for what thou art," they yelled, "a god! Is he not a god?" they screamed into the crowd, and soon the whole arena was calling Agrippa a god.

'And he didn't stop them. He stood, in glittering silver from head to foot, above him the criss-crossed ropes from which hung the flags and flowers. He stood still, hearing the mob making him into a god and not stopping them.

'Then he looked up and right above his head was an owl. In broad daylight, among thousands of yelling people, an owl. Staring down into his eyes in exactly the same terrifying way as the other owl, the first owl (perhaps the *same* owl) seven years before.

'Agrippa was as white as a sheet as he took his seat. The yelling went on, calling him a god and he did not stop it. It died away and the games began. Suddenly Agrippa clutched his stomach, in the most violent pain.

'It is recorded that five days later he bade a humble farewell to his friends, pointing out that "declared a god by men, he was now to die in a very mortal fashion and to be taken from this life by the real God".'

'As foretold by the soothsayer.'

'As foretold.'

8 Again Reuben, and Sarah

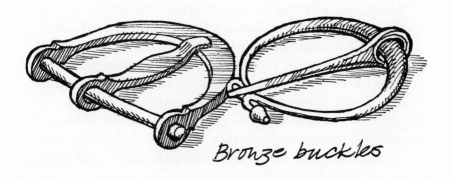

Bronze buckles

When Lucius was finished, I returned to Reuben for the continuation of his story. Reuben spoke tidily, covering no ground that he knew 'the Roman' would have covered. He had a certain respect and liking for 'the Roman' and Lucius returned those feelings.

'Although,' said Reuben, 'the Roman, for all his mild ways and his good manners, is a great cynic. However, as I was saying, if Agrippa's son, our present Agrippa, had been a little older when his father died we might have remained free of our procurators, our Roman overlords.

'Young Agrippa was seventeen, and in Rome, living in the palace, part of the household of Claudius, who was fond of him. The young man had all his father's shrewdness; the same skill with people; the same persuasiveness. His three sisters were here in Israel, the eldest, Bernice—you are acquainted with the various doings of that one?'

'Not many facts: street talk, dirty jokes, scandal.'

'Bernice was one year younger than her brother, sixteen. She was married to her uncle, Herod of Chalcis, her father's brother, who ruled in the north. Her sisters Drusilla and Mariamne were ten and six. There is a story that the two schoolgirls were abducted and violated by soldiers of Caesarea and Sebaste whose people bore some grudge against the late king. A stupidity, if true, for Agrippa—and Antipas before him—had treated both towns well. However, girl-ravishings or not, there were disturbances in both places and rude things said about

Rome and the just-dead king. When Claudius was told, he was very annoyed. His advisors told him not to send young Agrippa to succeed his father but to go back to rule by procurator till the young prince was older. Claudius agreed and sent to us Cuspius Fadus, who tried his best. Claudius was very anxious that this troublesome province, this Israel, should remain at peace. It was a bad time here in Israel during Fadus and the procurator who followed him, Tiberius Alexander. There was much famine in the land.'

'I remember it. I was about nine when it began and the rationing seemed to go on for years.'

'It did. Bad times. A strong man, Fadus. Better than his successor, who was a most careful choice by Claudius and seemed an inspired thought.'

'Why?'

'Tiberius Alexander was of most distinguished and wealthy family. An ancient *Jewish* family. He was the nephew of Philo the philosopher. He was well-educated, and could have been a great success. He was a great failure. There was much unrest in the country, all sorts of anti-Roman murmurings were beginning. All made worse by the famine and the inevitable black markets and inequality. Alexander received orders to calm things down just as Menahem and his brothers came back on the scene. His two brothers were arrested as ringleaders and Alexander had them crucified.

'Alexander, of Jewish lineage, was no Jew. He was raised and educated in Rome and followed no religion other than being "a Roman"—even down to the use of the cross. Menahem's brothers were well-known and liked. Leaders were emerging when leaders were needed. Menahem, who had been in hiding, came to my house about a month after the executions and there was a change in him. "It has begun," he told me. "God knows where it will end."

'Soon after, Alexander was replaced by Cumanus, who took over unrest and caused more. At roughly the same time young Agrippa's uncle, Herod of Chalcis, husband of Bernice, died and Claudius decided to let the prince take over his uncle's dominion. So Agrippa got both a kingdom and his beloved sister back. Bernice, a widow at twenty, with two children. The young king buried his uncle with great pomp. And the stories about Bernice and her brother began almost immediately.

'Cumanus was our procurator for about four years, and during his time there was a great deal of trouble. Eventually Claudius banished him for his bad rule. Bad indeed, for early in his four years took place the terrible Passover Riot of which you may have heard.'

'Yes, I have. Sarah of Masada—of whom *you* may have heard—?'

'Indeed yes. The whole camp knows of Sarah.'

'She lost her family on that day. All except a grandson.'

He was quiet for a moment, and then said: 'Why not let Sarah of Masada take up the story from here? For not only will she tell you of that day better than I, but,' with a smile, 'she will be less tired.'

'Forgive me, I am selfish—'

'There is nothing to forgive. It is not the talking, it is the recollection that talking brings to life.'

Soon I left him and went back to Sarah and the children. She was sitting outside our tent-house, enjoying the night air, the children asleep. I told her of my day.

'A good start,' she said.

'Yes. Silva was right. The background is important. Essential.'

'Are you tired?'

'Not very.'

'Do you want to hear the whole story of the Passover Riot?'

'Only if it does not cause you pain.'

A chuckle. 'It's nearly twenty-four years ago, lovey. No more pain. My husband was killed, and my son, and his wife, as I've told you more than once. No more pain. No, if I sit and talk about that day, comfortable and cool in the dark, and I laugh out loud, I won't have to look into your beautiful shocked face.'

'Laugh?'

'Lovey, your old Reuben, because he is old, and wise, sees things in their proper order and importance. Background. Where things start. Our Masada was the end of something. A vast rebellion, by a tiny country, against impossible odds. Reuben showed you all sorts of beginnings, starting points, first flames, yes?'

'Yes.'

'Well, *I* think the Passover Riot in Jerusalem began the war. It was twenty years before Jerusalem fell and half a life ago, but that's when *I* think it began. Will you accept that?'

'Yes.' A brand-new historian does not argue with a Mother Zealot who became a childless widow on the day in question. But in the words she used there was a lift of humour and I was curious. A 'laugh in the dark' had to be explained.

'Good. Now, my dove, if the Passover Riot began the war, what, you might well ask, began the Riot?'

'Tell me. I don't know.'

In the dark, her voice was warm and full of laughter. 'Perhaps I *should* have told you in daylight, to *see* your face! The Riot which started the war was begun by an enormous *fart!*' Her great laugh rang out and one of the children, startled, called out. In a moment she was silent and inside, with a word of comfort. She was right; I was shocked, as I later realized she meant me to be. 'Heroes,' she once told me, 'are people—and people are mostly ordinary, and ridiculous. God made us so.'

She was back. 'You knew Jerusalem, lovey, and the Temple. On the Big Festivals, the Romans stationed hundreds of soldiers round the top of the outer colonnades to keep an eye on the thousands of people in the worship area. The Romans did not like large crowds. They did not mix with the worshippers, but above, always, there they were. You must have seen it a dozen times.'

'Yes. Don't miss anything out.'

'Well, the tops of those colonnades could get very warm and the soldiers used to get both thirsty and bored—and the bottles used to pass. Down below we hardly gave them a glance. They were quiet and did not fidget much. Part of the scenery; part of the Festivals.

'Well, on that day, during the silent prayer part of the morning service, one of the soldiers called out something—most unusual, to *hear* them—and as people looked up he turned his back, bared his arse, and trumpeted forth!

'The crowd went crazy. Some of them started to throw stones at the soldiers, then it was seen that Cumanus was above, and they demanded that the soldier be punished. Some of the wilder elements in the crowd started to look for a way up to the soldiers. Cumanus lost his head and sent for more troops, the heavy infantry, with the big bows and longswords; the "macemen", who scared everybody. When they arrived the whole Temple area was full of angry screaming people. The troops poured in through the colonnades, holy ground or not, Passover or not, straight into the crowd. A panic started, and thousands of people tried to get out of the same exits, the passages down to the Huldah gates, the south gates. A tidal wave; a flood of unarmed people, who fell and were trodden to death. Trampled and crushed and killed in their hundreds. Nearly everyone I knew lost somebody. I was in good company, my dove. Come, let's go to bed.'

I put my arms round her and kissed her. Her cheeks were dry. Her hug was quick and warm. With her cheek next to mine.

'Not even a *Jewish* fart, lovey!'

By mid-morning the next day the twins, who seemed to know everything, were back with stories of packings up and sortings out, with rumours. That the camp was soon to move out; to move on; to Egypt, to Greece, to Cyprus; to sea, to the north, to the south. Sarah went off by herself to see *her* contacts. She was back for the midday meal.

'We'll be on our way back to Jerusalem by the end of the week. We are going home.'

We looked at each other, as the children danced and sang, happy to be going back to a place they had not seen for nearly three years. A place, when they had left it, of smoke and fire and the stench of death.

'Lucky we don't have much to pack,' said Sarah, and to the children, 'We'll make ourselves as useful as we can and not be a nuisance or get in anyone's way.'

After we'd eaten I went across the camp, and indeed there was a different feeling about the place. I went to the servants' part of Silva's house to see how Reuben was. My concern was not wholly for him: he had referred me to Sarah for the part of the story in which she had been directly involved—but I was sure he still meant to tell me more.

My message was taken to him by a young Syrian, slim-built and in cook's apron. His attitude suggested that Reuben had some status in Silva's household. He came back and took me along a passage to a small room. Reuben was sitting on a chair of wood and leather. He got up and gave me the chair, seating himself on the narrow bed which stood along one wall, under a small window. The room was cool and quiet. Reuben looked rather pale and old. He assured me that he was quite well, had slept his usual hour or two, and was free to speak to me.

'My duties are few, and simple, and easily performed by others. I have made a few notes. It would seem to serve no purpose, Ruth, to indulge ourselves too much in the long-past when the recent past is full of such rich episodes, of such importance, of such confusion.'

'Confusion?'

'Would you not agree?'

It had not occurred to me. He waited, his head tilted, his eyes on mine.

'War *is* confusion,' he suggested mildly.

'Yes, you are right.'

He did not pursue it. 'So. Cumanus had gone, banished by

Claudius, who two years later was himself gone, slain after some thirteen years as emperor. A sensible man, much ruled by his fourth wife, Agrippinna, at whose insistence the dreadful Nero, her son, was proclaimed heir. It was rumoured that Claudius was helped to his death by Agrippinna, who knew of poisons—as did Nero, who murdered many, including his mother, his stepbrother, and his stepsister (who was also his wife). A morbidly suspicious half-mad creature, of terrible lusts and cruelty, this Nero. He was eighteen when he became emperor, with power unlimited. For fourteen years he reigned, and the lunacy and cruelty of his court spread through his empire. Our procurators during his time became progressively worse. More and more like him. "Rome" under Nero became an intolerable burden to its subject peoples. He appointed men of his own depraved kind and gave them great authority; power over life and death.

'Fourteen years he reigned, and in his twelfth year—only seven years ago, Ruth my dear—our war began. Our war against Rome and its oppression was in many ways a war against Nero.'

'How did Agrippa get on with Nero?'

'Well. Our king, having inherited all his father's diplomacy, was able to handle Nero. He was about nine years older. Old enough to be a brother, not a father. Nero enlarged Agrippa's kingdom but did not take away the procurators. When Nero became emperor how old were you?'

'Seventeen, nearly.'

'Procurator Felix. Sent by Claudius to replace Cumanus.'

'Yes. Until I was twenty-three. My father said that Felix was once a Roman slave and spent his life getting his own back.'

'Near enough true. But not a "slave", not a servant, not a scullion. A man in bond, eventually made free, a freedman. He was coarse and violent. He was careful when appointed by Claudius, but when kept on by Nero, he changed. Myself, I think he had orders to crush all rebellion, all discontent. He killed thousands, and took pleasure in it. But for every rebel he slaughtered, two more appeared. And with every two rebels, two collaborators, and two more with different aims; and two who wanted rule by priests—and two who wanted no law of *any* kind. Confusion, Ruth?'

'Yes.'

'Your father had comment on this?'

'He said that all the Romans had to do was wait; we would destroy ourselves. My father was by nature an onlooker, not a participant. It was not said in despair, but with humour. When I became a "participant" he told me to allow for your "twos" and I did.'

'Good. Let us continue. With Felix, violence bred violence, as it must. Any sort of meeting or demonstration would bring out the soldiers, who were allowed to do anything they liked. Often the soldiers were alerted by the rival parties, who themselves soon took to arms—and the Sicarii were born, the Men of the Little Knives, who enforced their arguments and thinned out the opposition in their own way.'

'I know of the Sicarii. They were valuable.'

'They became valuable. At the beginning they included many who carried a knife to settle personal feuds; to kill and rob; to kill for a thrill. It was a time of lunacy, of desperation, of confusion. Every kind of party and secret society existed, anti-everything. Every kind of madman could attract followers. Do you remember the Desert Divines who led hundreds into the desert to receive gifts from God—and the Egyptian who gathered thirty thousand on the Mount of Olives ready to take over Jerusalem?'

'Yes, was it not during Felix's time that the troubles in Caesarea began?'

'Yes.' He gave a thin, rather approving smile. 'You have a tidy mind. But you are right; sequence, the right order, will be important in your book.'

He was thoughtful for a moment. 'There is a man, here in the camp, who does a clerical job in the stores. I hardly know him. He is of Caesarea. He was in the civil service or local government or something similar. He can be very unfriendly

I'm told, and has a particular dislike of the young Syrian who showed you in—who can be insolent. It seems the clerk hates *all* Syrians. Not surprising in someone from Caesarea. Ask your friend Sarah if she knows him; he could tell you more of the Caesarea troubles than I can. And your plan to find, as you call them, "participants", is sound.'

We spoke on, reviewing all that he had so far related, filling in detail when I asked a question. When I left, telling him that we were to move out of the camp by the week's end, he promised that we would speak again if I wished.

9 Benjamin

Carved Stone Lintel. Bath-house

9

I spoke to Sarah about the store clerk. She grinned. 'No, lovey, I don't know him. But I will. If you want him, you shall have him.'

'It is said that he can be unfriendly.'

'So can I, lovey. We unfriendly ones understand each other.'

She went off the next morning right after breakfast and was back in an hour. She beamed at the children. 'Judith is in charge. She will take you to the blacksmith who is making an iron cart with wheels and is very clever; he is expecting you. Ruth and I will be back by lunchtime.'

As we went across the camp she said: 'No trouble. He knew of me. Not only from here. He was in Jerusalem at the end.'

We went through an opening in a low wall which encircled a large area where heaps and piles of every sort of war-camp necessity were kept. To one side was a low building with a roof of tent canvas over poles. Inside was a long counter, divided into three cubicles, each containing a man. In the centre, a Roman sergeant, the other two in the drab overalls of the trusty-prisoner, the pressed man; one step up from slave. The sergeant, who was red-headed, started some coarse joke with Sarah, and then weighed me up, and stopped. A blight on honest vulgarity, me. Sarah, not inhibited in the same way, made an ending to his joke no less coarse—and building in a most scandalous reference to his hair. He roared, and turned to the man on his right.

'All right,' he said, 'two hours off! Round the back.'

The man got up without reply and ducked under the rough counter. We followed him out and round the building to the rear where there were some long forms against the wall below an awning made of woven rushes. He pulled one of the forms round so that it was at right angles to the wall, and we sat on it. He sat with his back resting against the rough wall.

All this he did without speaking, with an economy of gesture and movement. Sarah glanced at me with an amused glint, silent also. When we were settled she said:

'Ruth, this is Benjamin. Of Caesarea.'

He nodded. He was a tall man, rather lean, with a long jaw and deep-set eyes of a cold grey colour. His hair was thin and dark but with much white in it. The same ageing (he was somewhat over fifty) was in the lines of his face. His hands were large and strong. He gave off a feeling of strength, of good sense. His voice was rather deep, and dry.

'As the good Sarah says, I am of Caesarea. I was raised there, and educated there, and I was there through all its troubles. Well, perhaps not all, but certainly those of thirteen to fourteen years ago which brought Procurator Felix in among us.

'People remember "the troubles" in Caesarea more than they remember the reason. Especially since Jerusalem fell—which makes all the previous disasters seem rather trivial. But, believe me, the troubles in Caesarea had a lot to do with the war. Some folk think the war *started* in Caesarea. *I* think so.'

'Many would agree with you.' Then, as Sarah turned laugh-in-the-night eyes to me, 'Perhaps not Sarah. What was the reason for "the troubles"?'

'Well, as you know, Caesarea was one of those cities built by Great Herod, and its people were a very mixed lot, mainly Syrian and Jewish. It was a busy, prosperous place. An important port. I was in the tax department, a good place to watch a city grow—and to watch trouble grow. Because the city was the Roman procurator's headquarters, it had a certain Roman feel, but the industrial and commercial feel of the city was in no way Roman. For a long time the city had no clear identity at all. Then the Jews started to say that as Herod, a Jew, had built the city it should be regarded as Jewish and run by a Jewish council. The Syrians agreed that Herod had built it, but on the site of a town once called Strato's Tower, where not a single Jew had lived. Also, they said, he had put in statues and god-temples. Since both were against Jewish Law, he could *not* have meant it for the Jews. Well, it started with arguments, then public meetings and protests and petitions and marches, all getting nowhere. Then the "incidents" began, and militant groups started, and partisans, and terrorists. Soon there was fighting and bloodshed every day. The Jews were well organized and well equipped, but the Syrians were often helped by the soldier force, the troops trained and led by the Romans. Most of that soldier force were Syrian and of course felt it to be their fight.

'The procurator's men, the Roman prefects, arrested ring-leaders of both sides. There were whippings and long prison sentences. They stopped nothing. The riots grew worse. Felix brought in more troops and started to favour the Syrians. Many Jews were killed and their property stolen or confiscated. The other Jews fought the harder, now to revenge wrong. So Felix, having let the whole thing get out of hand, and having taken sides in the most blatant way, then decided to pass the whole matter up to Nero. He chose leading men of both factions and sent them off to Rome to argue it out there.

'Nero had little interest in the troubles of a far-off city and the business went on for years. Delays and postponements and deadlocks and all sorts of behind-the-scenes plotting.'

'What was going on here in Israel meanwhile, in Caesarea?'

'In Caesarea things quietened down to a sort of uneasy peace, with flare-ups every now and then. The tax-office where I worked was just across the way from the procurator's palace and we saw all the comings and goings. We saw Felix, who had started a seething rebellion that was spreading through the country, move out, and Festus, who was to kill so many of the rebels, move in. A strange man, Festus, with a certain intellectual curiosity about us strange Jews—and about the Jews who were also Christians, followers of the Nazarene. Festus took over many troubles, and also an important prisoner, a prisoner important enough to state his case before King Agrippa himself, who came to Caesarea with his sister Bernice, who went everywhere with him.'

Sarah: 'To bed also, 'tis said.'

Benjamin laughed, showing big teeth, more at the blunt delivery of the comment that at its information.

'Who was the important prisoner?' I asked.

'An unusual man. Saul, or Paul, of Tarsus. Of most pious family. When young a student of the great Rabbi Gamaliel, and when grown, a most violent and passionate persecutor of the Christians—until he saw some kind of vision and was converted overnight into just as passionate a disciple. He—'

Sarah: 'We know of him. He has no bearing on the war; on Masada. Am I right, Ruth?'

'Yes. Forgive us, Benjamin, we don't mean to be rude—'

Sarah laughed. 'Not we, *me*!'

'—but we want other things of that time, other parts of your memory.'

Benjamin, undisturbed: 'Festus lasted about two years and shed much Jewish blood. He made great show of trials and hearings and evidence, but to be caught was to die. To be a Jew was to be suspect. Jew and rebel began to mean the same thing. Appealing to Rome was pointless; his orders were from Rome. He was taken home this time of the year eleven years ago.'

'Taken?'

'He was dead. We had a short period without a procurator—about three months.'

'Which brings us to Albinus,' Sarah said grimly. 'It is eleven years since I first laid eyes on that one. In Jerusalem. State arrival of our new procurator. I knew his type at a glance. We had things like him in the market. Anything for money—and rotten to the core!'

'There was a three month gap.'

'A gap, my dove?'

'Between Festus dying and the arrival of Albinus. Benjamin just said so. It has bearing. Can we talk about it? No procurator. The start of the Wicked Priests?'

She looked puzzled, then her face cleared. 'Yes! Of course! I don't know about the *start* of the Wicked Priests. Old Annas had run things in the Temple since I was a girl—and he was no angel, believe me. He made the High Priesthood a sort of family business. Up till then he'd put four of his sons in and a son-in-law, Caiaphas, as top man!'

Benjamin said with a frown, 'He was a terrible man, old Annas. Great power, and enormously rich. When Albinus arrived, eleven years ago, the old man must have been in his eighties and pretty sure in his mind that God knew all about him and that he was on his way to Hell. In Albinus the old man found a wickedness to match his own—and seemed to go mad; to make certain of his place in Hell. Maybe he wanted to take it over, to run it. It was his way.'

Sarah laughed. 'How much do you actually *know*, taxman? Ruth wants facts. It has to be right.'

He looked at me. I said nothing. 'At that time,' he said, 'I worked in both Caesarea and Jerusalem. The revenue network was the most accurate news service in the country. As Zealots you must have used it a thousand times. Right: facts. In about a month old Annas and Albinus—to whom he gave huge money gifts "of welcome"—were as thick as thieves, which is what they were. They began a huge extortion operation, using fear and intimidation and violence—from which they would offer protection, at a price. The old man knew not only that pretty well everyone can be bought, but also that the Temple employees, the great priest force, were pretty well outside the law. Perfect for the lawless schemes he set them to work at. They became like gangs, absolutely controlling—and this is fact— the enormous quantity of produce given to the Temple as a tithe or offering. Its value ran into millions. Animals, grain,

wine, oil, fruits, vegetables—and money. Since the days of
Moses the tithe had supported the priests. Now it became what
bribed them—and paid them—for very *un*holy work. And if you
were too old or too honest for such work you would starve.
And many did. A fact. An uncle of mine was one. A fact. As
with the old man, Annas, so with Albinus. Everything and
everybody had a price. With Albinus, you could buy your way
out of prison or pay for someone else to be put there. Killings
could be arranged. Robbery, arson, destruction of every kind.
My old chief, John, of Caesarea, watched a friend of his, called
Mark, who owned olive groves, brought to poverty in eleven
months—his trees and his house burned down, and his family
injured and frightened half to death. A fact.

'Albinus was procurator for two years and in that time law-
lessness and violence and vice multiplied ten times. People
lived in fear.'

Sarah: 'Not all people. The Sicarii learned how to bargain
during that time. New games. Of kidnap, and ransom, and
prisoner-swap.'

This I knew, from Sarah. But her eye was alight and it could
bear retelling.

'When it's rotten at the top, lovey, it's rotten all the way
down, and it can be used. Many of our lot, the Sicarii, were in
prison. We had no money to buy them out because Annas and
Albinus hated them and the price was high. So we decided to
go into the kidnap business and started with a son of the old
man—a Temple scribe—and told Annas we would like ten
Sicarii for him and that he should ask Albinus to arrange it.
Great family man, Annas. We had our ten back in no time. So
we went on doing it.' She grinned at Benjamin. 'A fact.'

He did not return the smile; was again thoughtful. 'I think
often of that time,' he said rather sadly. 'We were like a lot of
children, out of hand. Or blind men, in fright. So much energy,
for the wrong things. So many different parties, factions, groups.
[I thought of Reuben's "twos".] Your Sicarii were no more
constructive than any of the others at that time. The unity came

too late—or maybe God never meant us to succeed. Maybe the Temple of Wicked Priests was the final insult to the Almighty.'

His eyes were lowered, looking at his knees. When I looked at Sarah she was awaiting my look, and serious.

'Benjamin,' she said, 'we know better than most about the lack of unity, the sinfulness. People are people. Tell us, friend, if you will, of the Leper Insult in Caesarea and then we must talk of Gessius Florus, who came after Albinus.'

I, purist, said: 'Florus came before the Leper Insult.'

Sarah: 'Yes, my dove, yes, but from others we can learn about Florus (we know enough ourselves, by God). From Benjamin, who was there, and involved, we should hear *now*, out of sequence, whilst we have him, of the Insult and what it led to.'

She was right, especially as after we left the camp we did not see Benjamin again. He told us much, in his dry calm voice, and all that he said is in these pages; but of the Insult, a little later, for before it came the terrible Florus, and it must be shown how that Devil made unchangeable the setting for our war.

The Wicked Priests and Albinus brought great misery and suffering; made possible all crimes, ignored law and order. But with secrecy, with plotting and subtlety.

When Florus came he made the others seem like angels in comparison. He was cruelty itself, an executioner, a rapist, a predator. A man without compassion, and of a cunning and greed beyond description. He did not bother with secrecy but trumpeted and displayed his wickedness everywhere. Whole communities were beggared and destroyed by him. Or by those of his kind made safe and rich by his leadership and example. He permitted and encouraged every kind of wrongdoing as long as he shared in the spoils. Many, many people left their homes and the country. 'Refugees from Florus' became almost an official description at the borders.

He was safe in his villainy. Nero, in his tenth year as emperor, was his friend. His wife, Cleopatra, was extremely close to

Nero's wife, Poppea. Indeed it was his wife who used her closeness to the empress to obtain the procuratorship for him. She was as wicked as her husband in every way.

Florus was our procurator for more than a year before the Insult and every day contained more misery than the one before. We have already heard how this or that incident, in the opinion of this or that person, started the war.

Florus made the war.

Florus took us, bleeding, beyond the point of no return.

Florus was a slavemaster, full of a mad hate, and we fought to be free.

Florus began a unity in us that we did not have. Too late perhaps, and to little avail, but we fought *together*.

Florus brought death to tens of thousands—and made war, and thus made Masada, where but one thousand died.

So recollect now, good reader, Procurator Felix, five years before Florus. Felix, who sent the Jewish and Syrian leaders of Caesarea to Rome, to Nero, to argue the rights of the Jews.

For nearly six years the arguments dragged on, with small interest from Nero, till his old tutor Burrus, paid well by the Syrians, persuaded him to find verdict against the Jews. Lucius related this in detail, but it is to Benjamin, of Caesarea, that we must give ear now.

'The verdict, and how it was obtained, made a big difference. What had been a sort of distrustful truce ended, and the fight was on again.

'My chief, John, was a wealthy man and much respected in the Jewish community. He had helped build the synagogue and was one of its Elders. He had been trying, with others, to buy the land next to the synagogue for a long time. It was owned by a Greek who had always refused—and who, since the verdict, had become as scornful of the Jews as the Syrians were. Once the verdict was known, he began to build a factory, of noise and bad smells, right up to and crossing the synagogue entrance, leaving only a filthy passageway for the Jews. Soon the fighting between the builders, supported by crowds of Syrian troublemakers, and the Jews, was going on every day. Suddenly Florus appeared, with his storm troopers and riot police. It was bloody. I lost my best friend that day. John met with a few others and they, knowing Florus well, asked him to stop the building and left five thousand gold pieces on his desk to help him remember their request.

'The next day was the Sabbath. I was the first to arrive at the synagogue. I lived near. I worked my way along the narrow lane left by the builders, a bit puzzled by the absolute quiet, for the building noise and shouting which went on seven days a week was usually louder on our Sabbath. Not one Greek or Syrian to be seen anywhere. I soon saw why. As I turned into the forecourt, there, ahead of me, right in front of the synagogue entrance, was a Syrian bent over an upturned earthen pot killing small birds and shaking the blood everywhere, defiling everything. Painted on the pot were the words JEW LEPERS. I could hardly believe my eyes. The sacrifice, as laid down in Leviticus, for lepers; small birds over an upturned clay vessel. The old insult: all Jews are lepers—and Pharaoh had got rid of us because of that.

'I'm a man of peace but I went straight in. The Syrian had a butcher's knife and I got cut a bit but I put him out of the bird-killing business for good. I lost quite a lot of blood and must have fainted for a few minutes. When I got up the forecourt was full of fighting people. Early worshippers and the crowd of Syrians who'd put the bird-killer up to it and had been hiding in the alley.

'It got worse and worse as the word spread. John and some others rushed over to the procurator's palace to talk to Florus —who wasn't there. He'd taken the money and gone off to Samaria, to Sebaste!

'Jucundus, the Riot Officer, turned up and said he would remove the pot and the dead birds and that we should calm down and start our service. By this time the Greeks and Syrians were all over the place, using animal blood to daub the same words all over the building. Jucundus was shouted down but he and some of our men got the forecourt cleared and the gate locked. Then we had a meeting and waited for John to get back. He told us that he and about a dozen others were going to follow Florus to Sebaste and that the synagogue was to be regarded as defiled and unclean. He told us to go in, remove the Scrolls of the Law and to take them to Narbata, a Jewish town about seven miles away. He asked me how I was and told me he wanted me to go with him to Florus. A woman washed the blood and dirt off my left arm, which was where most of the damage was, and bound it up and off we went. As we made our way across town to the stables it seemed that fighting was going on everywhere.

'We rode hard—it's about twenty miles; and we were shown in to Florus right away. We put our complaint strongly, with the feeling that he knew all about it. We asked his help, telling of the removal of the Scrolls to Narbata. He made no reply. Then John reminded him gently of the gold pieces. At this he stood up, overturning the table, and started to shout at the top of his voice. Soldiers came running and he told them to lock us up for daring to remove Holy Scrolls without his permission, for taking the law into our own hands! He would not listen to a word. As we were being marched out, very roughly, he gave an order and John and I were kept back. Then he told us that we were to go with an escort to Jerusalem and draw ten thousand gold pieces from the Temple Treasury! It was for Nero he said; a special taxing. He was obviously lying.

'We left right away. As we rode up into Jerusalem we could tell from the excited crowds that the Insult was known about. Our escort drew their swords and a big crowd followed us to the Treasury building. John was clever; he stayed on his horse and told the sergeant in charge of us to bring out the two top Treasury Priests. As they came out on to the steps, John gave the message from Florus in his loudest voice, for everyone to hear. The crowd went mad, a great mass of them rushing to the Temple to prepare a petition to Nero to rid us of Florus.'

'A few of the rest,' said Sarah, 'started a kind of insult in return. They rushed down into the market crowds, passing baskets round for poor penniless Florus who needed to steal all the time to stay alive. I joined in. A good laugh. Not very clever. Soon the baskets were everywhere, with notices saying "for poor Florus". Unmentionable things went into those baskets. Not clever.'

She stopped, and was serious. The memory of the few days following 'the collection for Florus' was enough to silence anyone. A memory for tears, for memorial prayers.

Florus, waiting in Sebaste, was told of the offence, and ignoring the strife-torn Caesarea came straight to Jerusalem, mad with temper, and with a small army of horse and foot soldiers. The crowds, who had calmed down, gave him a respectful welcome but the soldiers went straight through them.

By the middle of the next day a huge dais was set up outside the Palace and lined in front of it were all the important people in the city: the High Priests, the Sanhedrin, the rich men, everybody of influence and note.

Florus shouted down at them that he wanted the culprits right away—*all* of them! From below, the spokesmen apologized over and over again for the incident and the offence; said that the few wrongdoers, impossible now to find, did not represent the many—who wanted only peace.

Florus looked like a devil. He was ashen. His soldiers were everywhere. He screamed at them to fan out from where he was standing, right through the upper market as far as the Priests' Palaces and the Theatre—and to confiscate everything. Every house, every shop. Right away, with no warning—and kill anyone in the way. The panic is impossible to describe; the soldiers took madness from Florus and became beasts, mad for blood. Hundreds and hundreds of people were cut down where they stood—or were trapped in narrow streets, with red-wet swords coming from both ends. I can still hear the noise.

Then Florus had crosses erected in front of his dais, his 'judgment seat', and began to scourge and crucify. At will, without trial or question. 'For the market Jews,' he screamed, 'the sword and the mace. For the rich ones, the important ones, the Jews [with a crazed giggle] of "equestrian" rank, the whip and the cross!'

I looked at Sarah, and both she and Benjamin were sharing my recall of those first days of the War, for that was what they were. Only after, long after, did we see that Florus was forcing us into action, was kindling flames.

Sarah, knowing my thoughts as always, said:

'A thing comes to mind, Ruth, of that week. It is of Bernice, and perhaps should be written down. I am not fond of that one, but neither do I know too much of such people. They are not as you and I.'

Benjamin nodded. 'Bernice is more than one woman. I think I know what you are referring to. It should be written; it has bearing. Unless Ruth knows of it? Bernice in bare feet?'

'No. Tell me.'

Sarah: 'She was brave. And for once without the king, who was in Egypt. She was in Jerusalem on a sacrifice pilgrimage, in retreat. She was in the middle of the abstinence month; no wine or rich food, no dressing of the hair, no activity but prayer. When she heard about the killings she sent her personal guards with messages to Florus begging him to stop. He laughed. So she went before him herself, barefoot, with loose hair, like a market woman, and stood before the judgment seat and implored him to show mercy. He ignored her—except to make certain that people were tortured and killed in front of her—and let his half-mad soldiers insult her and threaten her with the same treatment. Had she not run back to the Palace they would have killed her.'

It was written down. Also that she added her voice in the magistrates' protest to Cestius, Legate of Syria, above Florus. About which protest Florus cared nothing. Indeed he provoked in the same week even more death and destruction. Cestius sent a tribune to meet the king on his way back from Alexandria and to tell him the contents of the protest. The people poured out of the city, meeting Agrippa seven miles south. The king and the tribune listened to the stories and when they entered the city saw the evidence '—of Jewish revolt against Rome,' said Florus into the king's other ear. '—Of Jewish rebellion,' he told the tribune; and wrote to Cestius similar lies.

The king was subtle—and weak. He could see that the people were indeed ready for revolt—and with good cause. But he was a king by permission of Rome, of Nero, friend of Florus.

Sarah: 'So he put his sister Bernice, who had earned our respect, up on the roof of the Hasmonean Palace and made a long speech telling us to remember we were a tiny part of the great Roman empire and should keep our voices down for fear of giving offence. He finished in tears and Bernice wept too. So we all calmed down and tidied up and buried our dead. Then the king called another big meeting and told us that we were to obey Florus until Nero saw fit to send us a successor. That did it. We told him and his sister to clear out of Jerusalem, to go back up north to his own lands and not come back.'

And he never did. In the war he fought on the Roman side.

Bronze pan & pitcher

BOOK
TWO

BOOK TWO

10 The Trek to Jerusalem

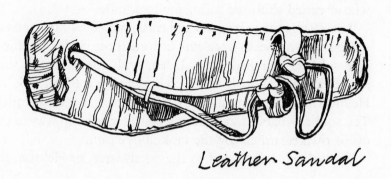

Leather Sandal

It was nearly seven weeks before we left the camp. As promised by Silva we went with the first group, but the operation was a huge one, and there were many delays.

Our group was large. There were about one thousand labourers, now released to return to their homes, all of them Jews. It
was our first sight of our fellow prisoners and we realized how
lucky we had been in the comparative luxury of Silva's camp.
Every face showed suffering; every body, the effects of insuffi-
cient food and too much work. Even though it was for them
the end of forced labour and the return to their families and
freedom there was little lightheartedness. They walked in
silence, husbanding strength, for the terrain was desert, and the
way hard.

Travelling with us was nearly the same number of troops.
About eight hundred, of the Tenth Fretensis Legion, including
camp-erectors, cooks, muleteers, and all the 'worker-soldiers'
whose varied skills we had come to admire.

There were many wagons and carts, pulled by both men and
mules. Such horses as were with us were those ridden by officers.
The soldiers marched heavy-laden, with spear, shield, shortsword, axe and short-handled pick, sleeping roll and food bag.
Helmets were worn at all times, as were breast and back plates.
The soldier's harsh way with the prisoner column was an echo
of his own treatment by the rank above him.

We walked. Inland and to the north-west, to Hebron, then

easterly, but still north to Herodium, then through Bethlehem and Bether to Jerusalem. The prisoners in the column were of those places and at each place the column thinned. The farewells were quiet and tired; people walked away, not looking back, to search for family, to begin again.

The children were remarkable; as if by some private agreement they had decided to be an example. Not to other children, for there were none, but to us who were often silent and aching with exhaustion and despair. Only when the five-year-old Sami was staggering with fatigue would he allow anyone to carry him. The twins' cheerfulness never waned and they heartened many. Little Simon marched with the troops, his six-year-old legs thumping. Judith walked with grace and a certain indrawn solemnity but always returned a smile, and wasn't so enclosed as not to notice an elder stumble and offer an arm. I was proud of my family.

Sarah was everywhere. She was known to many, for many came from Jerusalem. When I told her not to over-tire herself, she said, 'I'm on historical work, my dove. Looking for voices. Voices with good memories.' We walked from dawn till mid-morning and from mid-afternoon till darkness fell. The middle of the day was a purgatory of overhead sun—the only shade that which we could improvise ourselves. It was at this 'middle' time of the day that Sarah would bring me her 'voices'. And each person, chosen and found by Sarah, would find energy to recall in detail what might well have been till then, till Sarah, a hazy thing-of-the-past.

Shown how by Sarah we would make our sun-shelter of blankets and sticks, attaching the long edges of the blankets to the side of a cart. Others copied, and the carts would become the central anchor for a townlet of make-shift awnings. Privacy was impossible, but the children would ring us to provide a barrier, and I would listen to testimony given softly and make my notes and store detail in the mind.

I learned—and was reminded—of much on that journey. Of the 'Captain' of the Temple sacrifice priests, who decided after the Florus massacres that no 'foreigner' might sacrifice or have an offering made on his behalf. The first deliberate anti-*Roman* action. The emperor's offering thrown back in his face, rejected. I heard again of the terrors and fears the peace-at-any-price factions had at this action; of a city split and occupied by Peace and War parties. A War party strengthened by our Zealots and Sicarii. Of Florus I heard, standing in the wings, delighted that the flames were well alight.

A small man, on his knees under our low awning, told with glee how he and others burned down the lovely palaces of the High Priest and the king—and then took torches to the Halls of the Archives and the Records Office where debtors were registered. 'Anarchy, yes,' he crowed, 'but we wanted the debt-owers on *our* side!' My poor Jerusalem, offering real flames now for Florus to take pleasure from.

Then for Sarah, a find, a treasure. For me, pain. 'Itzhak,' she said, 'who was with Menahem seven years ago when he took Masada from the Romans and broke open the armoury and brought arms to Jerusalem when we needed them most!'

I listened to Itzhak and took my notes, for he was a fiery, thin man, who demanded my complete attention to his story. A story I knew, for with Menahem to Masada and back had gone my cousin Eleazar.

'My uncle,' Eleazar had said to me, in that calm deep voice, 'has waited long for this war, and is a practical man. He is not of priestly family, like the Temple faction, or a burner of buildings like the mob. He is practical, and knows that an army needs arms. So, my Ruth, we are off to Masada where Herod built palaces and walls on top of a mountain and laid in arms to withstand a siege. It has a Roman garrison but we know ways up that mountain that no Roman sentry knows. My uncle says they will die with surprised looks on their faces.'

It was as he had said. Menahem and his men returned bristling with arms and full of plans. As were the Captain of the Temple and *his* men. What a moment for unity was there— and what a lack of it.

Menahem, powerful and direct, put to death High Priest Ananias, a leader of the Peace party—and father of the Temple Captain, who'd gathered his men in an attempt to challenge Menahem, whom he considered a mere tyrant, and of inferior caste!

Menahem had seen himself as leader. Over all rebels; all factions. And behaved as such. And soon brought parting, and separation—the leader's nephew, my cousin, in flight, with only moments for a farewell.

'My uncle will be dead soon,' Eleazar had told me. 'They ambushed us in the Temple, at prayer. We were outnumbered ten to one and nearly everyone is dead. My uncle got away but they caught him and are torturing him, and eventually they'll stone him to death.'

The Temple was 'our' territory. The 'they' were our side, torturing their arms-bringer, their leader, to death. And the leader's nephew, a born heir to leadership, in flight. I'd felt sick.

'Where will you go?'

'Back to Masada. We are not many but soon there will be more. We can train people there—and who knows, one day we may need such a stronghold.'

Oh my cousin, my prophet.

To the awning came others of Jerusalem, who told of the new, armed Zealots—and of their wiping out the Roman garrison. And another who told of the slaughter, on the same day as the Romans in Jerusalem, of all the Jews in Caesarea, while Florus looked on and laughed—and laughed again as Jews rose in revenge throughout Israel. The land was filled with blood and terror, and Scythopolis, where Jew fought Jew, took its place in the story of disunity, of a people split and confused. A skeletal dark woman, whose eyes were afraid to close, told me of Scythopolis—'where no Jew survived'.

'The Jews of the town,' she recalled softly, in a haunted whisper, 'the townspeople against the Jews outside. And the townspeople told all their Jews to go into a grove to prove their loyalty—which they did, and on the third night were slaughtered, to the last child, by the people of Scythopolis.'

The nightmare in the grove started a chain of similar massacres all over Israel. Ashkelon killed many of its Jews, Ptolo-
mais also, and Tyre, and Hippos, and Gadara. In Egypt, in
Alexandria, the governor, Tiberius Alexander—our own part-
Jewish procurator of twenty years before—let loose two Roman
legions on the Jews, with orders to 'kill, plunder and burn'.
But the Jews, everywhere, were fighting back. The country
was in turmoil, and Florus laughed and fed the flames.

'It is said,' Sarah told me, 'that he bribed Roman officers not
to follow up advantage, to turn back, to wait over-long, Well,
perhaps he did, although I like to think we beat Cestius on our
own. Well, on our own and with God's help.'

Cestius of Syria. Roman legate who gathered his Roman
soldiers in tens of thousands and added thousands more of the
soldiers of Kings Antiochus Soaemus, and our own Agrippa.
Cestius, who swelled this vast force with the ready volunteers
of a dozen cities and set out for *our* city, Jerusalem. Roundabout
he went, into Galilee and Samaria, killing. Leaving desolation
and ruin. Smoke and ashes. He took Joppa and Aphek. At
Lydda he found an empty city, for its Jews had come to us, in
Jerusalem, to give thanks, for it was the Feast of Tabernacles.
So he burned Lydda and came after its people to Jerusalem.
For on Festivals and the Sabbath, he had been told, the Jews do
not fight, they pray.

But we stopped praying and we fought. We went out to meet
Cestius and we halted him, killing many and taking his pack-
mules back into the city with us. On Mount Scopus Cestius sat
and revised his opinion of the Jews and counted his dead.
Again he came, but stopped suddenly—advised to do so by
bribed officers, some said; halted by God, said others.

'If he'd made an all-out attempt that afternoon,' said Sarah,
realist, 'it would have been the end. But he didn't; instead he
called up to us on the walls and made speeches to tempt
traitors, offering them terms. So we were watchful and when
the traitors showed themselves we threw them down to him.

We threw *everything* down, and made it seem that we had a strength we didn't have, and the bluff worked and he turned away—and we went after him! We took on a Roman army and we *beat* it! We chased it and caught it up and ran alongside it and passed it and turned back on it. We surrounded it and cut it to pieces! In the night, in Bet-horon, the survivors got away, but we killed six thousand, and took back with us to Jerusalem great booty. The huge stone-throwers and missile projectors and quick-loaders that we used later against Vespasian were *Roman!*'

As always, when Sarah spoke of these early victories, her eyes glowed and her voice grew vibrant and full of energy.

Some of the tales others told us of the country-wide pogroms were strange indeed. In Damascus, said a man with one ear and fingers missing, the men of the city, hearing of the defeat of Cestius, decided to wipe out all the Jews in *their* city. But they had to do it with caution, being afraid of their wives, most of whom had adopted the Jewish religion!

Another man, with an educated voice and a cynical mouth, told of how Cestius used Jews who had fled from Jerusalem ('like rats from a sinking ship') to take the news of his defeat to Nero—and to blame Florus for it. 'Diverting Nero's rages to others was an essential ability in senior officers,' said the man.

The last part of the trek to Jerusalem was hard. There is no way to avoid the hills, from the south. As we climbed we grew more silent, each with memories and fatigue enough to halt speech and bring tears near.

And when we saw Jerusalem we did weep. Here was beauty raped and ravished with a savagery beyond description.

We came in through what was left of the Gate of the Essenes, in the past my favourite way into the city, for there to left and right had been the perfume factories and their flower gardens, the air full of beautiful scent. Now many of the small factories were in ruins and in the gardens grew vegetables, tended by sad-looking people and ragged children.

To every side, as we walked up through the Lower City, past the pool of Siloam, were smashed buildings or rubble-strewn open spaces where houses had stood. The great Stadium near the Temple South Wall looked shabby and damaged. To our right, low in the South Wall, were the Gates of Huldah, where Sarah had lost her family in the Passover Massacre: and the great walls themselves were rent and torn.

We stopped at the corner of the Temple Mount, where the South and Western Walls made their right angle. Below the Gates of Huldah the ground fell away to the plain of Ophel where Menahem was stoned to death. It looked desolate; a mourning place, in its soil the blood of a special man.

Leaving the others, Sarah and I made our way with the children up the broken steps to the gate in the Western Wall. Four helmeted Roman soldiers stood guard and looked at us searchingly, but saw no danger in two women and five children all in need of clothes and a good wash. We passed through them into the familiar wide open space, where we had fought so desperately three years before.

The twins said it first, in the same breath, in the same words. 'The Temple's gone!'

Who can describe the sight? Who can put down in words the stopping of the heart, the disbelief of the eyes, the feeling that the world had changed. As surely as the mind knew that our Temple had been the work of men, so did the soul know that God had guided those men, that God had had a hand in it, that God had lived there. In the Holy of Holies, unseen but there. Who could doubt it? Our mothers had told us so, our fathers, our teachers.

Now the Temple was a wasteland of rubble, wherein old men sat and wept into their beards. Where did God live now? Who could tell, in the vast field of ruin, even where the Holy of Holies had been? Where the great Altar, where the towering pillars of the Sanctuary, where the beautiful Gates of Nicanor, where the lovely Courts and Chambers had been? Did God himself now sit in the dusty stones, weeping?

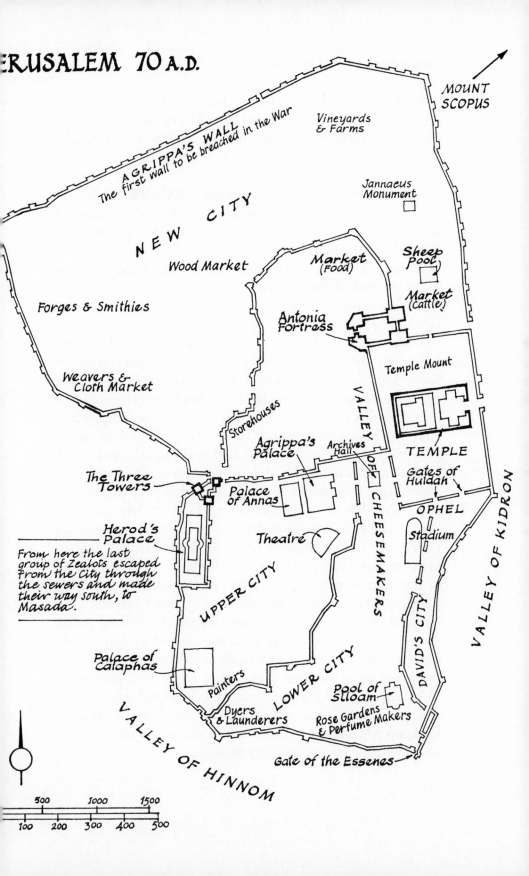

ERUSALEM 70 A.D.

MOUNT SCOPUS

AGRIPPA'S WALL
The first wall to be breached in the War

Vineyards & Farms

NEW CITY

Jannaeus Monument

Wood Market

Market (Food)

Sheep Pool

Forges & Smithies

Market (Cattle)

Antonia Fortress

Temple Mount

Weavers & Cloth Market

Storehouses

Agrippa's Palace

Archives Hall

TEMPLE

VALLEY OF CHEESEMAKERS

Gates of Huldah

The Three Towers

Palace of Annas

OPHEL

VALLEY OF KIDRON

Herod's Palace

Theatre

Stadium

From here the last group of Zealots escaped from the City through the sewers and made their way south, to Masada.

UPPER CITY

DAVID'S CITY

Palace of Caiaphas

Painters

LOWER CITY

Pool of Siloam

Dyers & Launderers

Rose Gardens & Perfume Makers

Gate of the Essenes

VALLEY OF HINNOM

500   1000   1500
100   200   300   400   500

Sarah stood close to me, her jaw like iron. Judith stood at my other side, with Simon's hand in hers. The twins were a little in front of us, silent. Little Sami, feeling that this was no time to be carried, wriggled and was put down, to stand, with serious grubby face, wordless.

I looked around. The colonnades which had edged the Temple Area, which had looked as if they would last for centuries, had great gaps, and in their remains people were living, in holes, like animals.

We picked our way along, the twins darting ahead. Ahead of us, at the end of the Western Wall, was the wreckage of the Antonia fortress. Impregnable, uncrushable Antonia. Mighty blockhouse. A ruin.

The twins, atop a heap of rubble in a gap of the wall, shouted and pointed into the city. We climbed up after them and looked down and across Jerusalem. Little impeded our view. The palaces were gone, even our last stronghold, the Palace of Great Herod, which had stood to the left of the Three Towers he'd built—to his brother Phasael, to his friend Hippicus and to poor tragic Mariamne, the wife he'd truly loved—and killed.

The Towers remained. Untouched. Left by the Romans to show future generations how noble a city had been humbled by them. The Towers stood; as though to point how little else stood. Whole streets were gone. The graceful Theatre, the monuments of Hyrcanus, of Jannaeus, of Huldah: gone. Many of the beautiful villas of the wealthy, in the Upper City, damaged in the war, were now, like the Temple, entirely destroyed. They lay, hills of debris, in their own over-run gardens.

Again from the twins, in unison: 'Where have all the people gone?' Indeed where, for we of Jerusalem were used to crowds, a teeming population of many tongues. Jerusalem was where the world came to worship and gasp. In the War people fled to Jerusalem—and the siege packed us even tighter.

The teeming crowds were gone. No worshippers, no sightseers, no pilgrims. No processions of priests, no royal guards, no merchant caravans swaying through.

'There are people,' said Sarah bluntly, 'plenty of people. All alive, all brave. Come children, we have friends to find, and a roof, and beds for tonight, and food for supper. Knocked-about old buildings we can look at any time.'

The children responded at once and we made our way round the huge mound of masonry that had been our beloved Temple. It was vast; a mountain. In many crevices wild flowers sprouted.

We went through the Northern Wall, through a gap; there was no sign of the old handsome gate and arch. We went down the hill to the sheep pools where in happier days the sheep were washed and made ready for sacrifice above at the Great Altar, to which they were taken through one of the many tunnels in the Mount.

Here there was more life to be seen, as always near water. A shanty town, a market place, a new beginning. Sarah brightened; she was among her own. In no time there was fruit in the children's hands—and in my hands too, for I was hungry. No money was exchanged, for we had none; but Sarah was of the markets and knew the language. She sat us all down and went away, chewing on a piece of smoked meat. A Roman soldier walked by, then another. A bird settled nearby and sang sweetly. Little Sami smiled and held out a piece of orange. I felt tired and drowsy.

Sarah was gone about a half hour, no more. And returned with good news indeed.

'Your brother is alive and well—and living in your father's house. God is good. Come!'

The children cheered and we set off. We found a gap in the stretch of rampart north of Antonia and went across the markets, where the damage seemed less. Perhaps the narrow streets and poorer houses of the area had not attracted such savage vengeance. Our house was between the Valley of the Cheese-Makers and the stores near the Three Towers. As we walked up the western slope of the valley I could see that many houses were missing, great storage buildings wiped away, whole roads pushed down the hill. But ahead of us, on the brow of the hill, some houses stood alone, seemingly whole—and one was my home. More than any other sight I was to see, the house of my childhood rekindled hope in me.

As we drew nearer I could see that such damage as it had suffered had been patched up. Life was there. The children, with an odd delicacy, held back, and I approached the door alone, Sarah a little behind.

Saul, my brother, five years my junior, had always been the closest to me, although before him had come another girl and after him two more. We were the most alike in our gravity and apartness. He had also a gentleness, which though real, covered great strength of will, and a family obstinacy. We had shared a love of learning and—in his case more than mine —the Scriptures. His decision to enter the Temple service was made when he was thirteen and he soon left home to live in the College of Priests. The life suited him perfectly, but he was no recluse. He had my father's calm foresight and saw clearly the terrors and nightmares to come. And when it was time to fight, he fought. He had a skill with herbs, and sure hands, and in the last days he tended the wounded. When it was the hour for the final hundred to leave for Masada, Eleazar asked him to come with us. He refused, with a courtesy like my father's. 'I have orphans to look after, and a blinded man, and people who are afraid, and an old priest who was my tutor.' He'd kissed me and we'd gone down to the tunnels.

I knocked on the door, and waited for what seemed an age. Then there were soft footsteps and a bolt drawn and the door swung back and my brother stood facing me. I could not speak. He was thin, with sunken dark eyes which flicked past me at the children and Sarah and then steadied, puzzled, on my own face, which was begrimed, my dusty hair pushed under a kerchief. Then recognition began, disbelief, a moment of closed eyes to thank God, and then his arms opened and I was home again.

11 Home

Decorated plaster ceiling
fragment from Bath-house

How wondrous is the resilience of mind and spirit. Before two hours had passed we were part of the household: with a place at table, with new friends, with a feeling of safety, of a new beginning.

Our new friends were those who shared the house with Saul. It was a large, roomy house, with a shady garden. In the War it had served as a dressing station and hospital. Sarah, who had so accurately foreseen such uses for it and had for a long period been in charge, was as at home as I, and as content. Almost by force of habit she fitted us all in, rough-tongued and bustling, but offending no one, which was skilful, for two elderly women lived in the house and were obviously used to running things. The first, Rachel, was in her seventies, bony and gnarled, with a hoarse voice; she was aided by her grandson, Abel, a rather frightened-looking youth of about eighteen, the only other survivor of her large family. Abel had seen the massacre that had left him buried in corpses but miraculously alive. Old Rachel treated him with a rough humour. With a story similar to Sarah's, she possessed a little of the same flint and glint.

The other old woman was called Leah. She was smaller, and thin, with no teeth. I knew her. She was a spinster, from the other end of the road. She had given her life to looking after an invalid younger sister who'd died in the siege famine. Her house had been smashed down by the Romans before her eyes.

Saul's other 'helpers', as he called them, were three in
number. The eldest was his old tutor, Simeon, whose long life
had been spent in the College of Priests—now, like the Temple,
a heap of rubble. I had never met him, but had heard his
name, spoken with love, a thousand times from Saul's lips. He
was small and plump, with ruddy cheeks and a bald head
ringed with a fuzz of white hair. His eyes were bright and
round, like a happy child's.

Never far from Simeon was a girl of about Judith's age,
fourteen, or perhaps more—or less—for here was a wild
creature. A swarthy, dark-eyed, unsmiling, tight-lipped gipsy
of a girl, who moved with the natural grace of a cat—and with
reflexes as fast. She had suffered much and seen terrible things.
She was from a small town in Galilee near Capernaum, which
had been wiped out by the Romans in Vespasian's 'subduing'
of the North. She had escaped to another village which had
suffered the same fate. She had made her way to Jerusalem,
like many, and lived by her wits in and around the markets.
When the siege began she had been about ten. A natural thief,
who stole to stay alive. A sharp-toothed lone soul with no
name. In the fall of the Temple she'd found herself with a hurt
ankle, half-suffocated and delirious, in a cellar with Simeon.
The old priest, one of God's comforters, looked after the girl
until he could take her to the only refuge he knew other than
his beloved Temple—the home of his favourite pupil, Saul.
Her wild dreams and half-starved illness went on for a long
time and the old man was the only one she would allow near
her. He would tell her Bible stories: 'I am your uncle Mordecai,'
he would say, 'and you are my Esther, a brave girl who
became a queen.' Of Naomi he would tell, 'Who suffered many
things but found happiness, because God is good. As you will
too, my little Naomi.'

She would listen unblinkingly, but say little—and less if
questioned. She never proffered her own name; but the old
man had infinite patience and a life's experience with young
people. So one day he said to her, 'I will call you Sim, which is

half of my own name. The front half, the best half. I want you
to have it. For you are half my life. The best half.'

And Sim she became. Silent, obedient, but never far from
Simeon; only he could bring from her one of her rare smiles.
When she and my grave beautiful Judith met, both the old
man and I knew that they would find a level with each other,
and they did. Each remaining alone yet each getting something
from the other.

The last of our 'new friends' was unexpected in that group
of washed-up-on-the-shore people. We'd arrived at the house
at midday and had spent the afternoon and early evening
settling in and talking (how wonderful to sit across a table
from a beloved brother and just talk, and touch hands, and
talk again). It was from Saul that I learned the stories of the
others, and that there was still one last person to meet. Of the
last, of Jesse, he said little. 'We owe him much. He comes and
goes. He will be here in time for the evening meal. He is never
late. Perhaps for the grace; never for the meal.'

He was in time for both, for we started late. The house now
had twice as many people, and two little ones. The bustle and
change in routine made for delay. As we gathered in the large
dining room there was the sound of hooves and a moment later
Jesse entered. A single sardonic look, which registered everything, and: 'Company for dinner. Nice. Good evening. My
name is Jesse. I seem to be in time for prayers. Ah well.'

He was tall with wide shoulders and a high-held head. He
looked about forty-five (he was forty-three) and clearly in his
prime. His hair was grey and crisp. It was cut short, in the
Roman way, and with skill. I glanced at Sarah, who mouthed
the name in my own thoughts: Silva. For this, from head to
toe, was a Roman. A patrician, with smooth-shaven, lean
cheeks and a bony nose. His eyes were deep-set under heavy
black brows. The eyes, however, were not Roman, but
Jewish. A difficult-to-define thing; of thicker lashes and a
warmer, darker gleam.

His arms were bare to the elbow and his legs to the knee.

Roman. As was the belted short toga, the thonged boots, and the heavy silver wristlets. But this was no Jew aping his conquerors, this was no slavish copier. This was a calm insolent decision by a strong man for good reason. Waiting for the reason, and to know more, was frustrating, for during the meal he listened more than he spoke. He listened with full attention; to relate one thing to another he would put in an incisive word, nod, and listen again. Such warmth as he showed was to old Simeon, and Saul—who obviously understood him perfectly. Sarah was as curious as I, and our Masada children fascinated, for anything remotely Roman meant the enemy, the all-powerful enemy, not someone who sat at table and obviously understood every Hebrew or Aramaic or Greek word.

When the meal was finished, Saul lifted an eyebrow to Jesse, as if to enquire whether he would remain at table for prayers; and on receiving a nod (and after a slow look at us of Masada) he began grace, adding in simple language thanks to God for our deliverance. I lifted my eyes to look across at Jesse and found his upon me, with a thoughtful gaze. I was confused.

Sarah and I saw the children and the moist-eyed Rachel and Leah to their beds and went back to the big room. We were tired but burned with curiosity about our Roman-Jew.

He sat at table still. At ease, with long legs stretched out, one wiry hand toying with a wine goblet that I remembered from my childhood (I had a sudden great yearning for my father). Near him sat Saul and old Simeon. All rose as we entered. As we sat, the dark-eyed Sim glided in with more goblets and Jesse poured. He toasted us gravely.

'To a happy reunion. And peace. Enjoy the wine. It is the best the Roman officers' mess can provide.'

Sarah, after a deep quaff: 'Beautiful. You're a man after my own heart. A good provider. You must know important people.' She waited.

Saul laughed. 'The Romans in Jerusalem couldn't do without him. He speaks seven languages and about a dozen dialects —both Roman and Judean!'

Jesse inclined a regal head, with a wicked glint just like Sarah's.

'He gives them good service,' said Saul, 'but charges high prices. Dozens of larders are stocked by him. He feeds a whole orphans' home. He can organize and arrange anything—for anyone.'

Sarah, slightly chilly: 'I understand.'

Jesse turned an eye to her. 'You don't, old battler, but don't let it spoil your appetite. There is a time to fight and a time to survive. I am a devious and crafty man—and have always been. By nature I always float to the top. And I mean the top. My schemes, for want of a better word, have never had much to do with the poor, they can't afford me. I deal with, or if you prefer, steal from, only the rich. Saul here, who saved my life, taught me a new game, *giving* to the poor. I enjoy it; it had never occurred to me before. I need very little money myself. I don't pay for much—and I live cheaply. Here. Wouldn't think of living anywhere else.'

Sarah, warmer: 'Working for the Romans, when do you find time for your stealing? And where are the rich to steal from? There can't be many left.'

'Very few. I steal from the Romans. Armies are rich—and after the blood this lot have spilled, very frightened. I comfort them, arrange their supplies, gamble with their officers, find baubles for their women and convince them they should take no action in this sad city without first asking me my expert opinion.'

'He *is*,' said Saul, 'rather an expert. On many things. He knows Jerusalem better than anyone, yet was not born here.'

Sarah laughed and said, 'Well, he certainly doesn't look as though he comes from round here. Looks like one of those Romans to me.' Clever Sarah; I also wanted to know why.

The laugh was general, with Jesse no less amused.

'It works with you too, old battler,' he said calmly. 'You won't forget me either. I ride a pure black horse. A royal Arab from her nose to her lovely tail. I won her at dice from the second-in-command to Vespasian himself.' He arched a quizzi-

cal eyebrow at me. 'I was a prisoner of war at the time. Taken
at Jotapata. Your good brother tells me you are writing a
journal of our recent troubles. I may have a thing or two for
you.' He turned back to Sarah. 'I dress like a Roman because
I think like a Roman. I deal with Romans and lived for years
in Rome. I am more Roman than Jew—'

'A little Jewishness remains,' murmured Saul.

'—and if a Jew dressed like a Roman aristocrat confuses their
little minds, all the better. I make my living from confused
little minds. If others think me a soft-in-the-head poseur, good!
It is a position of strength to be thought a fool—and not be.'

Sarah chuckled. 'I like you, Roman. What about the real
thing, the officer who *is* a Roman aristocrat, what does *he* say?
Quick with the scourge, some of 'em, handy with the shortsword.'

Jesse sipped delicately. 'So am I, grannie, so am I. Their
teachers taught me. In my jungle you need sharp claws. The
owner of my beautiful horse was a poor loser and called me
names. He did not call me cheat, for I would have knocked his
teeth down his throat with the edge of my hand and he knew
it. Rather a ruffian I am, if need be.'

Old Simeon spoke, in his light, rather high voice. 'Indeed
you are. A dreadful person. I am glad I am your friend and
not your enemy. Dreadful. Jesse, why aren't I more afraid of
you?' He chuckled, enjoying his joke, and turned to me. 'I
was also interested to hear of your plans to write it all down.
A big work.'

He was indeed interested, and asked many questions, showing a keen mind and good memory behind his pink gentleness.
As we spoke I sensed that Sarah shared my growing respect
for the old man. Saul and Jesse too seemed to notice a new
stimulation for the old priest in his recall of the times of strife
and struggle.

I sketched in for him the outline of the book so far and his
eyes shone as I finished with the defeat and rout of Cestius
nearly seven years before.

'Nearly seven years,' he marvelled. 'It seems at once much more and much less. Great days, after we sent Cestius running, great days. We felt invincible! Even we of the Temple. Old teachers, scholars, men who had not looked up from the Holy Scrolls for years, we all felt it. We were convinced that God was on our side, that we could not lose. We forgot that we had not deserved the help of the Almighty for some time. The younger priests were more practical than we were, I'm pleased to say. They saw more clearly than we did that Cestius was not the end but the beginning.

'There was a mass meeting in the Temple to appoint generals, each to be in charge of a province or district. The name "general" was rather grand for some of them. High Priests some were; or the sons of priests. My friend John the Essene—who'd lived most of his life in an enclosed community—was sent to look after Thamna, which included Lydda, Joppa, and Emmaus. But the idea seemed sound enough. Priests, men of authority, high-up men.'

'I was at the meeting,' said Sarah, with the hard note in her voice, 'when all Galilee was put in the charge of a very low man indeed. Joseph, son of Matthias. Now called Josephus, so they tell me. The whole of Galilee, in charge of a man of thirty, a lover of Rome and all things Roman. A man who believed that God lived in Rome and fought on their side. A born defeatist and an eater at Nero's table. Our beautiful Galilee in charge of a lying bastard full of prejudice and petty dislikes, a man who never had a brave thought in his life. . . .'

I put my hand on hers and she stopped, a vein in her forehead swollen and throbbing. Her colour was high and she was panting.

Simeon said, with a sweet and sensible tact, 'It is difficult to remain calm on the subject of Josephus. And I know from experience that changing the subject does not help. And certainly it will be of use to Ruth and her book if we speak of him. If you agree, Sarah, I will speak first, for I knew him well. He lived within the Temple for a while after his voyage to Rome, and was well known among the Pharisee congregation before he went.' The old man addressed himself equally now to me and to Sarah, who was calmer. 'I knew his father, who was a righteous man, and his brother, who was, shall we say, different from Joseph. Far less clever but rather more likeable. It is unfortunate, I think, for a boy to have both a surfeit of cleverness and an almost entire lack of modesty. Precociously clever children are often indulged by parents more proud than wise. Joseph was by nature a courtier, a flatterer, which people like. He had a perfect instinct for the action or person that would advance him most quickly.'

The old man was mild, gentle-voiced, and thus the more telling. 'There was, and no doubt still is, another side to Joseph's character, less well known. He was given to wild exaggeration, to enlargement, to romantic embellishment. Upon his return from Rome, for instance, he told us of his voyage there—in a vessel larger than we knew existed. Of its shipwreck, of hundreds drowned, of miraculous delivery. He had intimate tales of Queen Poppea, and of her husband Nero. He told of their great friendship for him, and of their gifts. He had stories of actors, of life at court; recalled his speeches in defence of poor priests. And at each telling the stories became richer and his part in them more heroic—and clearly, he came to believe his own words absolutely. You tell me, Ruth, that he is now an historian. I shudder for the accuracy of his writing—especially if he himself played any part in that of which he writes.'

Jesse sipped wine, his eyes amused. He spoke lightly. 'It's nearly seven years since he started to look after Galilee. About six since Jotapata. His story of that action must already be something worth hearing.'

'Ah,' said Saul, 'Jesse knows much of that time, Ruth.'

'And I remember every moment,' put in Jesse. 'But I'll not tell it now. Your beautiful sister looks ready for her bed. You too, old battler. Long day. You are home and safe. Tomorrow is another day.'

And indeed we were tired. We said we were not, we tough women of Masada, but the men stood and remained standing, and bade us firm goodnights.

Oh, the joy of a bed. Sarah and I shared a room—and a prayer too, that night. I am an inhibited and unsure person, with prayers inside me, softly said behind closed lips, but not so Sarah. She stood by the window, open-eyed and relaxed, and talked to the stars, to the sky, to God. 'Man to man, my dove. Simple words. No priest-words, no Pharisee-talk, no "forms of service". He understands market women.' Aloud she spoke, as unselfconscious as a child, and she spoke for us both, leaving out nothing.

I slept for nearly a whole day, waking in the late afternoon with the children and Sarah smiling down at me, bearing gifts of a cool drink, some nuts and a date or two. For a few minutes I was a queen, with every muscle and limb renewed and refreshed by sleep.

Jesse had been busy. The children were wearing new clothes, of a sensible and comfortable kind, and new shoes. 'Jesse said everything we had when we arrived was to be burned,' the twins explained, while Sarah nodded approvingly above their lively heads. For Sarah and me there were lengths of cloth of various weights and colour—and a local woman with skilful fingers to help us. The woman, 'Jochebed, like the mother of Great Moses', was a short, bustling, cheerful person, who had been a seamstress all her life— 'to the Court, my dears, when there was one. I knew all the palaces. I miss them.'

Those first few days back in my own home passed quickly. It was a place of routine, of order. My brother and old Simeon were involved in many things to do with the poor and the lonely and the bereaved. They had a way of getting people working together to help each other. People cultivated patches of open ground communally and fed themselves: they contributed their skills—for there were few jobs to be had. The house was a social centre, a school, a weaving workshop, a smithy, an advice bureau. My quiet brother, who had lived since a boy in the cloistered shadows of the Temple, had found in the blood and smoke of disaster an authority with his fellows that came as naturally from him as his breath.

We were quickly integrated. No one just sat in that house. People came and went all day. A number of them were known to me; Sarah known to nearly all. She was everywhere. 'Five orphans, my dove. There must be *somebody* related to them. A person should have kin—if only to fight with!' She didn't rest, my battler, it was a crusade.

You must understand, good reader, that there was a simple answer to the twins' question, 'Where have all the people gone?' The people were dead. Thousands and thousands and thousands. The Roman army had taken terrible toll. The best equipped, most highly trained troops in the whole world had been given freedom to kill all those who had dared to resist. People were not in hiding, they were dead. And not only those who had fought, or resisted. People who had never thrown a stone or shot an arrow had eventually died, within siege walls, of hunger and thirst, and much disease.

For weeks I hardly gave my book a thought. Saul and Simeon, whom I had told of our last days on the mountain, joined in a sort of pact to keep me occupied. I shopped, tended the vegetable garden, looked after children, washed and mended. All in a strict rota kept by Leah and Rachel, who were warders indeed in their own domains.

We saw little of Jesse. Often he would be away for days, for his 'field of operations' was wide. His letters of authority and safe-conducts were myriad, and he went everywhere. He made his own rules and kept his promises to everyone, Jew and Roman alike. The Romans (I think) laughed at him a little, but he (I'm sure) allowed for it—and made them pay more for laughing. When he slept at home he rose early and left the house after a good breakfast. He groomed his beautiful horse himself and it was at all times immaculate, like its master.

Sarah approved of Jesse. And on the few occasions he took the evening meal with us she showed it. He was amused by her but had a certain restraint. He was not as forthcoming about himself as on that first night. He told us of incidents in his journeyings and 'dealings' with a dry, knowing wit. Once or twice he asked me about the shape I planned for the book and I sensed that the question was not idle.

The months passed, and one day Saul told me with mild surprise that Jesse would be home for the Passover days.

'Really home. Unavailable to the Romans because he is celebrating the Passover. And that is the reason he has given the High Command. That he will not be available for four or five days because of a Jewish Festival of Remembrance. When they asked what it remembers he told them a release from slavery. Very risky sort of joke to make, I would have thought. Some of the worst troubles of recent years took place around Passover and the Romans get very tense at that time of year.'

I found I was looking forward to Passover. I had always loved the Festival as a child, with its wonderful stories and the feeling of newness and joy in the house. Now I was back in the same house and the same thoughts rose in me. The house, like the whole city, battered and shabby, my family far away, great sorrows to recall; but the sense of renewal was there also. The children, sturdier and well fed now, looked forward with no less anticipation to the holiday.

Sarah, meanwhile, had found an elderly aunt for the twins, and for my sweet Judith news of a farmer near Damascus who was cousin to her mother.

Sarah went to spend an afternoon with the elderly aunt and returned depressed.

'Ugly. Inside and out. Never been married and doesn't like children. The neighbours avoid her. She vaguely remembers a niece having twins but "didn't approve of the young woman" anyway. I may be wrong about everybody needing kin. The twins stay with us.'

When we told Judith of her Damascus relations she said little about it for nearly a week. We were used to our reserved young beauty and waited. She was of Jerusalem, of a large and well-to-do family, most of whom were wiped out when the Upper City fell. Only she and her mother had escaped. Her sweet mother, dazed with terror and shock and loss, carrying a child in her womb. How brave she was, how uncomplaining on the journey to Masada, yet safe on the mountain the terrors came back and when the child was born dead, so, quietly, she also died. Judith was nearly eleven. Now at fourteen, she pondered, and went about her duties with wide, thoughtful eyes.

Just before Passover she joined Sarah and me in the garden, in the cool evening. Sarah paused in the middle of a sentence, gave me a glance, and made room on the bench.

'Ruth,' began Judith after a moment, 'you've often called us your family, the little ones, the twins and me. Yet I don't think of you as a mother. Perhaps deep down I know that my mother still looks after me.'

'Certain of it,' said Sarah. 'How do you think of *me*? Grannie?'

Judith smiled. 'Yes.' She turned again to me. 'I think of you as sister, and I feel safe. I want to stay with you and be your sister. May I?'

It was said softly, with great simplicity—and our granitey Grannie wept first. And then we all wept, and then laughed and had a most satisfactory and feminine half-hour—and Sarah gave up forever her career as a searcher for kin.

12 Passover, and of Josephus

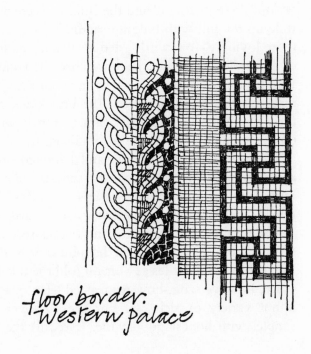

floor border.
Western palace

To prepare for the Passover, as it says in the Law, we cleaned and scrubbed the house inside and out till it shone. The males, heavily outnumbered, kept out of the way, Saul and Simeon busy anyway, and Jesse far away to the south near Beersheba, but positively returning for the Meal of the First Evening.

He arrived in the mid-afternoon. He had sent a message saying 'Presents for all' and the children were waiting when he rode up the hill with bulging saddle bags. Never was a horse more lovingly—or swiftly—led away and stabled and relieved of its saddle—and bags. Jesse watched the youngsters' activity with his usual sardonic glint but gave out the gifts with a great nicety as to precedence. First the little ones, then the twins, then Judith and the swift dark Sim, and then, with a manly clap on the shoulder, old Rachel's grandson, the shy Abel.

The old women and Sarah and I looked on, showing our approval perhaps too much, for the sardonic eyebrow went higher and Jesse said: 'Grown-ups get theirs later, when, it is hoped, their cooking will merit some reward. If not, not.'

The meal merited reward. And thanks to God, which were given. What a warmth and happiness was there. How we listened to the old tales as Simeon told them in his gentle high voice, how we sang, how we feasted—for quantity there was, if not variety or richness. But the Passover meal is better simple, with honest good wine. It recalls the Miracle of the

Departure from Egypt, and has its own magic. And our meal had safety, and reunion, and hope, and a feeling of a page turning.

The twins, natural comedians, became, with wine in them, hilarious. They had made up little rhymes about everyone, which they spoke-sang, with wickedly clever mimicry of each poem's subject. With Jesse one became, on all fours, a black horse and the other, astride and high-noised, 'General Jesspasian, nickety poo—without him the Romans couldn't do!'

Sarah's little doggerel was done with them both inside one of her old jerkins—and each time they moved, little knives spilled out. 'Sicarii—Sicarii!' they yelled, 'Sarah the Dare-er! Yellity—Zealoty!'

We roared and clapped and toasted them. Jesse had bribed them to do me last. Deborah stood with solemn face and a huge notebook—with pen to match—and expressionlessly entered the fearful disasters related by David, bandaged, limping, covered in red-dye blood. At last he fell dead—and the diarist looked down, turned the page, and made a note of it. It was marvellously observed and I laughed till tears ran down my face. It was the twins' greatest triumph, a superb finale—for my laugh, though rare, is infectious, and once begun, is difficult to stop—and is fed by others, who do not want it to stop.

At last I ceased, weak and relaxed (oh so relaxed, so released) against Sarah's shoulder. The twins came to me for a kiss of reward and love.

Across the table Jesse sat, with a smile in no way sardonic. He spoke to the twins: 'You will teach me please how to make your Aunt Ruth laugh, for it is very good to see—and does her no harm at all.'

How late we stayed at table, how reluctant we were to break the spell. Saul had given us all, we grown-ups, soft instruction that no child was to be chased to bed. And we were the richer for the children's company. Gradually their eyelids drooped and their heavy heads sank down. The twins fell asleep at table in the same half-minute and, closed-eyed, walked each other to bed. Judith and Sim then went softly away, and tall Abel assisted the old ladies, both vague with wine and old memories.

We sat on, Sarah on my one side and Saul on my other, his hand and my own enclasped. Jesse sat opposite, in sharp-beaked profile, listening with amused affection to old Simeon tipsily leafing over the pages of his long life.

At last we said goodnight and kissed each other with the soft wish for God's protection. Jesse's lips were dry and warm on my cheek.

'Sleep well, historian,' he murmured. 'I have been gathering a chapter or two for you. Till tomorrow.'

Jesse stayed at home for five days, and Saul and Simeon arranged their days so that they too were free. The weather was beautiful, smiling and warm, with cool breezes. For most of each day we sat at ease in the garden, and talked.

On the first morning it soon became clear to me that a kind of plan had been agreed upon by the three men, for our talk had a shape, a sequence, a comparing of memories, of detail.

'Your book honours many, Ruth,' said my brother. 'We owe it to them that it should be accurate. For most of them are dead.'

We recalled again the elation of the people after the defeat of Cestius seven years before. The huge losses of men suffered by the Romans, the vast booty and many war machines brought in triumph back into the city by cheering, jubilant Jews.

We spoke once more of the great public meeting in the Temple to celebrate the victory, when the 'generals' were elected to govern and protect the various provinces and districts. We found that we had all been at the meeting, Jesse too. When we recalled the election of Josephus, Saul and old Simeon sat back, leaving Jesse to continue.

'I came specially to the meeting,' said Jesse. 'It is my habit to look out for coming men. I attach myself. It is part of my way of life. You will recall that I told you I float to the top. I don't know that I really thought we would win against the

Romans but I thought it would be more pleasant to do what I had to do among the officers rather than the men.

'I was very interested in that meeting. Some of the men chosen to be leaders or provincial governors or whatever were to say the least a bit inexperienced. I knew hardly any of them, but Josephus I recognized right away. I'd seen him in Rome a year or two before. We'd met. We recognize our own, we floaters to the top. He mixed with some very important people in Rome, did our Joseph. Friends of mine.'

We laughed. Jesse smiled, thinly.

'Friends of mine. Business acquaintances, people I bought from, or sold to. All rich; all powerful. And there was our Joseph, about twenty-five or six, about ten years my junior, yet nearly as good at cultivating people as I was. You find a certain respect; you recognize a skill. So I wasn't too surprised to find him in the Temple among the group considered for election.'

Sarah snorted. 'When we gave Cestius a hiding it brought a lot of Rome-lovers out of their holes. For about five minutes they thought they'd backed the wrong horse. About two years before Cestius, when Josephus first came back from Rome, he'd spent a lot of time telling us how hopeless it all was and how mighty and beautiful was the Imperial Roman Empire. After a time we suggested he'd be much better off keeping quiet and living with the other defeatists. Which he did. Carry on, Jesse. We're listening.'

Jesse paused a moment, his eyes on Sarah's. 'Before I go on I want you and Ruth to know something—and you Sarah, to remain calm, like Ruth. Josephus is back. He is travelling the country, an official historian to Emperor Vespasian.' Sarah sat forward. Jesse smiled. 'He travels with a personal body-guard of about two hundred.

'Now where was I? Ah yes, the Temple meeting. I could see at one glance that Josephus was going to get Galilee, with its splendid Roman villas at Tiberias. Better than living in Italy. Also, let me remind you that the "elections" weren't any such thing. The choice of leaders was made by the Government, the Elders and the High Priests, and the Sanhedrin. I've been giving it some thought. The men chosen had a clearly defined job; to quieten things down, to stop what they called in private the flood of insurrection and rebellion. And it was a flood. The whole country was thinking in a different way. A suicidal way.

'High Priest Ananias and the Government were no fools. Galilee was boiling up, and those living there with most to lose were very worried indeed. So Josephus, an old hand at smooth talk and very much at home among such wealthy folk—and an eye-witness and compulsive describer of the might of Rome and so on, was chosen to pour oil. He was always a King's man, a natural collaborator, and had a great instinct for the winning side. Like me. He was my man. I attached myself. He found me on his staff fixing this and that for him before the cheering had stopped. Very close we became. Like brothers.'

Sarah and I glanced at Saul and old Simeon, ready to share the smile. There was no smile, and they kept their eyes, with a rather serious look, on Jesse, in whom there was now a sort of tension.

'From the day we left for Galilee until the fall of Jotapata was about eight months. Where Joseph went, I went. His reputation went before him and the revolutionary and resistance groups didn't trust him an inch. And there were many such groups—and some very brave men to lead them. John, of Gischala. Jesus, of Tiberias—and Justus too. We will talk of them all in turn and you will put them down, Ruth, for when Josephus is finished writing of them they will look different and be called by other names. John of Gischala saw Joseph for what he was and didn't stop saying so. And neither did Simon ben Giora of Idumaea. I wasn't here in Jerusalem at the last, I was a prisoner-of-war, but there is no doubt in my mind that John and Simon were worth having on your side.'

Sarah: 'They were. Ruffians both, but marvellous fighters. During those eight months Simon took his men down to

Masada and joined the Zealot group there, and later he brought
that force to Jerusalem, gathering hundreds more on the way.
They didn't get on too well, John and Simon, not at first, but
when the time came they stood together.'

Jesse paused before he continued, an odd expression on his
face.

'It would be a mistake to underestimate our Joseph. I did,
time after time, during those first eight months. Not so often
after Vespasian took Jotapata. Joseph will survive, mark my
words. A noble Roman, an honoured friend of the emperor.'

I was hesitant, but to direct the flow was essential. 'Will you
speak a little, Jesse, of the eight months? It is important.'

'How much do you have already? In parallel?'

'I know that after Cestius was defeated Nero took notice. In
public he ranted and screamed that it was Cestius' fault, not the
bravery of the Jews at all. He showed anger, and contempt, but
he was worried and looked for someone to handle the situation
and chose Vespasian, who had crushed the German rebellion
and had added the country called Britain to the Empire.'

'Britain?' said Sarah. 'I've never heard of it. What kind of
country is it? Where is it?'

'Far off. The other side of the world. Not much is known of
it. A strange people, very primitive.'

'Carry on,' said Jesse. 'Vespasian.'

'Vespasian was in his late fifties. Nero sent him to Syria to
concentrate the Roman legions and join them to the armed
forces requested of the nearby kings, who were in no position
to refuse. Titus, Vespasian's son, was sent by Nero to Alexandria to gather the Fifteenth Legion and take it north to join
his father's armies. Which he did, the forces gathering at
Ptolemais. It was an enormous army of about 60,000 trained
men, mounted and foot, with a worker and servant army of
nearly as many. Whilst the main assault was being planned and
organized Vespasian and Titus stayed in Ptolemais, leaving the
sweep attacks down through Galilee in the hands of Placidus,
who burned many towns and villages and killed hundreds. Yet

Placidus was stopped at Jotapata. He lost men and material and retreated in disorder. Shall I continue?'

'Have you *more*?' said Jesse. 'I am most impressed. Continue.'

I blushed. 'My job was intelligence. Vespasian decided that he would take over. He was ready. He marched out of Ptolemais with a very big force indeed. Cavalry, infantry and a big company of sappers whose job it was to set up the battering rams and catapults and other machines. There were trumpeters, the sacred eagle standards and the general's personal body-guard, hand-picked. They came over the border and paused to "make display", the tactic used to frighten.'

'It succeeded,' said Jesse, with a grin. 'Josephus and I and the rest of his staff and a company of troops had set up a camp at Garis near Sepphoris, south of Jotapata. A scout came in and told us of the "show of strength". We went, saw, and ran. We ran to Tiberias, for that was the full Roman might we'd been looking at. We felt like naked children. Carry on, Ruth.'

'Vespasian moved on to Gabara and took it without trouble. It was chosen to be an example of the revenge and punishment to be expected for the defeat of Cestius. He burned not only the town but all the little hamlets nearby—and killed every-body, leaving for some odd reason a few young children, who were allowed to watch their parents cut down.'

'Be calm, Ruth,' said Jesse. 'My turn. Josephus and I are now in Tiberias, with what's left of our men, who are quaking, and worse, talking. The people of Tiberias took one look at their provincial governor Joseph ben Matthias in obvious flight and the panic spread like fire. They worked out from the way he was behaving and speaking that he'd given up; he'd written off the whole thing. They were right. Also Josephus was certain that if he could fix it so that he could go over to the Romans he would be pardoned. He was positive; he told me so a dozen times. "To capture me," he said, "would be to capture the officer commanding all Galilee. A great piece of good fortune for them. A captive equal in rank to Vespasian. We could talk eye-to-eye!"'

'That's the way I want to talk to Joseph,' said Sarah. 'What happened next?'

'Well,' said Jesse, 'the cry of "Joseph the chicken-heart" began to be heard, for he was doing nothing. So he wrote a letter.'

'A letter!'

'Yes, old battler, a letter. To Jerusalem, describing the situation in detail and asking for an answer please by return. He said that if they wanted him to sue for terms he would; that if they wanted him to fight the Romans they should send an army. The letter went off by express messenger.'

'Are you joking?' asked Sarah. 'A *letter*? With Vespasian about fifteen miles away? What change could the letter bring about?'

'None.'

'I have never—' began Sarah.

'Do not,' said Jesse, 'underestimate Joseph, whose letter was a dispatch to base, a firm request to headquarters, a decisive action to quieten his critics. Also he knew that Vespasian would not come straight across to Tiberias leaving both flanks open to attack from north and south. In any case that fifteen miles is cut in half by mountain country; murderous terrain

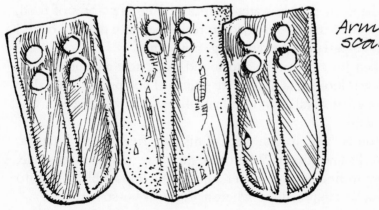

Armour scales

for an army. Joseph was playing general and doing it well. He worked out, rightly, that the Romans would strike first at the city nearest to them, Jotapata.'

'Jotapata,' from Sarah, with hard jaw.

'Not an easy place to take,' Jesse went on, 'or to get away from. High up; in the mountains. On three sides, deep gorges. From the north a sloping plain. Good solid defence walls on that side. Strong towers—and a lot of brave fighters with no-where to run to. For Vespasian, once up on that slope, a text-book job. Bring up everything, siege, blockade, starve out, for the city had no decent wells within its walls and it was May, with not much rain to be expected. But first Vespasian had to get his army up there. On bad mountain tracks difficult for infantry and impossible for cavalry. So he put his men to work, making the road before them.

'As soon as we heard of this delay Joseph announced to Tiberias his heroic decision. To go to lead the defence of Jotapata.'

Jesse paused, his eyes on Sarah's, who said not a word.

'We took a small force of scouts and foot-soldiers and approached the city from the side opposite the Romans. We were welcomed and the people took heart from Joseph's brave words.

'Joseph used many brave words, as did I, a senior member of his staff. Nobody used the proper words: that Jotapata had no chance at all. No water to speak of, no big stores of food, no great arsenal of any sort, no real experience of siege or real war. Vespasian had everything, plus time.'

Then Jesse fell silent, and so did we. I stole a glance at Saul who was looking at Jesse with a kind of compassion, and then I looked at Sarah, who sat with brows drawn, puzzled. She spoke first.

'You say that Joseph went of his own free will to Jotapata, which had no chance. Where to fight a way out was impossible, where to find another water supply was impossible, where to retreat was impossible—where *nothing* was possible?'

Jesse, who had been looking down, lifted his head as though it were a heavy weight. His mouth was bitter.

'Surrendering to Vespasian was possible,' he said.

Sarah let out breath softly, past tight lips, then spoke.

'First real fight of the War. Over to the other side with no waste of time. No accident. A plan. A worked-out decision. Using the circumstances. I *did* underestimate him. Bastard.' She looked at Jesse now in a different way, a knife-in-the-hand way. He waited.

'You went with him.'

'I thought like him.'

'You knew the plan.'

'I knew his mind.'

'—and the way he thought.'

'I thought in the same way.'

'Tell me how you thought.'

His voice was flat, detached. 'Personal aide to the general commanding, I thought. Senior officer, I thought. Ten years older than my general and an out-of-the-ordinary linguist, I thought. Very good chance of coming out of it alive—and maybe floating up a bit—I thought. All sound thinking. All came to pass.' His eyes went down again.

Sarah said, 'I also was in Jotapata. I also fought. I also was taken. But I got away. I killed men to get away.'

Jesse sat back, looking drained and exhausted. Saul moved nearer to him.

'So did I, old battler,' said Jesse. 'So did I. I killed Jews.'

It was a tremendous shock. Sarah's eyes were round and staring. My heart was pounding. Then Simeon's gentle high voice:

'There is more to tell. It must be told, and written down, and the words chosen carefully, and the happenings seen against their time. Or confusion and hatred—and madness—must ensue.'

Jesse said nothing for a moment, then continued, in a tired deep voice. 'When Vespasian arrived we were ready. Jotapata

gave trouble and its walls held and once or twice we even
drove the Romans back, but we were fighting troops who'd
had vast experience in crushing rebels like us. They knew
more tricks than we did—and had infinitely better arms. Joseph
was everywhere; all things to all men. Remarkable. A dozen
faces. A dozen ways of talking, and believing every word he
said. In a fortnight he knew every influential man in the city
(to them he used different words; a different voice) and was
looking over their houses for the strongest bunker.'

'What were his words to them?'

'To them he became like his namesake, Joseph, son of
Jacob. An interpreter of dreams, a man guided by God—and
in God's confidence. He hinted at signs and portents that
showed him God was now with the Romans, that no matter
how valorous and daring the various anti-Roman groups
fighting together in Jotapata were, it would prove to no avail.
He quoted at length from the sacred books and told the
prophetic meanings. He was hypnotic, because he was entirely
convinced and swayed by his own words.'

'You were too, by the sound of it,' said Sarah, roughly.

'Not in the least, but it is my habit to listen carefully, and in
among all the nonsense cold hard self-preservation was ticking
away; and when the visionary interpreter of dreams found in
his visions and dreams that some forty important and rich
people should gather provisions to last a long time, and with
his psychic help choose an almost impossible-to-discover
bunker, I got busy organizing it. The timing was perfect. The
forty moved into the bunker the night before the city fell and
Josephus and I joined them in the dawn mist as the Romans
came over the walls.'

'You missed something,' said Sarah. 'The Romans came at
dawn, in the mist, on a tip given them by a deserter who told
them that we were all so exhausted we could hardly stand—
and that in the last watch of the night even the guards couldn't
stay awake. It was true, God help us, it was true. The city was
full of Romans coming at us through the mist before we could

rub the sleep out of our eyes. You missed something. I was with a group that took over one of the wall towers and as the mist cleared and the sun came up we saw the Roman soldier at work. Most of the roads across the city end in a sheer drop into the gorge below. And that was the plan. Stand and be cut down or jump. Hundreds were slaughtered on that first day. Hundreds. Then the mopping up began, and the burning, and the pulling down. The hundreds became thousands. Our tower lasted no time. Five of us, all women, got away and mingled with a crowd of women being rounded up in the market square as captives.'

'Self-preservation,' murmured Saul gently.

'To fight another day!' roared Sarah.

'Don't defend me, brother Saul,' said Jesse. 'There is worse to come.' He looked at me for a moment, thoughtfully, with sadness. 'Take note, historian. I will speak slowly and clearly.

'In the bunker we saw nothing of the massacre and heard little. It was in a sunken garden and completely hidden. Impossible to detect. You had to know it was there. Well, one or two did: one of them a lady who at the last moment had not been invited to join us. When she was caught she talked freely and Vespasian was soon told that General Joseph was alive and well. He was also told exactly where the general was hidden. It had been Joseph who'd barred the lady, knowing exactly what she would do.

'So there we were, in the bunker, safe and warm and well fed. On the third day, in the afternoon, the Romans came. Now, the entrance to the bunker was a narrow passage through solid rock allowing only one person at a time. The Roman officers were wary, and shouted their demands for complete and immediate surrender from the garden end of the tunnel. Pandemonium. Joseph remained calm. So did I—and I didn't take my eyes off him. He said who he was in a loud voice but gave no answer as to surrender. The officers went away and returned later with another, of superior rank, called Nicanor, who asked to come through the passage, unarmed, to deliver a message from Vespasian. "I am known to you, Joseph," he said. "We met in Rome." He was known to me, too. An honest man, my age. He came through and assured Joseph of the goodwill of Vespasian towards so brave a leader. Valour was admired by the Romans, he said. "Have no fear," he said, "we want you alive and well and will keep you so. Your death is pointless and needless. These are the words of Vespasian!"'

'And then?' asked Sarah after a moment. 'What about the others? What about you?'

'Nicanor had no words for us and Joseph did not ask about us. No, his eyes opened wide and he went pale and he began to have visions, and words with God. It was impressive. "All now is clear and shown to me," he moaned, "all dreams, all prophecies, all the forbidden words. Now I know Lord, that it is thy wish, thou who madest the Jewish Nation and who hast now decided to level it with the dust, transferring thy favour to the Romans, now I know, Lord, that thou wishest me, chosen by thee to see the future, to surrender willingly to the Romans and live. But thou art my witness, Lord," he said in a louder, clearer, voice, "that I go over to them not as a traitor but because it is thy wish, because thou tellest me to."'

'I see,' said Sarah. 'Then?'

'He started to gather his bits and pieces together. Suddenly the forty woke up. There was their leader and prophet and dream-reader out of his trance—and packing. There was up-roar. I always keep quiet in uproar; that way you know which way to jump. The forty, knowing they were certain to be killed by the Romans, decided that killing themselves was more honourable—and that Joseph should lead them in this also. The roughest of them, a big man, called him names and re-minded him of how many he had persuaded to die for liberty's sake. To die rather than be taken. The rest agreed and joined in. "Be an example to us!" they screamed at him. "Better far to die as a Jewish general than live as a Roman slave"—and the big man put a sword in his hand.

'When the sword appeared Nicanor, unarmed, grew nervous. As more swords came out, I took him to the tunnel. I told him not to worry too much about Joseph and to set two extra places for dinner. As personal aide to my general I would share his capture and imprisonment.'

'How did you know? How could you be certain?'

'I did not know, Ruth dear. And the only thing I was certain of was that General Joseph wasn't going to join in any mass-suicide for honour's sake. The game wasn't over yet and my general was a master player, compared to whose skill my own wiggly little ways were like an innocent child's.'

'Yes,' said Sarah. 'So. The bunker is full of shouting people all keen on suicide. What now?'

'Now we are spoken to by our general in a reasoning, honest, philosophical way. Why are we so anxious to commit suicide? he asks, to part body and soul, joined together by God. "Certainly it *is* glorious to die for liberty," he told us, "but in war, not when the war is lost, or over." Were we dying for liberty's sake, or because we feared we were going to be killed anyway?

'Joseph went on at some length in this way. Open-faced, grave, chin up, honest. "Self-murder," he told us, "is contrary to the instincts of all living things, it is impious—and against God. It shows contempt to the All-Highest for his greatest gift to us. Life. It is for God to decide when to take back that gift. It is a valuable thing; in our trust; lent to us. By what right can we destroy it? No place in Heaven is there for those who murder themselves, any more than for those who murder others."

'I sat there watching how all this was working with the forty. Not too well. Joseph, aware of this, did not raise or quicken his voice. He became a priest giving a sermon; a teacher of philosophy; a master of logic and reason. His variations on the one theme seemed endless, spontaneous. But it wasn't going down too well. So he began a summing up.

'"Comrades," he said to us, "it is our duty to be honourable, and not to add to our human sufferings impiety towards our Creator. If we think it right to accept life when it is offered, let us accept it; for the offer bears no shame if it comes from those we have convinced of our bravery. But if we choose to die, how better than at the hands of those who conquered us?'' Then his voice took on a sincere, throbbing note. "I shall not go over to the Romans," he said, "in order to be a traitor to myself. It would be more foolish than to desert to them. To such deserters it would mean life, but for me it would mean death, my own death. I pray that the Romans prove traitors; and if after giving me their word they kill me, I will die happy, finding in such lies a consolation greater than victory itself.'''

'What the hell does all that last lot mean?' growled Sarah.

'Who knows?' said Jesse. 'It was meant to confuse and it did. But now there was a sort of madness in the forty. Swords and daggers were waved, great oaths were screamed. Every kind of crazed nonsense was spewed up. Absolute confusion. The one thing they were all agreed upon was that Joseph was a traitor and was in some way going to get away with it. They were cutting and thrusting at him. I am good with both hands and I had a sword in each and was looking after us both. Nothing heroic about it; I had absolute faith in Joseph getting himself—and me—out.

'I'd put him against the provision store in one corner and I was in front of him. Suddenly he was shouting and rattling an ivory box. The noise was unexpected and the shouting died away. When it was quiet he came round me and spoke in a firm, sad voice. "Very well," he said, "your choice is that we should all die. To kill oneself is fearsome and against God, so we will draw lots and number one will be dispatched by number two and he by number three and so on. Only the last one will kill himself but God will understand and forgive." He rattled the box. "God guided us to bring table games to the bunker to pass the time. Here is a game of ones-and-tens, with four sets of counters already marked from one to fifty." He thrust the box into my hands. "Jesse will count out one set and we will shake them up in the box and each will draw his number. Is it agreed?"

'They, beside themselves, shouted approval—and I pushed through them to the table and emptied out the counters and busied myself sorting one set. Joseph stood away a little to my left and slightly behind me. He stood with head up accepting the thanks and compliments of the forty, who now saw him for what they'd all along known him to be, a fearless Jewish general.

'When I'd sorted the counters in five rows of ten, numbers showing, four of the men checked them and looked at Joseph, who then also came over. He picked up the ivory box and I stood by his side and put the fifty pieces in. He handed me the box. He lifted his head to pray and the forty lowered theirs. "Inside the lid," he said in my ear. "Four blanks. Take two." And began his prayer.'

Jesse's head was down again, tilted, examining his sandal toe. No one spoke.

'It was easy. The blanks were in a pocket in the lining of the lid. I took two into my hand as I closed it. The prayer ended and I shook the box and put it back on the table. Each man in turn lifted the lid enough to put his hand in and with a little rattle selected his number. Joseph and I took our place in line and I gave him his blank. We put our hands into the box with the blanks in our palms and took our hands out with the fingers closed over them. It was easy.'

Sarah's breathing was noisy. 'Not all men can take a blade to another's throat. What about them?'

'I assisted them.'

'And who "dispatched" number forty?'

'It was not necessary. He and two before him were gibbering idiots by the time their turns came. We left them and went out to the Romans.'

'Enjoy your dinner?'

Jesse got up. He was deathly pale. 'Save your breath, old woman,' he said, his voice like a knife. 'To live is better than to die. And on the subject of Jesse's character it is unlikely that you will come up with new words. I've used them all.'

And he left us. The day seemed suddenly chill and the bright sun brassy and hard. I felt tired.

Simeon, after a while, began to speak, almost musingly, to himself almost. He recalled happenings of terror, of fear, of blood. He pondered aloud upon the actions of ordinary people in unordinary and nightmarish situations. He did not proffer subjects for discussion; it was the sleepy meanderings of an old man. But the mild light voice was not soporific; you listened, and proportion and priority returned. After a while Saul also left us; and old Simeon, seemingly, dozed off.

Sarah then got up and went and clattered and banged in the kitchen, ignoring the protests of the old women. I sat on near the old priest, and tried to sort my mind. 'Detachment is essential,' Silva had said.

After a while my brother came back and sat across the little table from me.

'He does not get drunk,' he said sadly, 'or take drugs, or in any way soften the edges of his life. He sleeps very little, and is at all times in control of himself and the situations in which he finds himself. He is feared, for he himself has no fear at all. He says that fear is really fear of death and that he would welcome death. I believe him. He has no peace. He will talk no more today but will join us for the evening meal.'

'Where is he? Perhaps I—'

'With his horse. Leave him.' Saul's tone was firm, wanting no argument. I went indoors.

13 Soothsayer to Vespasian

The defiant 'Year Two' (of the Revolt) shekels.

13

The evening meal was cheerful and normal. Jesse had changed his seat and sat at the head of the table with all the children at his end, the youngest nearest. Little Sami and the year-older Simon were Jesse's slaves, and he treated them like grown-ups. For the twins he did little impressions of high-up Roman officers and for Judith and the dark withdrawn Sim he had sardonic compliments and a flattering attention to their few words.

At the other end of the table sat Saul, and he kept our talk on light levels. Sarah, as always quick to pick up undercurrents, exchanged reminiscences with the old women and joked with Simeon about being a bachelor all his life.

The evening passed quickly. Jesse left the table first '—to gamble a little with the Romans. The Passover presents cost a lot, my children, I must get it back.'

As he passed my chair, he paused. 'At ten o'clock tomorrow morning we shall all meet in the garden. I have more for the book. Of Vespasian and Titus and the prisoner-of-war prophet Joseph. Goodnight, my historian.' And was gone.

When Sarah and I were in our room later preparing for bed, she said: 'I'm lost. On Masada we lived up in clean air, with room to move and a chance for the mind to get well again. I'd forgotten a lot, my dove, a lot. Who can help that one? Who can judge? Who is guilty—and who not?' She kissed me and settled on her bed. After a while: 'And we need him. He was on the other side, with Joseph. And if I know that one, he missed nothing. Goodnight, my angel.'

Indeed he had missed nothing. When we met next morning his eyes were shadowed and tired-looking but he was courteous and natural and we took our example from him.

'Sarah will begin,' he said. 'Fall of Jotapata; group of captive women moved out of the city to await further orders.'

'I waited till night,' said Sarah, 'and left for Jerusalem.'

'Just like that?' said Jesse.

'It's never just like that. But the news of Jotapata had to get to Jerusalem and I think I was the only one of our group still alive. The Roman soldiers were going to have games with that crowd of women, no matter what age, when night came. A soldier with that on his mind is careless, and who searches an old woman for a knife?'

'True. What did Jerusalem say?'

'By the time I got there it was known. Some fighters from villages to the east of Jotapata had taken the news. I was able to add some more. That a rumour existed among the women I'd left that Joseph was now with the Romans. The woman he'd sent out of the bunker seemingly knew him well.'

'She did. How did Jerusalem react?'

'Not with any great surprise but with great anger. It was good. It unified people, and the treatment of Jotapata by Vespasian showed us what to expect in Jerusalem. Now you, Jesse.'

He paused a moment, thinking where to begin. Then in a light amused voice: 'We came out of the bunker bespattered with blood like sacrifice priests. Nicanor and a detail took us not to Vespasian but to a captives officer who was in no way impressed with our high rank. He ignored our bloody clothes and called a smith, who chained us to each other, anchoring us then, with more chain, to a deaf-mute slave who was gross and disgusting. Then we were put in an outside cell open to the sky. It was nearly evening. There were guards inside and outside the cell.

'The next morning we were taken, deaf-mute anchor and all, before Vespasian and his son Titus. We were dirty and the blood on us smelt. We stood in the sun and the Roman general and his group of officers sat under an awning. Vespasian was brief. He told Joseph that taking Jotapata had meant the death of many Roman soldiers and had been a costly action in many ways. He told us that Emperor Nero was very angry at the vast ingratitude shown by the people of Israel in their desire for independence—and would now crush that desire for ever. He told Joseph that he would be kept chained and in the closest custody until he was sent to Nero. This to be as soon as possible.'

'Not the reception you expected,' said Sarah drily.

'Indeed not. Let me say again, old battler, do not underestimate General Joseph.'

'Chained together and smelly, with a deaf-and-dumb lump on the end of the chain. Impressive. Carry on.'

'Joseph stood still, looking into Vespasian's face with a strange, mystical, frowning expression. "I have little to say," he said, "but it must be for your ears alone." It was completely unexpected. The Roman after a moment asked everyone to withdraw except his son Titus, and two senior officers. He made a gesture inviting us to walk forward into the shade. Joseph didn't move, so neither could I. Take this down, Ruth dear.

'"It may be, Great General," said Joseph, in a priestly voice, "that before you you see only a Jewish commanding officer who did his duty to the end, fighting as bravely as would a Roman in like circumstance. But I am more. I am a messenger sent by God himself to tell you of the greatness soon to be yours. God spared my life for the work of bringing you this message—or else as a Jewish general I would have died with my men. For thus we die, we Jewish generals." I was fascinated,' said Jesse.

'So are we,' said Sarah. 'So are we.'

'So, I think, was Vespasian,' Jesse went on, 'although his

face showed nothing. He waited, and Joseph continued. "You say you are sending me to Nero. What for? Soon Nero will be gone, *and* his successors—and *you* will be emperor! And after you your son! Master of the Sea and the Land and of the whole world. These words are from God—and if they prove false, double the weight of my chains and let the penalties be heavy!"

'Vespasian and his son and the officers exchanged looks. Titus is about the same age as Joseph, maybe a bit older—and he was completely entranced by the idea. He and his father had no blood link to the throne whatsoever but were the darlings of the military junta. Vespasian was the great empire builder. It was a marvellous bit of long-shot thinking on Joseph's part —with a remarkable instinct for the Roman way of things.

'One of the two senior officers spoke first. "Did not your God tell you that Jotapata would fall?" he said, "And that you would finish in chains, lying to save your miserable life?"'

'Good point,' said Sarah. 'What happened then?'

'"I will say no more," declared Joseph. "Take my colleague here and question him in private as to my predictions, my interpreting of dreams, my reading of signs and portents. I am a priest, of priestly line. A soldier and leader of men by force of destiny." It was done. The smith came and the chain was cut and Joseph taken away.

'It is easy to convince people who want to be convinced. I enjoyed it. Wine was brought. We sat in the shade and talked of mutual friends in Rome. When I apologized for my stinking state, a clean set of clothes was brought, and scented water, and a slave to help.

'I told them the truth.' Jesse's smile was full of devilment. 'I told them I had known Joseph a long time and knew him well. That we had met in Rome, where we had shared a deep admiration for what we had seen. I told them that since returning to Israel, Joseph had predicted and foreseen in the most accurate way that he would be captured alive early in the War. I told them that throughout Galilee his predictions of defeat by mighty Rome were known and that many of the resistance groups hated him for his obvious psychic link with the Almighty. Even in Jotapata, I told them, he somehow knew that "he and one other would emerge unharmed into a garden from a place below ground filled with madness and blood." Signs and omens were like open books to him, I said, portents and the meanings of dreams were equally clear.

'"Keep him close, great Vespasian," I advised, "for this is no ordinary man. Do not scorn his words, incredible as they seem. Often, in prophetic transport, he speaks, inexplicably, in languages and dialects unknown to him in normal life. The translation of these pronouncements has been my work, for I am multi-lingual. It may be that I was sent by the Almighty to be by his side for this purpose. At all times."'

'How did that bit go down?' asked Sarah.

'Bait, hook and line. Soon we were free of our deaf-and-dumb anchor and living reasonably, with Titus friendlier with Joseph by the hour. We were closely guarded at all times and at first chained also.

'After the mopping up at Jotapata, Vespasian gathered his forces and went back to Ptolemais and then down the coast to Caesarea, which as you know is largely Greek. A big welcome —and great enthusiasm for killing Joseph and myself as members of the hated Jews. I'm not fond of Greeks.

'Vespasian rested his soldiers for a period, two legions in Caesarea and the Fifteenth in Scythopolis. He himself went across to King Agrippa and Bernice who were at Caesarea Philippi. They put on huge festivities in his honour and made him very welcome. Bernice, I understand, put herself very much at his disposal. A very attractive lady, I'm told, of about forty.'

'Didn't you and Joseph go with him?' asked Sarah.

Jesse laughed. 'It wasn't till much later that Joseph and Vespasian became such bosom friends. Vespasian was embarrassed by us. We had started emperor-longings in him. Dictator-of-the-world fancies, and he knew that we knew that he knew and so on. So he avoided us; left us in the other Caesarea, on the coast. Heavily guarded but fairly comfortable.'

'Where was Titus?'

'He went with his father to the king—and was shown similar hospitality by Bernice, so the story goes. Mess-room talk. What an old gossip I am, to be sure.' His voice was mocking; his eyes not. 'I gave a little time to thinking of the Roman general, whose stated policy was to wipe out as many of the troublesome Jews as possible, being entertained in some splendour by the nominal king of those Jews. Perhaps a word or two in your book, dear Ruth?'

'It is known to me. I have note of it. Do you know how long Vespasian stayed with the king?'

'Three weeks. A time of banquets, sacrifices to his gods for victory (a bit premature, that) and various other jollities. Then he was informed that Tiberias and Tarichaeae were in full revolt and he told the king that in gratitude for the jolly times he and Titus would go and wipe out the two towns. Which was done in about two-and-a-half months. Do you have material on that, Ruth? I have little.'

'I have enough. It was the first time that Titus led troops in a big action. He did well, for the troops liked him. He was about thirty. His father was pleased. In both towns the slaughter was terrible. In Tiberias the aged and infirm were herded into the stadium and killed to the last one. Thousands of the able-bodied were sent as slaves to Nero. Thousands more were sold as slaves by the king. Their own king.'

'What then?' asked Jesse firmly.

'All the towns west of the Sea of Galilee were then subdued, with the single exception of Gischala, far to the north. John's town. The least resistance was crushed without mercy. Many fighters made their way south, to Jerusalem. Everyone knew that we would be left until last. On the eastern side of the sea, in Gaulanitis, only the mountain town of Gamala declared itself anti-Roman. It was even more inaccessible than Jotapata and its inhabitants were determined and brave.

'The siege lasted one month. And many, many lives were lost on both sides. In Jerusalem we could see that a pattern was emerging; of highly-skilled engineers preparing the way for the armed forces. Nothing was too difficult for them. And the engineers could call on a huge labour force.'

'What after Gamala?' asked Jesse, with the same firmness.

'Gischala. Vespasian sent Titus to take it and he himself went back to Caesarea to plan the crushing of the rest of Israel. Gischala was soon overcome and John got away with some of his fighters, and came here to Jerusalem. He gave us problems but we were pleased to have him for he was a leader; people would follow him. We could have used you too, Jesse. People would have followed you also.' I regretted my words as I said them, for they touched a raw place, and needlessly I'd caused pain. He smiled.

'Ah. Yes. But then I would not have been able to tell you of the prophet Josephus and the mighty Vespasian. Now. As time passed and the whole country was overcome, Joseph seemed less and less an embarrassment to Vespasian. We were closely guarded at all times, though I'm not sure why; there was no danger whatsoever of Joseph trying to escape. So we became more and more comfortable. Titus would visit us when he could, and we found friends among the Roman officers. We were told little of what was going on but it was easy to keep up to date. Gamala fell in October and Gischala in November and that was Galilee done. The army went into winter quarters and began again in early March. Gadara fell and the army fanned out. Perea was "subdued", then the south, Judea and Idumea. By the middle of June Vespasian was at Jericho, fifteen miles from Jerusalem.'

'And what,' said Sarah, 'of the prophet Joseph during this time? How long, from Jotapata to all-except-Jerusalem-subdued. A year?'

'Nearly a year. Joseph took a wife.'

'A wife!'

'A wife. As part of making us more comfortable, at officer

level, as it were, ladies were available. Joseph was interested enough but having built up this reputation as soothsayer and reader of portents—and of an aristocratic priestly family—he thought he'd better not. So Vespasian sent over a virgin for him to marry. A nice child, captured at Jotapata. I thought it was a joke set up by one or two of the officer friends I gambled with. Perhaps it was, but Joseph took no chances. "If Great Vespasian has chosen this bride for me," he told a rather startled mess, "then it shall be." And it was. I quite envied him. All the comforts of home!'

Sarah. 'Didn't Great Vespasian send a virgin over for you, too?'

'No. It seems that in Rome soothsayers and virgins are inter-linked—if you will excuse my clumsy use of words.'

There was laughter. It was good.

'Enough of the Romans,' said Jesse. 'What of the Jews in that year?'

Simeon sat forward, his eyes round and bright. 'Ruth dear,' he said, 'Jesse is right. It is of value now for us to speak in parallel. Jesse of Rome and the Romans, and we of Jerusalem—and Masada.' My brother nodded, and I was grateful for the plan, to which it was obvious they had all given thought.

'Sarah—?' prompted Jesse.

'Gischala fell and John was in Jerusalem in early December or late November,' said Sarah, who had fought under John and admired him. 'He cut away a lot of dead wood and got rid of the lot who'd elected the so-called leaders. He started to call things by their right names. Inside Jerusalem people felt safe. Big walls; God in the Temple; huge defence towers—and lots of people: refugees arriving every day. John made us see we weren't so safe. He started stockpiling every sort of weapon, from bows and arrows to big rocks. He issued orders about training and sentries and guard-duties and rationing. He made enemies right and left but he made sense. Ruth, how long did you say it was between Jotapata and "only Jerusalem left"?'

'Jesse said it. About one year. Vespasian began again in early

March and by late June only the fortresses of Machaerus, Herodium and Masada were holding out. And Jerusalem had not been approached at all.'

'Ah,' said Jesse. 'June. Everything ready for the big push—and then the one thing that could stop everything happened, and *did* stop everything. The violent death of Nero—at a time of nearly as much unrest and rebellion in Rome as there was here in Israel. Galba was brought home to Rome from Spain to be emperor and Vespasian sent Titus to him to get instructions about Israel. Whilst Titus was on his way, by sea, news came that Emperor Galba had been killed, after six months, and that one Otho had taken over. So Titus came back to his father, both of them looking at Prophet Joseph in a decidedly respectful way.'

'During that period of Galba,' said Sarah, 'Simon ben Giora, who'd done so well in the defeat of Cestius and had brought so much booty and munitions back to Jerusalem, was very busy indeed. When earlier Vespasian had gone south with his armies to "quieten" Idumaea and Peraea, a lot of the Idumaeans had taken to the hills—which could hide a million. Masada is only one of the mountains down there by the Dead Sea—and not the biggest by a long chalk.

'Now, using Masada as a base, Simon set about gathering Idumaeans and turning them into an army. Then he brought them up to Jerusalem—although that was not until about six months after Galba had been killed.

'With them, with his own fighters, came Eleazar.'

'An important and eventful half year,' said Jesse, settling himself. 'After Galba, Otho—who was emperor for only about three months! He committed suicide, after losing a battle with Vitellius, who also wanted to be emperor and was general over a great many soldiers who agreed with him. So after Otho killed himself, Vitellius set *him*self up.

'Vespasian, also a general with a lot of soldiers, was not pleased. He had just as much right to be emperor and his personal soothsayer Joseph had said he would be. How could he give his mind to little Israel when the great Roman Empire was being usurped by an obviously unworthy person. An opinion with which Joseph and I made it our business to agree at every opportunity, loudly. The game was nearly won. Mind you, Vespasian's officers did not need much convincing—and it was true, by all accounts, that this Vitellius was a nobody compared to *our* general.

'Well, I don't know whether Joseph started it, but soon there was a decided "movement" among the officers—indeed among the whole army—to proclaim *our* general emperor. Vitellius was called a lot of nasty names and his soldiers even worse ones. *Our* general suddenly became a clean-living, home-loving, honourable husband and father, perfect for the post. Joseph and I were like two great spoons; we never stopped stirring.

'Then the senior staff officers who had been with Vespasian in all his great campaigns exerted heavy pressure and—after not too much hesitation—he agreed. Especially when they pointed out that his nomination would be backed by some three legions, all the armies lent by the nearby kings—and all the parts of Europe out of Vitellius' reach. Also, they said, he had many supporters all over Italy—and in Rome itself. Indeed in those troublous times Vespasian's own brother was entrusted with the control of the city, a great asset for a candidate.

'Now,' said Jesse, in a different tone, 'Vespasian, I think, when faced with being emperor, was *not* too keen. A dangerous job. Also he was nearly sixty and far more used to the battle-field than to the Palace and the Senate. But he was a first-rate tactician and knew that just calling himself emperor might not be enough. So we all went not to Rome, but to Alexandria. Not to Italy but to Egypt.'

'*We* all went—?' said Sarah.

'*We*,' said Jesse. 'Without chains, with personal bodyguard, and a certain status, undefined but definite, on the staff of the emperor-elect.'

'What about the young Mrs. Joseph?'

'The marriage was dissolved before we left. Joseph thought it best. His new position required a more distinguished lady. He was quite right, and the girl was well out of it. Don't look shocked, Ruth.'

'Why to Alexandria instead of Rome?'

'To be master of Alexandria was to be master of Egypt—which supplied Rome's corn. No fool, Vespasian. Also, in Alexandria were two more legions to add to all his other supporters. There was one more thing. If things went badly, that part of the Nile delta was marvellous Vitellius-fighting terrain.'

Jesse paused again, with an amused glint. 'Joseph, man of destiny, didn't miss a trick. When he heard about the corn, and Egypt, he right away had a vision in which his own namesake Joseph appeared, and the seven lean years and the seven fat years, and corn, and Egypt, and a great warrior-king with the face of our beloved general.

'By the time we arrived in Alexandria the governor, Tiberius Alexander, one-time unsuccessful procurator of Judea, had fixed everything. Total allegiance to Vespasian by everybody. Vespasian, emperor of the Romans, monarch of the World.'

'Tiberius Alexander,' said Sarah slowly, 'who crucified Menahem's two brothers. Joseph was in good company. What was going on in Rome?'

'Vitellius and his army were being beaten into the dust by Mucianus, sent there by Vespasian to do just that. Vitellius was killed outside the Royal Palace. He was drunk and gorged with food at the time. Emperor about nine months. Mucianus put Vespasian's other son, Domitian, on the throne to keep it warm until his father arrived. The news of all this came to Alexandria at roughly the time that the rest of the world had accepted Vespasian. Great news—and celebrations to match. Alexandria, after Rome the most important city in the world, was well able to put on the great show such an occasion demanded. My favourite bit of the show was a little private ceremony, when the Prophet Joseph was brought before Emperor Vespasian who was attended by his senior officers, some friends, and his son Titus. With the prophet, his translator and fellow-prisoner, Jesse. "It is wrong," said the new emperor, "that this man, who prophesied my rise to power and is the mouthpiece of God, should be still treated as prisoner and captive. Let him be set free." Then Titus stepped forward. "Father," he said, "instead of the traditional Removal of Fetters to betoken a freed captive, let there be the Cutting of the Links, which means free pardon, removal of all disgrace, and full grant of all civil rights." Father said good idea and an axe was brought and a bit of chain was cut in half.'

'To remove a disgrace,' said Sarah, 'they should have hit Joseph with the axe.'

'Please,' admonished Jesse, 'Detachment. A calm gaze. Like our beautiful recorder. Am I to go on, Ruth?'

'Yes, please. Did Vespasian go to Rome after the celebrations in Alexandria?'

'No. Not right away. He spent the end of the winter months in planning the end of the Israel campaign, as it was called. And there was Joseph's wedding to attend, of course.'

'What, another one?' said Sarah. 'Busy little man. I've been thinking about that girl-wife in Jotapata. Joseph was already married. Here in Jerusalem. A woman in my unit was a cousin of his wife.'

'Perhaps he knew, with his psychic powers,' said Jesse, 'that he would not be coming back when he left Jerusalem—or that he wouldn't need her any more. He's still got the Alexandrian one. Shall I go on, Ruth?'

'How do you know he still has the wife from Alexandria?'

'Tell you later. Now. Where are we? Yes. The War to be finished off. Titus was to be in charge of the assault on Jerusalem, with the pick of the legions. Since the death of Nero: about a year and a half. A pause in the War; a breathing space for Jerusalem. What had gone on here meanwhile? Ruth?'

'Argument and disagreement on the subject of leadership and what best to do. A lot of people were afraid. A lot hoped that the War would not come; that Rome would pass over us like the Angel of Death in the time of Moses in Egypt. Quite a lot of the rich people thought that some sort of terms could be worked out; that Rome could be bought off. Simon and John did not get on well. Their men and followers split into separate factions and a lot of energy and effort was wasted. We knew a little of what had happened in Rome and Alexandria and that Titus would be in charge of the attack. We knew also that the Twelfth Legion which we had beaten under Cestius was coming back for revenge—'

'Typical Vespasian, that kind of thinking,' said Jesse. 'Continue please.'

'—and that the Tenth was coming down from Jericho and the Fifth across from Emmaus. We did *not* know that Titus was coming from Caesarea with three more legions.'

'*And* more too. Troops from the Egyptian and Euphrates garrisons. Ruth dear, Joseph is going to write up this War as if Titus was a prince of God on a white horse all by himself, but *I* tell you that our emperor's boy was taking very few chances. Thousands and thousands of men. When we marched out of Caesarea it was a sight to see, Ruth, a sight to see.'

'Describe it, please.'

'An advance guard of Roman and allied troops. Next the road-makers and camp-constructors, then the officers' baggage —with armed escort. Next, Titus with spearmen and cavalry. Then the engineers, the towers, the missile-launchers, the rams. The standards next, and the Royal Eagle, with trumpeters. Then the endless columns, six abreast, each legion with its vast supplies—and servant corps. Last of all, the mercenaries, with Roman rearguard. Two days' march to Jerusalem, overnight stop at Gophna. The base-camp was made in the Valley of Thorns, about three-and-a-half miles east of here. During the night of the base-camp building, the legion from Emmaus— the Fifth—joined us, and soon after the Tenth, from Jericho. Titus then ordered camps to be built nearer to the city, heavily fortified and less than a mile away. One was across the Kidron Valley on the Mount of Olives.'

'We know,' said Sarah; 'we interfered with the work quite a bit.'

'A lot of planning and looking down on the city was done from the top of my favourite hill, Mount Scopus. It was during this "looking down" that Titus decided to level and clear all the ground between the hill and the city and the sappers went to work. I must tell you, old battler, that good Titus was often put out by the amount of coming-outside-the-walls-to-fight that the wicked Jews did. He really thought that the "display of might" would frighten you all to death.'

Sarah laughed. 'We were frightened. And when the camps were brought nearer and we *did* see the full strength, all the argument inside the walls stopped like magic. From the city, Jesse, those three camps were very visible—and looked like cities themselves. East, west and north.'

Jesse nodded. 'We were in the west one. Army command. It may be of interest to you, Ruth, to know that the commander of the armies was our old procurator friend Tiberius Alexander. I don't know why; he was no military man. Perhaps he was to be the one to take the blame if Titus messed it up. Son of the emperor must not be wrong, and so on.'

'Why were you and Joseph with Titus?'

'Special adviser with prophetic powers, and his personal aide and translator. It will emerge in Joseph's History that he himself played a most heroic part in the taking of Jerusalem. A maker of mighty speeches, stressing to the wicked ones within the walls the hopelessness of their resistance, the positive fact that God was on the Roman side and the great kindness and mercy of those same Romans.'

'Really?' said Sarah. 'Those kind and merciful Romans, when the starvation began, waited for the people who crept down into the valleys looking for food and crucified them in front of our walls. But not right away. First they tortured them and then nearly took the skin off them with scourges. There were a great many of those crosses.'

14 The End of the City

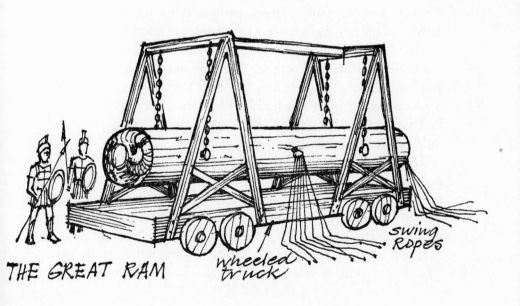

THE GREAT RAM wheeled truck swing Ropes

14

Aand so we talked. In a sunny garden, at our ease. We recalled terrible times; from a three-year distance and from
different viewpoints and it made for accuracy. I have given
much thought to the elements and factors in the battle for
Jerusalem; for they were many. It was the Roman engineers
and builders who beat us. They built the attack towers and the
engines which sat on them. They built the mighty platforms
along which rolled their catapults and missile-throwers. They
made the roads up to our very walls and constructed the
mighty swing-rams which knocked holes in those walls. They
worked fast, superbly skilled, protected by the shields and
arrows of the troops they were preparing the way for.

The first wall to be breached was the one to the north,
furthest from the city proper. The wall started by Agrippa I
and halted sharply by Rome; but over the years finished and
made strong. Agrippa, a builder like Great Herod his father,
had made the wall a great half circle to enlarge the city, to provide new areas, more space for people.

The wall was breached three weeks after the legions arrived,
and from the new areas, the 'New City', came the thousands to
the Old City, with any possessions they could carry. As they
rushed to the safety of the inner walls, so our fighters went
through them to meet the Romans.

It had been a pleasant place, the New City, where cloth was
woven and sold in booths and small shops, where the iron-

smiths had done their skilled wrought-work. Small fruit farms had been there, the woodmarkets, the grazing lands and pens for the sacrificial sheep, the arcaded pools where the sheep and cattle had been washed and made ready, the beautifully kept monuments to Jannaeus and Hyrcanus. Up on the slope north of the Temple Mount had been fine villas, with shady gardens. It was difficult to believe that all had now become a rubble-strewn wasteland.

'The fighting in the New City was rough,' said Sarah—who had been in every fight and was a good judge. 'But in four days they'd broken a hole in the second wall—and had started to build four platforms! Two against Antonia and two across the valley by the Three Towers—whilst we were holding them away from the Old City Wall and the Temple! We fought out-side the Old City and the Temple for five days—and that plat-form-building didn't stop! The platforms were for the Ram, the biggest wall-batterer I've ever seen. Like a nightmare, eh, Ruth?'

A nightmare indeed. A tree-trunk as thick as the height of a man supported between wooden towers on chains to hang level, and swing; the towers themselves on a great wheeled truck. Its striking end was enclosed in iron, rough carved into the head of a curled-horn ram. Its enormous blows were made by companies of troops pulling its ends in turn—and at the height of the backward swing moving the whole structure, with a great yell, forward to the wall. The sound of the impact as the iron head came down and forward could be heard all over the city and was like the fist of God.

But John of Gischala was quick to learn; with Eleazar and Simon, now firmly by his side, no slower. As, outside the Antonia fortress, the attack platforms were being built, so, from inside, our tunnellers were at work, undermining the platforms with underground passages propped with wood soaked in pitch and bitumen. When the moment came the props were fired and the passages collapsed, the Roman plat-forms falling into the craters and adding to the flames. A superb, heartening success, with smoke rising to heaven. The Romans were much put down by this, for timber was scarce. Two days later, Simon and Eleazar, waiting till the other two platforms had rams on them, led a huge torch-bearing attack outside the Upper City wall and burned both rams and platforms—and many Romans.

'We took *that* fight nearly to the Roman camps!' said Sarah. 'A great shock to them, that was! We lost a great fighter that day. "The Cripple." A club foot and shoulders like a giant. He went through a ram platoon with a pitch torch in each hand. Those he couldn't burn he clubbed to death! And the Zealots behind him became like him! A thing to see, a thing to see.'

'There were courts-martial that night over that skirmish,' said Jesse with a grin. 'Titus was rather rattled that soldiers told to storm the walls of the Jews should spend part of the day defending their own walls. He'd lost a lot of men, and worse (his own words) a lot of very scarce timber! When he calmed down he called a full council of war. Everything was discussed; every suggestion—by some very experienced senior officers— talked over. More platforms; a ring of men right round the city; leave the city to starve—for Joseph painted a picture of various factions killing each other within the walls. "All we have to do is wait!" he said. One of the tribunes, who did not like our Joseph, observed that inside the walls they might quarrel but outside they fought side by side like devils. Titus made up his mind. "No!" he said. "No waiting. And no platforms for a while; the timber is far away. And no ring of men; a ring of men means thin lines of men, open to surprise attack— and the Jews certainly know ways through such lines—"'

'So we will build a wall,' ended Sarah.

'Right round,' said Jesse. 'With every single soldier and sapper and worker doing his full share. Right round the city. About four-and-a-half miles. Up hill and down dale. It was a mixture of very hard discipline and inter-legion, inter-company competition. Big prizes—and big punishments and disgrace for slacking. Titus wanted glory and his papa's approval as

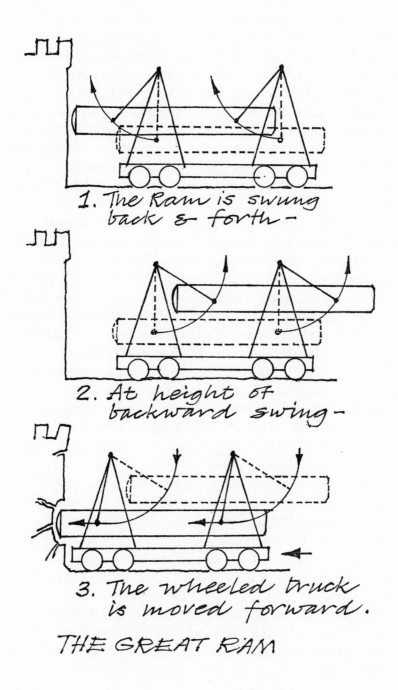

1. The Ram is swung back & forth —

2. At height of backward swing —

3. The wheeled truck is moved forward.

THE GREAT RAM

soon as possible. No fighting to be done; only building.'

There was a little silence, and then my brother spoke, half to himself, half to Jesse. 'I think that when the wall began we admitted the thought we had been suppressing; that the food was nowhere near enough. The produce of the New City and the laden markets of the Inner Wall areas was gone for ever. We were going to starve. We were vastly overcrowded, not only with New City and Market Area people, but also with thousands who'd come to Jerusalem for the Passover and had been trapped by the Romans' arrival. And we had refugees from other places too.'

'The wall and the starvation did another thing as well,' said Sarah. 'It showed us that as a fairly nasty death was pretty certain, there was nothing more to lose by *fighting* to the end. It was during the wall-building, by the way, that our Joseph paid us a visit. I was with a unit up on the rampart just south of Herod's palace. He came forward from the wall-builders on the west and started some sort of speech. I made our lot keep quiet and he came nearer. Then our best slingman let him have a rock right in the ear. He dropped like an ox. Great moment. I was sure we'd killed him. There was cheering right along the rampart. Some of the lads wanted to go out and get him but the Romans were quicker. I was told that when they gave the news to his mother here in Jerusalem she wasn't too upset. I think she knew her Joseph very well.'

Hunger, despite Sarah's words, is in no way ennobling. There were a great many shameful acts. In a vastly over-crowded community, when the food runs out very primitive laws of survival take over.

A lot of people left the city. They went across the open spaces between our walls and the Roman wall and gave themselves up. Most were killed and their bodies stripped of everything. Jesse told us a rumour started that many of the Jews had secreted or swallowed their gold and the Syrian and Arab mercenaries—and the Romans too—ripped open the bodies by the hundred.

John and Simon, who were alike in getting their priorities in the right order, ordered the Temple stocks of sacred corn and holy oil to be broken open and rationed out. Hoarding and overpricing was punished by death. Life was cheap—and thousands died. People gave up hope, and sat apathetically until death came. There were few burials. People hadn't the strength for such work and there were no sites. The bodies were given prayer and dropped over the eastern wall of the Temple, where the deep Valley of Kidron runs, banked on its other side by the Mount of Olives. In the beautiful valley, the piles of bodies rotted and stank.

'Once the encircling wall was well started,' said Jesse, 'a lot of the Roman soldiers and the worker force were sent out foraging for timber, for an all-out attack on the Antonia fortress was planned, and four more ramps were to be built.'

'We went out to those platforms more than once,' Sarah told us, 'but we got nowhere. *They* fought *us* with fire! Thrown from behind troops in full armour. They brought up the Ram on July the first, a month after they'd started the wall, which was finished. We threw everything down at them. Fire, arrows, stones, boiling oil, everything! They just went on, with sappers digging away at the foundations under a roof of shields. They were clever, and looking for the passages we'd dug the first time. They found them and used them. First to weaken and bring down one of the Antonia outside walls— and three days later to come in by! They came in the night, as silent as cats, but with trumpeters; and on a signal, it was bedlam: suddenly the invincible Antonia was invincible no more!'

Indeed not. Now it was a building in the north-west corner of the Temple Mount full of Roman troops and noise. Then every inch was fought for with a starving desperation, for this was the beginning of the end. The Romans were now inside, within the Temple compound, for the two-storey colonnades which ran along all four sides of the Temple area joined Antonia. They were part of it; provided entrances and exits to it, both at ground level and along their flat roofs. From it the Romans could pour out and encircle the Temple, *our* fortress.

'So we burned a gap,' said Sarah, 'to stop them coming out—and then they burned a gap the other side to stop us getting in!' She was serious again. 'But they came out. Again and again.'

And soon all the beautiful colonnades were charred and blackened and the fighting crept towards the Temple itself. Outside the walls, day after day, the ram thundered and fear drenched the very air. The great walls surrounding the Temple Area held, but their gates gave way to fire, and the flames roared and devoured—and on the inside of the walls the colonnades burned anew. One month almost to the day after Antonia, as the sun went down, the Temple was ringed with fire. The Romans drew back, into Antonia and away from the walls, as if they knew, like we did, that tomorrow the Temple would fall. On the same day of the year as centuries before it had fallen before Nebuchadnezzar of Babylon.

'Our Joseph will say, in his Titus-adoring history,' said Jesse slowly, 'that the Temple was destroyed against the wishes of Titus. Rubbish and nonsense. Titus knew all about Nebuchadnezzar—and the anniversary date! He knew it from Joseph, who never failed to make such observations. Titus didn't need too much pushing to see himself as the Roman Nebuchadnezzar. Also his whole staff agreed that if it was the Temple that made Jews fight like that, the quicker it was destroyed the better.'

It was done with fire—and by Romans mad for revenge. Thousands and thousands of Romans. And as the Temple flames mounted to heaven, so from all over Jerusalem a cry went up, a choked scream of loss—and people began to run up the slopes to the Mount. Ordinary people, poor people, starving, unarmed people. In the Temple itself, a place of many courts and chambers and halls, a multitude had hidden, a great mass of people who'd felt safe and sheltered in the Sanctuary of God. In the huge complex of buildings hundreds of our fighters had been based. Its very solidity had made it a fortress, the only fortress facing Antonia.

There was much in it to burn and the flames trapped a great many—whose screams added to the nightmare of sound which echoed back from the hills around. The Romans were like crazed beasts, looting and killing without rest. The whole Temple area, the whole Mount, was carpeted with corpses.

Simeon spoke in his high voice, in a sort of wonder. 'I did not want to leave the Temple, but Saul said it was time. I had known very little life outside. The Temple had everything for me. To live inside the Temple was to be surrounded with beauty. Ruth dear, the last thing I saw before the break-through to the Upper City—that saved so many—was two of my friends, gentle priests both, hurling spiked pieces of orna-mental railing down at the Romans from the Sanctuary roof. Then they fell backwards, by choice I think, into the inferno.'

The 'break-through' had been by the main Zealot group under Eleazar through the massive Roman concentrations round the inside of the Temple compound walls, blocking all gates.

'Had we not got through,' said Sarah, 'they would have caught both John and Simon—and Eleazar too. The fight wasn't over yet. The Temple was gone but there was still the Upper and Lower City. Still plenty of Romans to kill.'

The Zealots fought their way across the Upper City and we barricaded ourselves in the Royal Palace, near the Three Towers, the last fortress. The Romans swept down into the Lower City and the carnage was dreadful. The Great Ram was now brought round to the west and set up against the Palace wall. Then the Romans came up into the Upper City with no pause in their slaughter and the Palace was surrounded.

It was late August.

Then it was that Eleazar called his meeting, in one of the gorgeous salons of the Palace. Seven Zealot units were repre-sented; we numbered about four hundred men and women. Eleazar was brief.

'Jerusalem is finished,' he said. 'But what was here in Jeru-salem, what has always been here, the belief that our only king is God, will continue. The resistance will go on. At Herodium, at Machaerus, and at Masada. Zealot and Sicarii groups are already there and more have left in the last weeks. All three places are strongly fortified and well provisioned. There are weapons. We will leave the city tonight and tomorrow night. We will use the underground passages that the Romans do not know, and the sewers. They reach beyond the wall. There are lists. You will see that parents and children, whole families, are on the lists. It is not a mistake. I will be in command on Masada. My brother Judah will lead a detachment to the fortress of Machaerus and share leadership there. My brother Simon was to have gone to help defend Herodium but he is dead. Are there any questions?'

I have said little of Eleazar, for this is not the story of Eleazar, and even after this long time I do not speak of him easily. Jerusalem, in the five years from the first positive action of revolt against Rome to the destruction of the city, was a melting pot, wherein people were changed, remade, forged anew. Leaders emerged, as did cowards, and traitors, and heroes. Men of peace found they were fighters; men of study, tacticians. Lone people found a new life as members of a team, a unit, a platoon.

Eleazar was one of three brothers, the sons of Jairus, who was cousin to my mother. Eleazar was the eldest, and the quietest, and most studious. Simon, the youngest, was flashing-eyed and handsome and laughing, and a great favourite in the family. The middle son was called Judas, a heavily-built, gentle, good-humoured man, who was rather shy.

Although our families were related we saw little of the brothers as we grew up. My father, for all his gentle humour and wisdom, was essentially a lonely man, who lived a little apart from his fellows. For a while after my mother died, we had visits from such female relatives or friends who esteemed themselves as marriage-brokers, but they became discouraged and stopped coming. A widower by preference was unusual—

almost ungodly—but for my brothers and sisters he was enough.

I became a Zealot seven years before Jerusalem fell, and Eleazar about two months later. I had not seen him, or his brothers, who joined at the same time, for some years. Soon they were part of an action group, whilst I remained in intelligence, in recruiting, in our 'sandal-maker headquarters'. When Menahem took Masada and brought back its arms, and also men from the Dead Sea area, Eleazar was with him, his brothers too. When Cestius was beaten before Jerusalem they were captains of men, leaders. When John fought his way out of Gischala to come to Jerusalem, Eleazar fought with him. When Simon gathered and trained his Idumaeans in the hills around Masada, Eleazar and his brothers, using the mountain as a base, gave aid and strength to the work. The 'sons of Jairus' were famous, for they were rarely apart—and fighters of rare cunning and skill. When Sarah and her grandson, the amiable Seth, became Zealots, two years after I did, it was partly because they wanted to be among those led by 'The Sons'. A year later, in the fight that routed Cestius, she showed how much a market-woman grandmother could learn of soldiering.

Her grandson adored the brothers, and in the terrible hand-to-hand fighting around the Temple when the Romans came through Antonia he fought by their side. By Simon and Judas he fought—and with Simon he died. Sarah took dreadful revenge that day, and later, back in the Temple, bloody and exhausted, wept in my arms like a lost child. Then Eleazar came in, with dead eyes, to give comfort to Sarah, and to others with losses that day. It was early July, one month almost to the day before the Temple burned. One month after, we left the Royal Palace and Jerusalem by way of sewers—and exchanged one Herodian palace for another.

Of all the horrors of the war the journey through the sewers was the worst. We were not the first to think of the sewers as a shelter or refuge or way out. Or as a place to die. I had noticed many times how people dying of starvation had dragged themselves with their last vestige of strength to a hole, a crevice, a corner. The sewers were choked with distended corpses, of every age, that watched us with lifeless eyes as we picked our way past in the smoky light of our own torches. The torches gave off an acrid smell, that we blessed, and made our eyes water, so that we saw mistily—and we thanked God again.

We came out far below the Pool of Siloam, through a new-cut passage that branched from a sewer just before it became an open trench. We were in a wooded part of the lower hills, where sheep grazed. It was the break of dawn, and cold. We were filthy and stained beyond description. Sentries were set and we slept like the dead for most of the day. We moved on again at night, in small groups. There was little danger. The country was full of people on the move, looking as we did. Homeless, displaced, refugees. Roman patrols out in the countryside were few. We took different routes and found no lack of food in the hamlets and villages we passed. We gave the news of Jerusalem and the Temple and were fed by people who wept as at the death of a loved one.

Thus we came to Masada.

15 Of Survival, and Masada

Stonemason's marks
on Palace-Villa

I draw back a little from speaking of our first days on Masada. Indeed all of the time on Masada has for me this sensitive, to-be-touched-carefully quality. So let us stay a little longer in the garden of my father's house and hear the fifth day's talk, a day like the other days, calm and golden. We had relived much together, with Jesse a still and absorbed listener to the stories about our side of the wall.

Simeon, who had let tears run unhindered down his cheeks when we spoke of the destruction of the Temple, spoke first on that pleasant morning.

'Our hearts died with the Temple. It was over. Thousands upon thousands of prisoners were taken by the Romans. Any who even looked as though they might make resistance were killed. The old and infirm were killed. People who informed were killed and those they named killed. The tallest and hand-somest prisoners were put aside for the triumphal processions in Rome. Of the others, those over seventeen were put in irons and sent to hard labour in Egypt. Those under seventeen were set aside to be sold as slaves. Thousands more were put into huge compounds for "the shows" which at that time I did not understand, being newly out of the Temple, as it were.

'Jesse has told us,' said the old priest, 'of Joseph's love of portents and "signs". Well, he will find many such in the memories of the survivors here, or the slaves elsewhere that came from here. As the war came nearer all sorts of voices were listened to, all kinds of stories. We heard of a great star, like a broadsword, pointing down at the city. On another occasion, on the Eve of Passover, it was said, in the pitch dark of the night, around the Altar and the Sanctuary, was a glow as bright as the midday sun. During the same Festival, a story ran, a cow awaiting sacrifice gave birth to a lamb. Others told of others, who had seen, at midnight, the East Gate of the Sanctuary open of its own accord. A gate of bronze needing twenty strong men to make it move, and barred and bolted with iron into stone. Chariots and regiments were seen speeding through the clouds by people ready to swear their words were true. Do you make note, Ruth?'

'Yes. Do *you* swear to anything? What did *you* experience?'

'A great noise and a movement in the ground underfoot. At Pentecost—when, 'tis true, the mind is perhaps receptive to strange things. We were in the Inner Temple, at night, for the last ceremony of prayer. A movement underfoot and a great noise, half thunder and half voice. We shared the experience, twenty-four priests of the Inner Temple. No one else.'

After a moment I told Saul, for the hundredth time, that it was a miracle he was spared, especially now that I knew of the murderous disposal of the survivors by the Romans, with slaughter and slavery—and selection for triumphant marches.

'And for sporting events,' said Jesse. 'Ruth dear, your gentle brother is tight-mouthed on the subject of his own survival, but I suspect that he has a little of old Jesse's cunning inside that priestly goodness.'

Saul laughed, and then was serious. 'Certainly to be a priest or to be dressed like a priest offered no protection at all during those last few days,' he said sadly, 'but to be a corpse was to be unnoticed, a commonplace, among a thousand others. During the last fighting, for the Upper City, and for a day or two after, the Roman soldiers were like mad dogs, with all orders ignored—or none given. So during those days of madness and massacre, to stay alive you acted dead. The moneyed dead were stripped and robbed so I lay among the poorest corpses I could find. I wasn't the first to think of the ruse. On one occasion in a house of corpses there were as many alive as dead. I also discovered that the Roman soldier has a superstitious fear of rats so I lay always with a dead open-eyed rat on my chest.'

'Worthy of Jesse,' said Sarah in sincere admiration. 'You too, old man?' she asked Simeon.

He nodded. 'And Sim also. She was hurt and had to be looked after.'

'Finding the house standing was like a smile from God,' said Saul. 'After the group left the Palace for Masada there was bad fighting in the Upper City. We fought our way out and split up. Then I went looking for Simeon and the girl and the one or two others I'd hidden here and there. And we started to live with the corpses. For days. A bad time. The plan was to work our way down the inside of the Middle Wall to the Valley Gate and up the other side to what I thought would be the remains of our house; for after the fighting was done, and the sorting of slaves, and the killing of the useless, the pulling down of the city and what was left of the Temple began. But our house was still standing. A miracle.' He turned to Sarah. 'You saved us. When the house was a hospital you hid oil and grain in the roof. I remembered and we found it. We lived in the roof space for a week and a half. Then we came down and started to clean up. The Tenth Legion, which had been so murderous, was now the occupying force and back under discipline, so we were not interfered with. The destruction of the city slowed down and stopped when every part had been damaged in some way. People came up out of holes like pallid worms. There was much to do. The rest you know.' He smiled. 'It's past. Ask Jesse what he meant by "sporting events", Ruth. I've talked enough.'

All this of death and destruction and men mad for loot and booty was told in a garden full of sunshine and birdsong. It was, even to us who had shared such things, unreal, of other people, far off.

'Pulling down the city and the Temple ruins was by order of Titus,' said Jesse, 'to show what mighty and civilized Rome

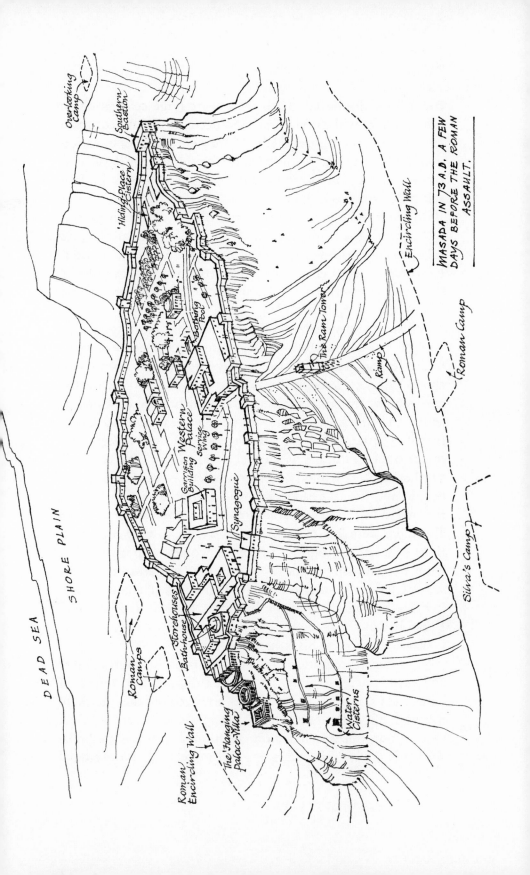

MASADA IN 73 A.D. A FEW DAYS BEFORE THE ROMAN ASSAULT.

DEAD SEA

SHORE PLAIN

Overlooking Camp

Southern Bastion

'Hiding Place' Cistern

Bathing Pool

Garrison Building

Western Palace

Service Wing

Synagogue

The Ram Tower

Ramp

Encircling Wall

Roman Camp

Silva's Camp

Roman Camps

Storehouses

Bathhouse

Roman Encircling Wall

The Hanging Palace-Villa

Water Cisterns

could do if disobeyed. Then there were huge celebrations in headquarters with promotions and decorations and congratulations given out right and left. There were sacrifices to various gods and great feastings. It went on for about three days. Then the various legions were posted—the Tenth to stay in Jerusalem and so on—and we went back to the coast, to Caesarea. Both John and Simon had been taken alive, and their journey to Rome for the triumphal marches together with all the carefully selected prisoners had to be arranged. All the spoil had to be sorted to see what was trophy for the processions in Rome and what was convertible into currency. Tons and tons of stuff. Impossible to detail, Ruth.'

'What did you mean by prisoners selected for sporting events?'

'Well, to go by sea to Rome was dangerous since the summer was over, so Titus decided to have a few processions and shows of his own. Such shows are a traditional Roman entertainment where large audiences sit, well protected, round an arena, and watch how groups of people get on when attacked by wild beasts; or how they manage when forced to fight each other to the death, the winners allowed to stay alive and fight another day. This kind of entertainment is very wasteful of people, and Jewish prisoners were ideal for the purpose because they were in the news, which made for good audiences, and also there were lots of them. Occasionally, to vary the attractions offered, a group of prisoners would be burned alive. Titus put on many of these great shows. In Caesarea Philippi *and* in Caesarea-by-the-sea. Also in Beirut. To celebrate things; like his brother Domitian's birthday, and his father's, too. Enough, Ruth?'

'Enough. What of his father, Vespasian?'

'A rapturous reception in Rome, which saw in him stability and common sense after the recent troubles. The return of Titus the Conqueror to Rome was arranged for the middle of the year after Jerusalem fell. During those seven or eight months our journeys and shows continued. It was a long tour ending in Alexandria and taking in another look at devastated

Jerusalem on the way down. Both Titus and Josephus, his friend, made long philosophical speeches over the ruins. Josephus made note of both orations.

'In Alexandria huge preparations were put in hand for the voyage to Rome. Seven hundred prisoners, the tallest and handsomest of both sexes, were sent off, then shiploads of spoil of every description. With these plunder-ships went Simon and John, under special guard, both looking ill-treated and half-starved.

'Titus's own vessel, on which *we* sailed—as part of his confidential staff—was magnificent. The voyage was made in perfect weather, and when we arrived we were met by Proud Father Vespasian and the whole Senate, with the date of the Victory Procession already set. You wish to hear of this, Ruth? You look pale.'

Sarah spoke roughly. 'Another time. It has no bearing. Josephus, great historian, will no doubt write of it in loving detail. Was it in that procession they killed John and Simon?'

'Simon only, in the temple of Jupiter Capitolinus. John was put away in chains for life. Soon after, Vespasian announced plans for a Temple of Peace, wherein would be exhibited treasures from the world including those of the Temple in Jerusalem. The golden vessels and candleholders and bowls and lamps and so on. He told us however that the crimson curtains of the Inner Sanctuary and the Scrolls and Writings of the Law would be kept safe in the Palace.'

There was a pause in the talk, with some quietness and a feeling of depression. Then Sarah, recalling Silva, asked Jesse whether it was during that 'triumph' period in Rome that streets were renamed and the arches and arcades built.

'Yes,' he said, 'standard practice. To commemorate victories.'

'But not yet victory at Masada.'

'No.' He was careful with her. 'It was some little time before Masada began to be considered important. An unfinished job. A slight loss of face. It was one of the mopping-up operations to be done. In order. After Herodium and Machaerus.'

Machaerus. Where the Zealots gave up the fortress above the town to save the life of one of their bravest and the Romans, let in to the town below, slaughtered nearly two thousand of its people. Where, in the Forest of Jardes, the Romans trapped what was left of the Machaerus Zealots and killed them all. Where the Zealots fought to the last man, led by Eleazar's brother, second of 'The Sons' to die, my gentle cousin Judas.

Lucilius Bassus it was who took Herodium and Machaerus. Bassus, governor of Israel, who died in Israel.

My brother said, 'Bassus lived long enough to set in operation an order from Vespasian requiring every Jew in Israel to pay to Rome the yearly offering he used to pay to the Temple. No longer an offering; a tax. With no excuses accepted.'

'The replacement for Bassus was carefully thought about,' said Jesse. 'Israel was regarded as one of the places similar to, but less important than, Germany and the various Gallic countries who had also been in revolt—and had also been subdued. Was Israel to have for its new governor an administrator or a military man? Then someone remembered a recent report about Masada. Like Machaerus, a well-nigh impregnable fortress on top of a mountain. But, unlike Machaerus, unconquered. A symbol of resistance, with Zealots in residence, seemingly well-provisioned. *And*, by all accounts, experienced guerrilla fighters. The subject for some behind-the-hand bitcheries at court receptions when Titus waxed too "conqueror-of-all" in his dinner conversation. So a military man was chosen. The General Flavius Silva. I never met him. You and Sarah are ahead of me there. For my part, when I'd had enough of Rome, I came home, largely overland, with short sea voyages, taking my time, seeing things. By the time I arrived, nearly two years ago, Silva had been down at Masada about a month. He is now in Caesarea. He doesn't come to Jerusalem.'

Sensing a sadness in both Sarah and me, caused by his light-voiced description of the appointment of 'a military man' to get rid of the subject for 'behind-the-hand bitcheries', Jesse's tone changed to one most strange for him—tender almost.

'Tell us,' he said, 'of Masada. Of the first time you saw it. Of its beauties, of the life. We know of the death. Tell us of the life. Did you see it first by day? What kind of day? Tell us. Come, Sarah, you have words. And you too, Ruth dear. Share the good memories, and the bad will fade a little.'

It was most unexpected, this warmth of voice, this concern. I was not far from tears and sniffed—matched immediately by a similar sniff from Sarah. It was a good moment, and we exchanged damp smiles.

'We saw the mountain first as the dawn came,' said Sarah. 'We, our small group, had taken the route ordered by Eleazar. Down to just above Hebron and along the river bed to Ein Geddi on the coast of the Dead Sea. Then we went south, using the lower slopes of the hills edging the sea, taking part of a day and sleeping in a tiny village for a few hours, and going on whilst it was still dark. As the sky lightened we saw the whole line of mountains, of which Masada is one, and there was no difference in its appearance from the others. Then as we got nearer, the two Masada Zealots who had led us from Ein Geddi told us what to look for. The flat top, and the walls and look-out towers running round the edge.'

The elder of the two Zealots had been a tall, quiet man, not young, with a sinewy hard look about him. But he had been courteous, and gentle with our young ones. We were a party of some twenty or so including our four orphans and Judith with her mother.

As we began the inland walk to the base of the mountain, the sinewy man stopped. The top edge of the mountain now had a line of sun along it, the lower slopes still in the shadowy pink of the dawn.

'Look,' he said, pointing up to the tip of the plateau nearest to us, 'a palace in the sky.' At first I thought he meant the mountain refuge itself—and indeed I called it by that name in my mind from then on—and I looked too high, at the edge-wall and towers. But then I saw it. The Hanging Palace. Cut out of the rock and set below the wall on three levels. Even from far off, and far below, as we were, we were aware of its beauty and size. Marble glowed and gleamed from column and balustrade. Metal glinted. Colour was there, in the friezes and roofs.

Sarah had grunted, and had taken a child's hand in each of hers. 'From one palace to another! Come children, it looks a hard climb. Sight-seeing when we get up top.'

It was a hard climb, but with many rests. The path wound and turned upon itself a dozen times and we were in the full sun the whole time, which in September is soon very hot—especially in the Dead Sea area, which is said to be below the level of the rest of the land.

The sinewy man, whose name was Avrom, and who had been of great aid to Judith's mother, pregnant and so recently and violently widowed, told me during one of our rests in a rare patch of shade that Herod made Masada the luxurious fortress it was. 'But Herod was not the first to fortify Masada,' he exclaimed. 'The Rock was given its name and first made a stronghold by Jonathan, of the line of Judas Maccabaeus, great Judah the Hammer, whose spirit I swear lives on in Eleazar, who brought you out of Jerusalem. When Menahem came and took Masada from the Romans his "rod and his staff" were his nephews, Eleazar and his brothers, the Sons of Jairus. It is like losing my own brother to hear of the death of Simon. But across the Salt Sea'—he gestured at the still water far below—'in Machaerus, *our* Judah holds out.'

When we arrived at the top it was nearly midday and the sun burned straight down. We were parched and covered in dust. The path levelled for a short way and ended at high gates of wood and iron, which were opened as we approached. Eleazar himself stood there, with many others. We were surrounded and taken straight to shelter, food and drink.

'That was the sweetest water I ever tasted,' said Sarah. 'To be greeted with water to drink, and wash in, and cook with up on that sun-baked flatland in the sky was part of the staggering surprise of the whole place. We were there on Masada nearly three years and we were never short of water. Great Herod's architects were men of genius. The rain came maybe a dozen times a year—but like the heavens being emptied on us. Very little got away. There was a gulley and aqueduct system—using the sides of the mountain—that collected the rain water in enormous underground cisterns dug out of the solid rock. Great lofty halls—big enough for five hundred people to stand in—full of water. A miracle, eh, Ruth?'

Indeed, indeed. How often in our history water figures in miracles. Great Moses struck it from a rock—and parted a sea with a wave of his staff. As did Joshua also. Iron axe-heads floated on water for Elijah, and water turned sweet at his command. The purification of the body—and soul—by immersion, is part of our Law.

'So many miracles,' said Sarah. 'You know, Jesse, it's hard to describe Masada to someone who has never seen it without it sounding like one of the exaggerations Simeon says our Josephus is famous for. On the flat top of that mountain was a place truly fit for a king. For a king, and his court, and his servants, and his officers and his soldiers. Nothing was shoddy, or roughly put up "with anything to hand". Everything was planned and carefully built and beautifully finished. Down in the desert, in the middle of nowhere, above a great lake of water too salty for anything to live in, Herod had prepared a place to run to—either from his people, who didn't much like him, or from Cleopatra, who was greedy for empire. But it was to be a home from home, a citadel royal in every way. How we looked and wondered, eh, my dove?'

It was completely unreal, and remained so for days, for weeks. We had come from terror and battle and fire and smoke —and ceaseless noise. On Masada it was quiet, so quiet. Jerusalem had been a place of hills which allowed sight of other hills outside the walls. Inside the edge-walls and towers of Masada only the sky was to be seen. We lived in the sky, in a palace, in a place of palaces. All the newcomers were affected in the same way. The change was vast, dreamlike, too big to absorb—especially for such as we, light-in-the-mind with near-starvation and exhaustion. Standing dreamily before a wall-painting or an exquisitely finished piece of stone carving, I would turn and find another, or more than one, in similar wonder.

'—enormous storerooms,' Sarah was saying. 'Of stone. Each for a different use. This one for grain, that one for wine. Others for dates, for dried fruits, for vegetables, for olives, with presses for oil, the oil kept in yet another storeroom. Every kind of dwelling on our mountain; from barracks to palaces! The very edge-walls themselves were houses! An inner and outer wall, with windows and roofs. Big rooms and small. Dozens and dozens of rooms. We used them. There was a beautiful swimming pool, deep sunk, with wide terraces and steps for lying on. There was a bath-house, in the Roman style, with a room to get very hot in and a room to cool off in, and a little pool to plunge in, and everything was tiled and there were pictures painted on the walls. Gorgeous. We made use of the hot room, not like the Romans do, naked and being rubbed with perfumed oils, but as a warm place to sit. We had a man who had helped build the Roman bath at Caesarea and he knew how to heat it.'

16 The Hanging Palace

Corinthian capital
from Palace-villa

It was strange how the Zealots on Masada preferred to live in the bare rooms of the edge-walls rather than in the beautiful villas and palaces. Or, if they made use of such a building, they would use only a corner of a salon, or part of a courtyard. It is difficult to explain. Certainly the Zealot needed discipline and a certain down-to-essentials outlook. He was, both from a religious and from a way-of-life point of view, scornful of show and ostentation; of needless 'glorification', as he would describe the Herodian way of doing things. Eleazar was practical always. 'Live where you will,' he said. 'Within call; out of the wind; under a roof, near water, near others. Everything will be rationed, every need met. Everybody will work for the common good. Everybody will live by the Law. There will be rules because there must be, but those rules will be sensible and agreed by all.'

Indeed we lived in remarkable harmony. Eleazar's 'sensible' rules were few but clear. We were on his side. Masada was not a place of hiding for 'poor refugees'; it was a place where anti-Roman fighters were making a stand. This was known to the Romans. Disunity among ourselves would have been the greatest stupidity. There had been enough disunity in the early days of the Revolt, as Eleazar would gently remind us. 'My uncle,' he used to say, 'the great Menahem, who took Masada from the Romans, and supplied Jerusalem with the arms of those Romans, was himself killed by people of Jerusalem who saw in him a danger to their way of life. Maybe my uncle was wrong in some of his ideas for the leadership and preparation of the country, but his terrible death, my brave friends, was the result of disunity.'

Wise Eleazar, who made his points with calmness, without heat, simply. And wise Jesse, to start us talking of our mountain. How the words came! How the mind picked among memories and chose those to offer and share. Jesse was right; we talked of our first days—and the last days lost their nightmare. We recalled our gentle welcome, the willing hands to help us find a place in the community, the tears shed over our orphans, who soon found comfort from a dozen sets of parents, all with children of their own, all with love to spare. Masada, good readers, was full of love. We arrived with no possessions; in small groups, all from Jerusalem, and joined the Zealot garrison already there, themselves survivors of a score of Roman massacres over the four years since the War began, since the defeat of Cestius.

We were people lucky to get away alive. Those of us who had known wealth were the same as those who had owned nothing. Artifice had no place on the rock. The regimen made for unselfishness. Sharing, and caring, was our way of life. We were no saints; temperament—and temper—we had in plenty, but also we had Eleazar, who possessed a marvellous instinct for the moment to intervene, to arbitrate, to listen—or to let the argument reach a screaming climax, noisy with curses and tears—and then, with him to lead, reach a new end, of laughter.

'There was so much to do and see and wonder at *in*side the walls,' recalled Sarah, 'that it was about a month before I even remembered the Hanging Palace, as I called it—which was *out*side the walls.'

She spoke the truth. The first sight of the Hanging Palace— it could have no other name—from below, in dusty exhaustion, had left a dream-like impression, swept away by our first weeks on the plateau. For from the flat top of the mountain the Hanging Palace was invisible. At the end of the plain were the storehouses and the Roman bath-house and a large administration building. Near them the ever-present edge-wall and towers. The Palace was on the other side of the wall—and *below* it, out of sight. If its dream-impression had gone from the mind, no part of it was to be seen to bring back its reality and existence.

In the number of other things to 'see and wonder at' Sarah also spoke truth. At the opposite end of the plateau, which was diamond shaped, was a second great pool, and near to it one of the huge underground cisterns, with a long flight of steps down to it. The only cistern with access within the walls. The cistern where we waited for the Romans to come. And at the point where the walls joined at that southernmost tip of the summit, there was a powerfully built bastion from the top of which the guards could see for miles.

'I've got my own ways with the Almighty,' said Sarah, 'but on Masada in the matter of worship and prayer everything had to be just so. Our synagogue was against the north-west wall, nearest spot to Jerusalem, sort of. Herod built it, the Romans knocked it about and we put it right and made some improvements. We were strict, but when some of the Covenanters of Qumran came down the coast from their settlement to visit they made us feel like heathens! Frightening lot. A rule and precept for every minute of the day, but as with us God was their only king. And like us, if need be, they would fight. After Machaerus fell they abandoned their settlement and dispersed. Some of them came to join us, bringing their holy writings which they kept in a special little room in the synagogue—as being the only place holy enough!'

They were strange indeed, these men of Qumran, with their mystical ways and their speech full of allegory. Of the Seekers of His Will they spoke, of Teachers of Righteousness, of the Terrible Ones, of the Manual of Discipline, of the Princes of Light and Darkness. Sadly it was not to me they spoke of these things, for I was a woman and thus outside their mysteries; not to be confided in, or indeed looked at too much. A pity, for they were full of interest. It was from others that I learned that

Menahem had an heroic place in Covenanter thought, and by direct relationship, Eleazar too.

'Now, we weren't as lavish with the water as Herod was,' said Sarah. 'He had hundreds of servants running up and down the mountain to bring it up; but we managed well, all the same. And neither was the ritual bathing forgotten. Two very nice "mikvas" we had. The Zealots built them, purifying the "brought" water with a few drops of rainwater "flowing direct" which was collected in little pools next to the dip pools. Clever —and permitted. Did you know?' Then she roared. 'Great God, two of the three of you are *priests*!' She went on, telling story after story, with a natural talent for making the happening live again.

Jesse said, in a pause, 'Tell us of the Hanging Palace, Ruth', and I was surprised that I had not done so—and found in myself a reluctance to speak of it, which was momentary, and linked I think to how I felt about talking of the Western Palace, where Masada died, and the Great Cistern, where we'd waited with the orphans, alive. It was odd, this link to such memories, for the Hanging Palace stood in my mind with no overtone of tragedy or sadness. Sweetness rather, for I saw it first with Eleazar, the two of us alone, on a cool morning, with silver in the sunlight.

The memory of the morning helped the telling, but who can describe, with voice or pen, the Hanging Palace? It was said that the Western Palace, up on the plateau, was Herod's 'official' residence, where he ran his affairs and ruled like a king, but that in the three-terraced Hanging Palace he rested and relaxed and took his pleasure. It was easy to believe: a three-level villa to delight the eye and refresh the spirit. The terraces had shade always, and were protected from the wind by the whole mountain. The air was still, and fragrant. Hushed also, which was strange, for above, on the plateau, the sounds from below were clearly heard.

We had approached the upper level through an ornamental small gate easy to miss, for it lay behind the great storerooms and the Roman bath-house. Once inside the gate there was an immediate feeling of difference, of a lighter touch in the design of everything. Slimmer pillars, more delicate arches, more fanciful metalwork. We went into what was a small group of rooms built round an open court surfaced with white mosaic, which reflected light into the rooms. The walls of each room were painted with great skill, and depicted different themes. The floors were inlaid, using many colours. We walked through and out on to a semi-circular balcony with a waist-high balustrade, giving views that took the breath away. Far below, the Salt Sea stretched away into the distance, glistening, grey-purple. Eleazar pointed out to me the white roofs of Ein Geddi, the plains of Jericho, far, far off.

We looked downward over the balustrade and saw the villa's two lower levels. The one immediately below us was circular and open to the sky, with a roofed area behind, as big as a house, which joined the rock face. Eleazar touched my arm and I followed him to where the balustrade curved back to the outer wall of one of the rooms. There was an arched opening which led to steps going down. There was a little landing and then the stairs were spiral, cut into the solid rock. It was dark except for narrow slits cut through to the flank of the mountain. It was necessary to be careful.

We came out into the roofed court we'd seen from above, half of its area comprising two chambers, which were pillared, with decorated walls. The floors were marble and of intricate design. The pillars of the shady court were Roman in detail with Acanthus capitals and fine bases. These features had been copied in the half-round pillars carved out of the rock face, the spaces between them perfectly flat and painted with country scenes. The work was masterly. The wall pillars, like the pillars surrounding the court, were of sturdy proportions, for they supported a considerable roof of carved wood and heavy clay tiles.

The circular, open part of the terrace was ringed by two low walls upon which were spaced pillars of the same design as those that supported the roof but lighter and more delicate in every detail. They supported only a carved frieze, which like the pillars and twin walls was finished in white plaster, making the blue of the sky and the scorched light browns of the desert and mountains the richer, the more vibrant.

We were silent, in tune with the atmosphere of the villa itself and with each other. We again descended, again down a spiral stairway, this time cut in the outside face of the rock and enclosed by a curved wall of the same stone. The masons must have been men of cool nerves, for the drop was sheer.

The lowest terrace was the most ornate and ambitious of the three—and must have been the hardest to construct. It was over a hundred feet below the top of the mountain and was more spacious and grand in dimension than the terraces above.

'This lowest terrace,' Eleazar had said to me, 'is one of the reasons I should like to have known Great Herod. The whole of Masada is an astonishment, a wonder. And this villa that steps down a mountain part of that wonder. Herod, masterbuilder, has been dead seventy years. He died diseased, hated, and mad. Yet there was a time when his mind was full of beautiful structures and superb buildings—set perfectly.'

'Why do you particularly admire this lowest terrace?' I had asked.

'Look around you, Ruth. You stand in a centre courtyard, on all four sides of which are colonnades. Cloisters, with Roman columns on either side, with painted ceilings and carved stone. Three of the cloisters are open; the one against the mountain, like the terrace above, uses the rock to provide columns carved to match and panels for the artists. The plan of this level is square to complement the circular plan above and the half-circle above that. This square is wider and heavier in its design, as it should be. But it stands on a spur of the mountain narrower than itself! It is not an impossible building problem, but near enough impossible at the top of a desert crag. Imagine how many experts must have told Herod that the lowest level could not be done, or was unneccessary, or should be made smaller, narrower. But no, it was done as he wished, and below it, as though to add another "impossible" to the list, is his own private bath-house, with a cold water pool, a tepid room, and a hot room! The same way of heating as up above, and even more expensively decorated. Come, I will show you.'

It *was* beautiful, and stays in my mind, like that whole morning, with great clarity. We went up through the terraces slowly, marvelling a second time. We sat awhile on a stone seat near the small gate to the villa and Eleazar spoke again of Herod.

'A dozen men in one. To choose a mountain in a wilderness and to have clear in the mind what it would become. And to make it come to pass. What could such a mind not achieve? The whole of Masada is a monument to a fantastic obstinacy!'

Eleazar had been quiet then for a while, and spoken in a different tone. 'It is said that hundreds died in the building of Masada and in the ceaseless toil of running it. A legend exists that Herod, murderer of many, brought death to Masada, and that it lurks here still, taking periodic toll from those who live on the mountain!'

I did not tell Jesse and the others of these words of Eleazar about the legend. To what purpose? Eleazar spoke often to me of death and dying. We had seen so much death. Death without dignity or quietness, death by great violence—or starvation, which is truly horrible to see. To me death has a ghastly leer, a mouth dripping with blood—and screaming, with foul breath. For Eleazar, who had experienced far more than I in every way, who had killed, who had lived in blood and stench, death did not have such pictures.

'We don't understand the patterns of life and death,' he once said. 'How can we? God alone decides such things. If a man is to die, the way he dies does not seem of great importance. It is time; his end has come. It is written. Even when a man decides to end his own life—a great sin say the Elders—how can we be certain that the Almighty has not so guided his mind?'

About these words also I kept silent in the garden. Jesse

asked about the state of repair of the buildings on Masada, most of which were nearly a hundred years old.

'Remarkable,' said Sarah. 'It must be the very dry air or something. You got the feeling it would all last for ever. Maybe because everything was built in the best way, with a careful finish. Remarkable. A bit chipped, a bit shabby, a bit faded, but in no way a ruin. There were pieces missing here and there; the Zealots took bits to do their own building with. But everything was usable. The place may have been there a hundred years but there had always been people living there, it was said. Not hard to believe. The only place with a water supply for miles and miles! With water the desert will grow anything and our mountain had not only good soil but a lot of good farmers! We had a man who wanted to cultivate flowers because he missed his bees and loved honey!'

She talked on, of the everyday life, the community meetings, the teaching of the children, the rota systems for guard-duty, the expeditions by small groups down the mountain to nearby settlements for special needs and news. She told of the rationing system, the careful observance of the Sabbath and every Festival and Fast. Then she was a little sad, and told of the silent reception of the news of the fall, first of Herodium, and not long after, of Machaerus—with the death of our Eleazar's brother, known to many of us, sweet-natured Judah.

Eleazar had sat by himself for the whole of that day in the small room in the Western Palace that he used. We kept away. Suddenly the War was near to us again. We kept silent, and avoided the thought uppermost in all our minds. Typically, it was Eleazar who gathered us together after his day away of silence and brought the thought into words.

'Masada alone holds out,' he said. 'We are next. Lucillius Bassus, who took Machaerus, is, by all accounts, a sick man, so we have time. To examine every inch of our defences—and to have no fear. We are a fortress, well-armed and self-supporting. We must match our own strength to the strength of our walls.'

From then on, scouts and runners went out every day, in

different directions—and I was back in intelligence. Machaerus was on the other, far-off shore of the Salt Sea and further north. There would be a period of re-grouping, of mopping up by the Romans, and then their movement up and round the northern shore and across the Jordan. Hill country; dry country.

Then news came that Bassus was dead and that a replacement was expected.

'Your "military man",' said Sarah to Jesse, grimly. 'General Flavius Silva. We were given a number of pointers as to the size of the operation that was going to be mounted against us. I for one didn't give them the importance I should have, or put them together carefully enough. Did you, Ruth?'

'No. Jerusalem was one thing, we were another. We were a fortress in a desert.'

'What were the pointers, Ruth?' asked Jesse.

'Roman patrols started to spread through Nabataea to the south of us, rounding up forced labour. Every place, large or small, was ordered to provide workers. Farm labourers, masons, bakers, all kinds of people. Then, all round Masada, in every direction, the Roman hand was suddenly heavier. The least thing was punished by being rounded up for "forced labour unspecified". Each place was told that its contribution to the occupation forces of Idumaea and Lower Judea would be increased, as those forces were to be increased. In addition Roman quartermasters began to tour, counting crops and paying a fair price, with delivery date and place left blank. Wood merchants had their entire stocks impounded by Roman order.

'Perhaps,' said Sarah, 'we didn't want to put two and two together. And we were busy ourselves. We were quarrying stone to make balls. Small ones for the slingers and large ones to roll or drop over the walls. Everyone big enough to hold a bow was taught to use one. We built up huge stocks of arrows. Oil-soaked torches were made ready in piles. Braziers were set up on the battlements, with cauldrons for boiling oil. Y'know Jesse,' said Sarah, 'I'm a great believer in boiling oil as a deterrent.'

He looked at her with great affection. 'So am I, old battler, so am I. When did the two's and two's start adding up, Ruth?'

'It was in April or May, about twenty months after Jerusalem fell, that we saw the first Romans down below. Far away. Very few; in small groups, scouting or surveying. Over about four days they had examined us from every side. The nearest they came was to the Tower, built by Herod down below on the western side of the mountain to guard the White Cliff, the only natural rock bridge to cross the ravines of the west, rising to within five hundred feet of the summit. We did not man the Tower, for the five hundred feet from the join of the cliff to the top of the mountain was a hard climb and easy to defend.'

'What happened after the scouting parties went away?' asked my brother.

'Nothing. For about ten days, perhaps two weeks.'

'And then?'

'Try to imagine,' said Sarah, with no smile, 'getting used to looking down day after day at empty desert. Other mountains nearby, like ours, and deep valleys and ravines between. To the east, the sea; to the west, the desert. And then, one morning, all our look-outs giving the same report: large columns approaching. Down from Ein Geddi along the coast road, up from Nabataea, and from the west in three directions; from Beersheba, from Hebron, and the largest column from the Jerusalem-Jericho area. Y'know, looking down at large numbers of people far off is strange. A moving smudge with an edge and tail of dust. The smudges sort of float. True, Ruth?'

'True.' Sarah and I had walked round the battlements at the tops of the walls with Eleazar and his ten leaders, his 'centurions' as he called them—'each responsible for a hundred, a correct term'—and we had watched silently. In a similar way, on similar walls, we had watched the gathering of the enemy around Jerusalem, but much of the sight had been obscured, by hills and trees and the corners of buildings. On Masada there were no such obstructions. We saw everything.

The hours passed, and the smudges became vast numbers of

people. The columns from the Hebron and Jerusalem directions glinted and sparkled in the high sun.

'The old enemy,' Sarah said. 'The Tenth Fretensis Legion. And auxiliaries—and as many slave-workers, coming from all over. The survey must have been done by experts, the thousands of troops and workers split up and moved to eight different sites all round us and the camp building began right away. It was an odd feeling, being so high up. As though all the activity had nothing to do with us. This feeling continued; I couldn't shake it off for days. I felt that the thousands down below hardly gave us a glance. Only one of the camps bothered me. It was a small camp due south, across a deep valley on the tip of a plateau higher than ours. They could look across and down at us. No more than a quarter of a mile away. I didn't like it.'

The camps went up very quickly. Two, quite close together, were built on the plain near the White Cliff not far from the Tower. On the other side of Masada, the sea side, were three camps, grouped, one large and two smaller. Another was due north below the Hanging Palace.

17 The Encirclement

Cosmetic pallette
(Red sea shell)

No action was taken against us at all. Silva himself spoke to us, but that was much later. One of the qualities of Masada and its life was the quietness. A bird calling in flight far below could be heard and savoured in perfection. We lived aloft and in quiet. We were most of us from cities and used to turmoil. Masada made us quiet-voiced, and simpler.

But the acoustical perfection of the bird-call now brought to us every sound from below, and those of us with the sharpest ears became a new sort of wall-guard. 'Sentries with closed eyes,' Eleazar called them. But they gleaned much, for there is much shouting in forced labour and much bad temper in thirst —and those below were severely short of water. There was no living off the land either. Food and drink had to be brought from far away. Much of the slave-labour force was Jewish. Thousands. Men and women.

The camps were square, in the Roman fashion, soon complete, and soon with their own disciplined life. I could discern no logic in the positioning of the eight camps, which left large gaps. They were in no way equidistant; indeed, to the east, a large one lay behind two others. Eleazar himself was puzzled, for we knew many escape paths down the mountain for which moonlight was enough.

It was one, and then a second, of our listening sentries who gave the solution. 'A wall. Right round. Connecting six camps. The two largest outside.'

It was begun two days later and employed thousands. To the east, towards the sea, where our secret paths were, the wall had towers every hundred yards. The wall encircled us entirely, here and there built on slopes that a goat would refuse.

Eleazar called us together. 'This will be no siege, like Jerusalem, for we are better off in every way than our enemies below. We have water and stores of many foods and we grow more. This will be no siege, for they will burn in the summer sun and freeze at night. With all the camps and the wall, the White Cliff is still five hundred feet below us, and stone-throwers and rams and archer towers of the kind used at Jerusalem are useless. But they are here to wipe us out. Make no mistake. This is an operation regardless of cost, of human life, of effort. Their preparations are not complete. They cannot be.'

The 'completion' began the same week. Our White Cliff, which joined the western face of our mountain to the lower level of the desert across the ravine, was to be built upon. It was to be the base for a gigantic slope, a ramp. A man-made hill.

The speed of the building was astonishing—and thorough. This was no heaping of dirt and rubble. In a barren, dry-wadi desert, vast loads of timber started to arrive, of every kind, from the stunted bush trees of the mountainside to wide sawn planks. As the earth and sand was piled, the wood was used in a dozen ways, expert ways, to bond the great mass together.

Eleazar observed everything with little comment. The Roman workmasters stayed well away, at the bottom of the slope. The ant-like activity, involving thousands, in lines and groups and gangs, was performed by the pressed labourers, the slave-workers. In the main, Jews. We rolled no stones; we shot no arrows; we poured no oil. We watched, and waited.

'Watch, and wait,' said Eleazar. 'Every new activity down below to be reported. Remember, many masons were pressed into the labour force, many ironworkers and smiths, many carpenters. The Tenth Legion itself has a big force of such artisans—as we know from Jerusalem. Why more? Watch. Tell me everything.'

About three weeks later, Eleazar again: 'The slope of the ramp is not steep and points to a spot still well below our plateau. It is a straight line, like a road, but of an earth surface —and soft. Who has comment?'

Absa, a 'centurion' and a stone-carver, said: 'To the right of the ramp, at its base, large blocks of stone are being roughly squared as they are quarried. They are very big. Pulley work; rollers. Our brothers there must think they're back in Egypt.'

One of the younger men, with the sight of an eagle, said: 'Behind the hillock, at the end of the ramp, a wooden tunnel is being constructed. Of square section. Only the end can be seen. I think it is bigger at one end that at the other. The building noises suggest metal as well as wood. Smiths are edging thick discs of wood. They could be wheels.'

Sarah said abruptly, 'The Ram is here.' Heads turned; eyes grew serious. If Sarah said a thing was so, it was. She would not speak of so important a thing were she not sure. 'I am sure,' she said. 'It is on a low truck pulled by mules and hidden under branches and other rubbish but yesterday some fell away and I saw the iron head. I have had my suspicions about that truck for nearly a week. It is far off, near the big camp to the north of the ramp, Silva's camp.'

It was a puzzle, for the ramp rose to a point well below us. Were the Ram on the same kind of swing as at Jerusalem it would bang harmlessly against the side of the mountain.

The solution to the puzzle soon emerged. The great stone blocks were for surfacing the ramp, their own weight bedding them in and pressing them against the one behind, for the work began at the bottom. As the surface came up towards the top, so another course was laid on top, and then another. One of our own masons gave his opinion. 'The surface, of stone, now higher, is still not enough, if the top line is drawn with the eye, to reach our level. No, the surface is of stone because it is to take great weight.'

We watched and waited. The use of manpower moving the stones on rollers up the ramp and putting them in place was prodigious. As the work drew nearer to us and we prepared to take action, the work stopped. Now all the ants clustered round the hillock, with tripod cranes and pulleys and ropes. Every person on Masada stood on the walls that day.

And slowly the wooden tunnel behind the little hill was pulled into view and came forward, on trucks and rollers, till it lay on the stone-surfaced slope, its narrow end nearest to us. Then the work with ropes and levers and pulleys was renewed and the tunnel slowly stood up and became an enormous tower! It had sloping sides, and a base slanted, on wheels, to match the angle of the ramp. It was armoured with iron plates, with archer platforms and arrow-shooting engines. It had stone-throwers, and in the upper third of its height an arch through back and front.

'There,' said one of our carpenters, with bitter memories of Jerusalem, 'the Ram will swing.'

Our mason, again called to measure with his eye, confirmed what you did not need to be a mason to see. The Ram was now in line with our wall.

The plan was simple. The tower would protect the workers as they completed the surfacing of the ramp with stone—and would come up the ramp yard by yard as the stone was laid. Our stone balls did little damage and our arrows made no impression on the iron. The tower archers made our least activity upon the walls hazardous. The stone-throwers lobbed great missiles without warning on to our plain. One of our sharp-eyed children discovered that a system of signalling existed between the south camp, which looked down on us, and the tower, which could not yet see over the wall. We had no way of escaping this surveillance, for our high buildings were at the other end of the plateau.

'That blasted tower,' said Sarah, 'took on a sort of monstrous personality of its own. A giant in armour who waited for his next step forward to be prepared. Then when all was ready

his army of midgets pulled him uphill and his engineers
shifted the huge wedges behind him and he waited for another
step to be made level. Then there was the day that the Ram
was hauled up and hung in the arch—and it became a great
tongue sticking out of a black mouth.'

'You are a poet, Sarah,' said my brother gently.

'In no way,' said Sarah, 'but the last few days had a quality
of nightmare, of a mad dream. In Jerusalem we went outside
the walls to fight, to set things on fire, to upset plans, to pull
things down. On Masada we could do none of those things. It
went,' said my beloved old battler, with a break in her voice,
'against my nature.'

'What did Eleazar do, Ruth?' asked Jesse.

'He thought logically, as always. "The Ram can go forward
or back," he told us, "we know exactly where it is going to
strike. Our wall is double, with space between. We will fill the
space with walls of wooden planks an arm's length apart and
fill the spaces between them with earth, loosely. When the
outer stone wall gives way the Ram will hammer at a structure
that will give a little each time, compacting the earth and growing stronger at each blow. The tower will then be very close to
our wall. The Romans have to use the tower to reach the wall.
They have no other way. The tower is their attack point and
it is the only one." '

'But an iron-armoured protection for every soldier on his
way up,' said Jesse.

'Yes.'

'And thousands of soldiers.'

'Yes.'

'Archer-platforms and stone-throwers above the Ram.'

'Yes.'

'Scaling ladders also.'

'Yes.'

'The top of the tower well above your wall when the Ram
is in place.'

'Yes.'

'No chance of surprise.'

'None.'

'No chance of outside-the-wall fighting.'

'None.'

Jesse moved his eyes from mine to Sarah's. 'No chance at all, old battler.'

Sarah was grim, but without heart in it. 'Only to kill Romans.'

Jesse: 'Had an offer been made you—any surrender terms, Ruth?'

'Yes, by Silva, when the earth ramp was nearly finished. We rejected it.'

He paused a moment. 'Did your earth and timber wall behave as foreseen?'

'Yes. The stone wall fell, and revealed the mass of wood and soil. It seemed to be no great surprise. We had forgotten their look-outs in the south camp that could see our every move. They

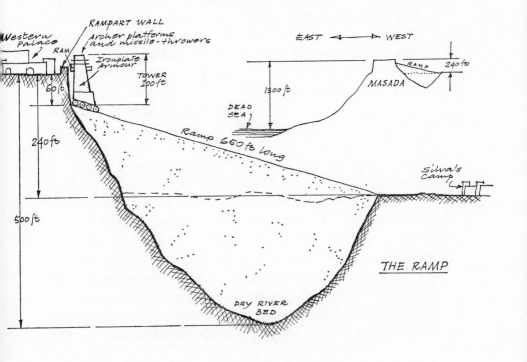

THE RAMP

did not waste any time using the Ram. Arrows were packed and wrapped in pitch-soaked rags and shot into every inch of our wooden walls and then others sent after them, already alight. The fire was immediate and huge. The wood was very dry, as was the earth packing. We watched everything from either side of the tower, along the top of our wall.'

'Eleazar . . .?' asked Jesse.

'He stood with his head up, slightly on one side. "The wind," he said, "the wind." And as though he'd called it up, the wind was there, the April wind that comes from nowhere and everywhere, that runs around the desert like a puppy; in every direction. It was strong. Across our plateau east to west, blowing the wall of flame straight back at the Tower, licking and roaring at the soldiers like the very breath of God. We cheered and shouted and began to show ourselves; our own archers and slingmen active and accurate. The light was beginning to go. It was late afternoon.'

'Then the wind changed,' said Sarah, flatly. 'It just stopped, and the flames steadied and the smoke went straight up; then it started again, as strong, from the opposite direction. It is a cursed wind, the desert wind, a wind without a home.'

I saw everything. I was on a part of the wall that jutted forward to a blunt point, between the Synagogue and the Tower on the ramp. I saw the first wooden wall turn to ash and fall away, releasing the earth behind it and revealing the next wooden wall, which ignited right away from the flames blown roaring at it by the wind. The dusk was well begun.

The Roman soldiers made no attempt to put their scaling ladders into position—or take any other action. There were orders shouted above the roar of the flames and the archer-platforms cleared. More orders, and the catapult-men and Ram swingers withdrew, clattering down the inside of the Tower. The flames bit and tore at the wall with noisy breath. The wind was steady and strong. A night-guard of archers in armour appeared on the top walkways of the Tower, and an officer of high rank, who observed the furiously burning defence wall in silence. After a few minutes he disappeared. Far below the soldiers poured out of the openings at the bottom of the Tower shouting noisily about 'finishing the Jews in the morning', about 'showing the Zealots some *real* swordwork—and the Sicarii some *new* tricks with small knives!' How clearly we heard them. 'And there are women and girls up there!' they yelled. 'We'll kill *them* a different way —and no "officers first" either!' The obscenities were detailed and positive. 'This time tomorrow we'll be sleeping in palaces and having a share-out!' We were silent, listening. 'Only about a thousand in all, the south camp says, and that includes the women and children! A thousand! A morning's work—and the fire is opening the wall for us!' The voices died away and the sun went down.

We were not a thousand. We were nine hundred and sixty-seven. We were people from large cities and tiny hamlets. We were scholars and priests and cattlemen and farmers. We had workers in metal and in wood, a dealer in precious stones, a court hairdresser and a jeweller. We had a muleteer, who missed his mules sadly but was a patient teacher of small children in the ways of the Fathers. A scribe we had, and a mathematician, and eight who could not read or write. A perfume blender was among us, and a plumber; a basket-weaver and a cloth-dyer. We agreed, and differed, bound by one thing. All on Masada had at one time or other taken the oath, made the declaration to show zeal for God. To be Zealot!

18 Josephus

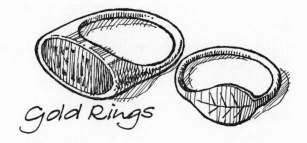

Gold Rings

In the telling of the sun going down on the last night of
Masada, our own sun in the garden of my father's house
had also lowered. A coolness was in the air, and a sadness also.
Sarah looked pale and strained, and I was conscious of tension
and fatigue in my own limbs. The men sat very still, with concerned frowns. It was quiet.

Simeon it was, gentle old priest, who found a way to halt
this opening of old wounds (*old*? no, not old, never old, never
healed). He rose to his feet.

'Listening is exhausting work, I find. I will enjoy my supper
the more if I rest a little. Let us *all* rest a little before supper—
and at supper, with the children and the old ladies, we will
amuse them with talk of lighter things. We will sing Passover
songs and—more softly—Zealot songs. Come friends, no more
talk. A rest before supper—and after I will say the Grace and
add a little prayer for us all.'

His 'little prayer' was like him. Gentle, undemanding of
attention, soft-voiced. He had said the blessings, with 'a little
prayer', a number of times during the months we had been
home, and the children loved what he did. His communication
with the young was remarkable. Jesse, on one occasion, said
at the end of one of Simeon's 'little prayers', 'It is good of
you, old teacher, to let us grown-ups remain at table while you
talk to children. One can learn much.'

Simeon was brief in the prayers before eating, and more

leisured in his thanks to God after. 'A child—of any age—has more patience for God if his stomach is full.'

He stood, pink and smiling, with eyes of an innocence that could be taken, mistakenly, for childishness.

'Lord,' he said, 'thank you for the good supper, and for giving Rachel and Leah the energy and patience to make it. They thank you too, Lord—and so does Abel, who ate enough for two, but today did the work of two. Thank you too for the presence at our table of our children and our beautiful young ladies, Sim and Judith.

'Now Lord, a word about our grown-ups. We have all known terrible times, Lord, and things are not all that splendid even now. We are surrounded by reminders of the cruelty and folly of men. Up on the Mount your own wondrous Temple is a heap of rubble and your own place, the Holy of Holies, is gone. Protect us, Lord, from thinking that you too have gone. It has no logic sometimes, Lord. Help us not to look for logic. It is beyond understanding just lately, Lord. Help us to stop trying to understand. Help us to live for today, with hopes for tomorrow. And Lord, if it's not asking too much, let yesterday fade a little. We thank you, Lord, for the gift of memory, but a way of turning it off would also be useful. Sarah and dear Ruth have a travail to come, Lord, which has a little to do with memory—' Sarah's head came up and our eyes met. We looked at Jesse, who was looking down at his hands in untypical piety, '—with the past a little, with bad times. Support them, Lord, let them find tolerance and strength. Amen.'

The table said, Amen.

Sarah: 'Amen. *What* travail? Why tolerance? Strength we have; why tolerance?'

Jesse, pouring wine, 'Later, old battler. We promised to play riddle-dee-dee with the children. Their riddles first, yours after.'

I looked at my brother across the table, who lifted an eyebrow and smiled, looking a little worried. I sat, and joined in the guessing of clues and gathering of facts that was part of the children's game. The old women and Abel cleared away, refusing help from Sarah and myself with compassionate glances. Sarah half rose to follow them but old Simeon murmured, 'They don't know,' and Sarah, cross, sat down again.

Judith, who was as wise as she was beautiful, told the children that the game would be finished out in the garden by the kitchen window, 'so Abel can join in'. Sim, dark and silent, moved nearer to Simeon, but Judith took her hand and led them all out.

Sarah looked stormy. Jesse looked at me.

'Questions, Ruth?'

'Yes. This has to do with Masada, with Josephus?'

'Yes, it has.'

'You told us he was in the country, and so much of him, and when I asked you how you knew certain things you wouldn't say.'

'I said I would later.'

'Is now the later?'

'Yes.'

Sarah said roughly, 'What is this, a game? The bastard's in the country. Where?'

'Caesarea.'

'Well?'

'You and Ruth are to go to him and provide facts about Masada for his history. It's an official order from Vespasian, countersigned by General Silva.'

'How do *you* know?'

'I spent a whole day with Joseph about ten days ago. Good place for Passover presents, Caesarea.'

'And for meeting old friends.'

Jesse was mild. 'Remain calm, Sarah dear. He is not my enemy. We shared many experiences. I know him better than anyone living. We had a hand in saving each other's lives— when such things meant more to me than they do now. We are very alike in many ways, as I've shown you. And another thing—'

'Well?' from a sorely tried Sarah.

Jesse grinned. 'Would you rather go to Caesarea on two army donkeys, with a troop of Roman foot-soldiers, or in the way *I* have arranged? With *me* as your escort. The devious and crafty Jesse, who can arrange *any*thing! Another question, Ruth?'

'Yes. You know so much of Josephus. Are you not in danger?'

'From him?'

'Yes.'

'The position is an odd one. He *believes* in the image he has created. It is impossible for him to see me as other than the one chosen by God to share his remarkable psychic experiences.'

Sarah spluttered, her mouth working in anger. 'But he—he is a—you said that—'

'Simeon here knew him as a boy,' said Jesse evenly, 'a fact-twister and fancifier who believed his every word by the third telling. Josephus is a man without self-doubt. You will see no sign of guilt or regret. A fascinating and complex character. Unique. Prepare yourself. I am in no danger from him, Ruth dear—or he from me. He is in more danger from you—if your book is ever read by those who believe Josephus to be an instrument of God. It is, I fear, unlikely.' He paused. 'Silent, Ruth?'

'When are we to go?'

'As soon as possible. I didn't argue. It would be as well to put it behind you. We will go the day after tomorrow. Jochebed the seamstress will accompany you as female attendant and you will travel in a covered conveyance, horse-drawn, with mounted escort of four officers, all gentlemen, who have a few days' leave owing. Their batmen will see that we are well looked after. We will not hurry and will stay overnight in Antipatris.'

Sarah chuckled. 'Rather grand for an old market woman and a penniless young lady—both ex-Zealots.'

'Not really, old battler,' said Jesse. 'As I pointed out to

Joseph's tribune-in-charge, you are both known to General Silva, at whose table you have dined. One of you is related to the family of Menahem whose character, oddly, is admired by the Romans. Perhaps they feel a certain kinship, as like so many of their own, he was killed by Jews. And you, Sarah, as I reminded the good tribune, are one of the famous women fighters of Jerusalem.'

'Famous? Me? Who made me famous? You?'

'A little recognition, even by the other side, is not out of place here,' said Jesse with affection. 'Do you not agree, Ruth?'

'Indeed. You are such a scamp, Jesse.'

'Possibly. I am a salesman by instinct—and rather proud of my friends. Understand, ladies, that among the things I am expert about is the Roman way of thinking. They will enjoy the arrival of our little procession. Don't disapprove, Ruth. I could as easily have brought Joseph here. Caesarea is nicer. At this time of year, beautiful. A little sea air for you both. Very beneficial.'

Saul and Simeon, now the news was given and the tension over, joined in, and the talk became easy. We did not speak of Josephus but of the journey, and Caesarea—like Masada, built by Herod—which we had never seen. A city-port, where Jews had been massacred under Procurator Florus, and where the Leper Insult had taken place. We did not sit long at table.

In our bedroom Sarah was thoughtful and I did not disturb her silence. Indeed I was thoughtful myself; our journey was to part us from the children for the first time in nearly four years. A feeling of nervousness began in me.

'I feel rather nervous,' said Sarah, the other half of my mind. 'Not afraid—except of my own temper, for I shall kill Joseph if I get the chance, make no mistake—no, not afraid. Wound up, like before an attack, or a sortie outside the walls. You too?'

'Not quite. I feel that we are coming to the end of something. Telling my brother and Simeon and Jesse about Masada is one thing. Telling Joseph will be another.'

She looked at me with a very serious face. 'You haven't really told it *all* to *any*one, my dove. Not to Silva, or your brother, *or* Jesse. It worries me.'

I had no reply for her. None was necessary. One can lock away things in the mind, but not from someone who has the key. She didn't pursue it. Then:

'There's another thing about telling Joseph—'

'What?'

'It dirties it.'

'It must be done. And done with truth, for his history will be in Roman archives, or he will publish, being a person seeking fame, and the story will thus be known.'

'Will ours not be published?'

'Who knows? It will be written; it will exist. Under the present regime it is revolutionary writing of the most dangerous kind.'

'Yes, it is. That had not occurred to me.'

She became silent again and we prepared for sleep. She went to the window 'for a few words with the Almighty'. I sat on my bed and watched her in profile. The short grey hair, the strong, lifted chin, the square bulk of her. I loved her.

Her few words took in our coming trip—'Keep an eye on the children, please'—and our meeting with Josephus: 'Help us speak clearly, Lord, and help that traitorous dog to put it down right!' She finished and stretched out on her bed. After a pause:

'Will Jesse be present when we talk to Joseph?'

'He didn't say. I hope so.'

'So do I. Goodnight, my dove.'

Our 'little procession' turned out to be an apt description for the officers mounted on fine horses, the fast-marching platoon of soldiers, our own 'conveyance' and four other wheeled vehicles—and the magnificent Jesse on his black Arab. The officers, determined not to be outshone by Jesse, glittered and gleamed in breast-armour and helmets, with side

arms. Their short woollen capes and thonged boots were spot-
less. They took it in turns to ride alongside and provide
company and conversation. At the meal stops and the overnight halt in Antipatris we got to know them well.

Antipatris was interesting, with many trees. We slept at the
largest inn, where we were expected. We received curious
looks, for despite Jochebed's skill, we had resisted any but the
plainest cut in our garments, and wore no ornament (Sarah to
Jesse: 'Tell the bastard we're in mourning!'). Thus we fell
into no clear classification. Prisoners-of-war do not have their
own conveyance, their own woman companion, their own
bedroom. And it must have been obvious to everyone that
we were not 'officers' women'. Well, nearly everyone . . . .

Our bedroom was large and shady, with a smaller room
adjoining for Jochebed, who was enjoying every moment. We
were shown in by a sour-faced muscular man who had made up
his own mind as to what we were. Sarah grinned at me behind
his back and held a finger to her lips. We said no word, and I
thanked him in pure Greek, not the *Koine* Greek of the streets.
He muttered in Hebrew his name for such as we and turned to
go, blocked squarely by Sarah, whistling softly through
strong square teeth the fighting song of the Sicarii. He backed
off, looking down at her hand for the little knife. She clapped
him on the shoulder and exchanged Jewish ruderies with him
in the same tongue as his own. Then the high-nosed Jesse
looked round the door, every inch a Roman, and the man left,
sorely puzzled.

The youngest officer was named Aelius and had something
of the size and shy humour of Seth, Sarah's grandson, who
had fallen with my cousin Simon on the day the Temple
burned. I was careful not to point out the resemblance to
Sarah. But five miles out of Jerusalem she said, 'The youngest
one has a bit of Seth in him. I've taken to him.'

The other three officers were older and harder. They did not
stay in the mind, for truly the mind was much occupied with
the meeting to come. The officers were correct and witty, and

seemed to do everything Jesse wanted—without ever knowing it. A patrician authority had Jesse—and great subtlety. He never intruded—and seemed never more than a dozen yards away at any time. He seemed to take no rest of any kind.

We entered Caesarea in the early evening and were met at an army check point by two grizzled centurions with orders to lead us to one of the smaller governmental buildings on the coastal plain.

As we approached the low white villas set in their own well-kept grounds, Jesse reined up alongside.

'It is a kind of small palace, for the use of important visitors from Rome. Josephus regards himself as such—and has a liking for such recognition. He thought it only right.'

'It *is* only right,' grinned Sarah. 'Ruth and I are *used* to palaces.'

At the gates in the wall encircling the estate, the four officers took their leave, one after the other, with some formality. Aelius, the youngest, last. He had obviously taken to Sarah as she had to him. 'Come to supper,' she told him. 'Jesse knows where we live.'

With the officers went their soldiers and vehicles, leaving only our wagon and its driver.

We watched them go, and Jesse turned in his saddle.

'Nothing this evening. Tomorrow mid-morning. You will be very comfortable here, and after you have bathed and rested and the sun has gone down, dinner will be served in the smaller salon. A beautiful room. It would give me pleasure, ladies, if you would invite me to join you.'

'It will give us pleasure too.'

'Thank you, Ruth. All right, old battler?'

'*Always* a pleasure, my Roman. Food good here?'

'The best. The chef is a friend of mine. A Syrian Jew. The Romans burned his restaurant and I fixed him up here. His kitchen staff is his family. They live in. A satisfactory arrangement. Come.'

Our quarters were part of a group of rooms set around a

square garden. The rooms were softly lit and obviously designed for women. Jesse saw us installed and went away, 'to a suite suitable for one so close to the soothsayer of Vespasian. Very luxurious, complete with Greek masseur. It seems only right. See you for dinner. Say two hours.'

The small salon where we ate was indeed beautiful, with slender pillars and a floor of marble. The walls and ceiling were painted in pale tints, with much decoration picked out in gold. The table, chairs and other furniture were of black wood with silver embellishment. The glass and cutlery were delicately designed and most pleasing to the hand and eye. At dinner the lively Jochebed joined us and, encouraged by Jesse, regaled us with stories of court life. 'Nobody notices a dress-maker, dear, any more than they do a hairdresser, or a cupbearer. You hear some remarkable things. Very enlightening.' Of Bernice she told us, 'More than one woman, that one. Made her own rules —about everything! Once I heard her having a bitter lover's quarrel with her own brother—over Titus!'

Jesse added malicious and funny gossip about life in Roman higher military circles, and Sarah, joining the game of not talking of the morrow, was outrageous about the markets. The food and wine were excellent, but the day had been long and we were suddenly drowsy and ready for our beds. We took our leave of Jesse, who promised to come for us a few minutes before the appointed time the next morning.

19 Eleazar

Wooden
comb

19

I slept well and woke refreshed, thanking Jesse in my mind for filling my glass more often than usual with the same firmness that he had shown in guiding the table talk. I woke early and lay awhile listening to the birds, feeling strange at having a bedroom to myself. Sarah was next door, with Jochebed on the other side. It was quiet, and I tidied my thoughts for the meeting to come. I found I could not recall Josephus in any detail. At the great Temple meeting he had been far away—and after election soon gone. Jesse's stories of his experiences with Josephus had been remarkably graphic, telling of a man for whom thousands bore a deep hatred; yet I did my best to be detached in my thoughts about him. It was difficult.

I thought of the last night on the mountain and of the years before and was aware of great sadness, as always with those thoughts. 'Waste,' Silva had said, coldly. I prayed. Dear God, Father Almighty, let it not be waste. Let it be known for what it was; what it is. So many mistakes, Lord, so much folly. So much blood, so much misery. Your Temple gone, Lord, your Sanctuary, your Altar. But was Masada the end of the matter, Lord? Let it not be waste, Lord, let it not be the end of the matter. If we sinned, Lord, on the mountain, forgive us. Treat us as you will, Lord, thy will be done, but let it not be waste.

Sarah came in, smiling—and in a moment was across the room, my head on her breast.

'Tears, my dove? Back on the mountain, my beauty? No one can touch it, my Ruth, no one can make it dirty. I've also been having a think. The scriptures are history, eh, my scholar?'

'Yes.'

'Handed down, exact, careful. Spoken or written, open or hidden?'

'Yes.'

'Well, *we* are history. *We* are scripture. It happened. We hand it down. Written, hidden. The children. A solemn trust. We are scripture!'

She was jubilant, and not quiet. A tousled Jochebed put her head in, asking if we'd called.

Calmness returned and we broke our fast and prepared ourselves. Jochebed stood back at last and eyed us critically, head to toe.

'Not elegant, but with a certain dignity, which is right. While you are gone, I'll tidy up.'

Sarah smiled and then looked past me with a raised and approving eyebrow. Jesse was crossing the inner garden. He wore a full-length toga with a heavy silver belt and shoulder clasp.

'Bless him,' murmured Sarah, 'my Jewish senator.'

He came in smiling in his usual sardonic way, but his eyes flickered across our faces and missed nothing. He assured himself that we had rested well, had eaten, and were ready. And we left.

Crossing the garden he said: 'Sarah, you are to be searched. Ruth, you are to be asked if you will submit to search. The meeting will not be prolonged. It will take place in the Room of Council. Big heavy table between brave Joseph and you assassins. His personal bodyguard of four Alexandrian mercenaries will be present. Ignore them. Speak only Hebrew. I will be there the whole time. Two scribes also will be present.'

We were searched in a small ante-room by a rather embarrassed middle-aged centurion who was careful and respectful, making clear that no disrobing would be required. He was shorter than I, which increased his discomfiture. I bent my head for him to gently prod my hair and he was relieved to be free of me. Sarah was bright-eyed with laughter and swayed toward him with a shocking vulgarity, speaking street Greek. He and the young officer looking on blushed, and Sarah purred deep in her throat and the laughter came. Jesse came in with head shaking in mock disapproval and we followed him out and along a short corridor towards ornate doors, which opened inwards as we approached.

The room was large, but well-proportioned, with a formal feeling in its colours and appointments. Around the walls were heavy carved and gilded chairs carrying the insignia and eagle motif of Imperial Rome. The largest feature of the room was a huge, wide table across the end furthest from us as we entered. It nearly reached from wall to wall. It had obviously been moved from its central along-the-room position. Sarah glanced up at Jesse between us but he looked straight ahead.

At each end of the table sat a scribe with writing materials. Behind the table, on either side of a throne-like chair standing on a low dais, were four fierce-looking men, heavily armed, with spears.

In the chair sat Josephus.

It was not until the next day that I remembered that he and I were the same age, thirty-seven. In manner, appearance and posture he could have been my senior by fifteen years. He was of medium build and dressed in a similar way to Jesse, but the colour of his toga was of palest beige rather than white and of thicker material. He wore his hair to his shoulders and a full flowing beard. Both hair and beard were shot with grey, in streaks rather than all over (Sarah thought by artifice). His eyes were deep set under heavy eyebrows. They were strange and compelling, but like the frowning set of the forehead and brows, consciously so. His skin was very pale and smooth, and his hands, which rested judiciously on the table before him, manicured and white, with dark hair nearly to the knuckles.

We stopped before him just in front of the three chairs set a little away from the table.

Jesse said: 'These are the two women of Masada', and gestured for us to sit. Josephus made no sign other than to move his eyes back and forth from Sarah to me as we settled ourselves. I was aware that he looked as much at my body as at my face. I sat in the centre chair with Sarah to my left, and Jesse to my right.

Josephus was a still man, with a great control of his movements. He looked down at some writings for a long moment and then looked up and spoke to a place in the air somewhere between Sarah and me and above our heads.

'As my friend may have made clear to you, I am engaged upon a History devoted to the recent War. As the period covered is a long one, a large number of interviews such as this one will be held. My aim is exactitude, and truth. Great Vespasian himself has deep interest in this work of chronicle, and the Valorous Titus also. These interviews will, as it were, fill in gaps, for my personal knowledge of this country and of the period to be chronicled, that of the War, is considerable. Also I am in the fortunate position of having been an active participant in more than one area of operations.'

'And on more than one side,' said Sarah, agreeably.

His eyes did not flicker in their examination of the spot in the air. Her remark he completely ignored. 'I understand that you both have first-hand experience of the fighting within Jerusalem, but there are many such, and I will not trouble you with questions upon it. No, the subject of this interview is to talk about the last night upon Masada.'

'Do you need anything on Jotapata?' asked Sarah helpfully. 'Or do you have enough?'

He lowered his gaze to meet hers. 'I have discovered in the interviews that I have conducted so far,' he said calmly, 'that when there are two witnesses, as in your case, it is best to hear one very fully, using the other for added or overlooked detail. We will follow the same procedure here.' He looked at me.

'*You* will speak of that night please, as fully as possible, and your friend will add detail as required. I have from General Silva knowledge of you both that would suggest such an arrangement would be best.'

'Does he keep well, the General?' asked Sarah, '—and good Lucius—and the nice young woman and her handsome artist. All well?'

Josephus looked at her without answering, his face without expression. She was quite unaffected, and prattled on: 'Of course, the General could tell you a lot about the last few days at Masada. Very observant man, the General. And a man who shows respect. . . . You could learn a lot from him.'

The expressionless eyes moved to me. 'Begin when you like.' The voice was modulated, well-used, but not warm.

I remained silent, suddenly aware of a great tension and strain in myself. A cold shudder went through me, shaking me visibly, bringing Sarah's head round with a snap, her eyes concerned, sharp.

My hands were trembling and I could not trust myself to speak. I tried; twice, but could make no words. I looked at Sarah and then at Jesse, helplessly.

'The good Josephus,' said Jesse, 'having experienced so much himself, will readily understand the mental stress caused by the recollection of great and tragic events.'

'The good Josephus will wait a minute whether he understands or not!' said Sarah—and came to me. The guards stirred, but at a glance from Jesse, became statues again. Josephus made no move or sound. Sarah knelt, her face level with mine. 'Speak, my dove. Tell it all. Free yourself of it. It lives in you like an unquiet spirit, a curse. This is the time, my darling. Trust me. Tell it for *me*, speak to *me*, not him. To hell with him, he's a nothing, tell *me*!'

She went back to her chair, but only to drag it, with a loud squeak, nearer to mine. Again the guards stirred, but she swore at them and they blinked and became still again.

I steadied myself, my hand in Sarah's, but Josephus spoke

first, with a strange mystical look on his face and in a voice as
if in prayer. I looked at Jesse, who was waiting for my look
and gave a tiny nod, as if to say 'Not yet, you have a respite.'
The respite was from God, although strange in the extreme.

'Give this young woman peace, O Lord,' intoned Josephus,
'as you have given me peace. For in the peace you have given
me I recognize that all my words and actions were by your
wish. As you guided me, so I walked. Your words I spoke,
your actions I performed. Your choice of Great Vespasian to
be Monarch of the World I proclaimed. It was as written and
foreseen. Obedience to your wishes, O Lord, giveth a man
peace. And thus I walk in peace.'

'Like hell he does,' said Sarah in my ear.

'But here in the country of my birth,' prayed Josephus,
'I, who spared no effort to avert catastrophe, to avoid destruction, walk alone, surrounded on all sides by hostility and
hatred. It is forgotten, Lord, that I created armies of tens of
thousands, arming them from my own armouries, training
them in the Roman fashion—'

'Jesse's right,' murmured Sarah. 'He *believes* it.'

'—and many are the places I fortified with great walls.'

'All in eight months,' gritted Sarah.

'But now wicked men heap calumny and insult upon me in
their writings, and those who cannot write or read prate in
their ignorance of matters they comprehend not. Grant this
woman calmness, O Lord, to tell me of Masada where, as at
Jotapata, you guided men to die rather than submit.'

Sarah released breath slowly, through clenched teeth, her
eyes murderous. 'To *me*, Ruth,' she said, her head to mine, 'talk
to *me*. You've just heard how this bastard is going to use
Masada to ease his own mind about the forty at Jotapata. He
doesn't matter, my dove, speak to *me*!'

'As you used me, O Lord,' continued Josephus, in the same
voice, with the same unfocused eyes, 'to show men a way to
your loving and forgiving embrace, now let us hear of another
such as I—'

'Keep quiet, please!' My own voice surprised me with its sharp loudness. 'Keep quiet! Eleazar was in *no* way like you! Stop it! Stop this talking to God. He can't hear. Sometimes he doesn't listen—or turns his face away!' Now the eyes had focus; unblinking, upon my face. 'The wall was burning! It was burning . . . it was of wood . . . the wall was of wood . . . and the flames were yellow against the red sky. The wood burned and the earth dropped away and the wood burned again—'

'The earth dropped away—?'

'Keep *quiet*, Joseph!' rapped Sarah. 'Tell me, my dove—'

'—the sky went purple and then it was dark and the flames lit the Tower. Then some of our men were running back and forth, shouting. "A meeting! A meeting! Eleazar says everybody to a meeting! In the Western Palace, near the gap in the wall, a meeting! All the men, without exception, and all single women. No wives or children. A meeting! In half an hour!" You made a joke, Sarah; you said, "All the men and all the single women, maybe Eleazar is going to marry us off!" D'you remember, Sarah—?'

'Yes, my angel. What then?'

'We met in the service wing courtyard, open to the sky but hidden from the spies in the overlooking camp. We were private and everyone brought lit torches. It was bright and we could see each other's faces. One or two of the wives came. Nobody spoke much. We could hear the noises from the camps down below. It was an excited sound, to do with finishing the job soon, and with wiping us all out. We couldn't hear words but we knew. And then cousin Eleazar was there. He looked taller, and pale. He got up on an old bench and told us all to sit down on the ground. He waited till the last shuffle and murmur had died away before he began to speak. As he began, the wind, which had run around the mountain like a mad sprite, stopped, and seemed to wait and listen like the rest of us. Even the noise from below in the camps, brought up by the wind, lessened. The flames too, without the wind, lost their roar and also gave ear. Then Eleazar spoke—but what use to tell someone the words when they cannot hear the voice that spoke the words, and see the face and feel the compassion and courage. What use, what use—'

'There is use, there is reason,' said Sarah, her grip on my hand warm and strong.

Her voice steadied me and I paused, aware of a tremor in my limbs and a feeling of chill upon me. I turned my head to Jesse, who was looking at me with great intensity, his body turned in his chair, ready it seemed to move to my help if necessary. How un-Jesse he looked—and the thought brought a smile, which he returned, and his eyes dropped to my breast, where lay a stain caused by a tear, joined by another as I looked down. Into my mind came my father's voice: 'We do not weep, you and I. We get on with it.' I looked at Josephus, who sat perfectly still, waiting, the white hands interlinked. He glanced briefly at the two scribes and then back at me.

'The accurate recollection of your leader's words,' he said, 'will be of great use—as your friend says. Accuracy and truth, that is the aim. Continue when you are ready.'

It was very quiet in the room. I could hear a bird singing through the open doors that led to a terrace. It was a sweet, lonely sound, pleasant to the ear. It was peaceful and I relaxed a little, seeing pictures in my mind.

Sarah squeezed my hand. 'Ruth?'

I gathered my thoughts. 'Eleazar called us friends, and it was said in a way that made us listen. And again, "Friends," he said, "brothers, sisters, what I have to say to you must be said. It must be put into words, and will at once be no great surprise, even logical, but also a great shock. How to begin, my loyal friends, my brave friends, how to begin?

' "Long long ago we made a resolve to serve only God. No kings, or Roman overlords; only God. We were among the first to revolt and we are the last stronghold of resistance. Tomorrow morning the Romans will take Masada. We have given them great trouble but their object will be to take us alive, for exhibition, to make us slaves, to violate our women before our eyes and to torture and maim our children because that is their way, as we have seen in action a million times in our poor little country. How we die, if we are taken by them, will be as they decide. If we are taken by them. We cannot in any way prevent their capture of our mountain in the morning, but until the morning how we die is in *our* hands entirely.

' "Our wives have never known the treatment so many Jewish women have suffered at the hands of the Romans; our children know nothing of slavery. For our wives and children to die rather than suffer such things is for them to receive a kindness given with ungrudging heart. And we others, men and women, without families, who have fought so hard and so long, how can *we* accept slavery? Let us die free, wrapped in our own freedom as in a glorious winding sheet, a shroud of glory." '

Who can describe in words, to a silent man with white hands, backed by swordsmen, attended by scribes, the feel of night air, the exchanging of looks by Zealot warriors sitting on the ground listening to a man whose authority they never doubted, from whose love they drew strength.

Eleazar paused and waited, his ten, his 'centurions', as still as he. The Zealots exchanged looks, to one side, then the other. The looks held disbelief, a growth of fear, of horror. The first to speak was a big fair man, of a simple and un-sophisticated way. A much-liked Samson of a fighter from a small village where he had been the smith.

'Eleazar,' he said slowly, 'do you have *doubt* that we would fight to the last man, the last breath? We will kill six for one, we have done it before!'

Eleazar and the Ten stood like statues, waiting for others to speak. The big man looked round, meeting heads which shook at his lack of comprehension, eyes which frowned into his own. He spoke again, his voice husky.

'You mean we are *not* to fight? Die *without* a fight? *All* of us? The women and children also? How?'

Suddenly there was a hubbub of voices which died away, replaced by a realization of horror so tangible it had a feel on the skin, a taste in the mouth, an odour like the turned earth of a grave.

'We were born to die,' said Eleazar, his voice calm and thoughtful. 'We and those we brought into this world. This is the way of things. In this the most hapless and the most fortunate are alike. The rich and poor, the scholar and the fool, the cowardly and the brave. It is the law of nature, the law of God. But to see our wives and children led away to shame and outrage and slavery—this is *not* a law of nature. We can suffer this or prevent it—it is in *our* hands. As we have lived here on Masada with our loved ones, thanking God for every day, for every meal, for every good thing, so here can we die. Honourably, in freedom, together, thanking God also for this chance to do so. A unique chance. A privilege given to us by God. It needs courage. Great courage. We have it! We have proved ourselves courageous a dozen times. It needs resolve. Great resolution. We have it! There is no cruelty in this thing, my beloved friends, pity rather. Pity the young whose bodies are strong enough to endure prolonged torture; pity the not-so-young whose bodies will break. Pity the wife as she is violently dragged away; pity the father, bound and fettered, whose child's cries of 'Daddy' grow fainter as the distance between them grows.'

Then Eleazar was silent for a few moments, and the Ten with him. The compassion and strength in his face was in theirs. Like him, they had suffered great loss. They were fearsome fighters; men of the sword, but now they stood like priests before a congregation, silent and sad-eyed.

The crowd was also still. Here and there a murmur would begin; and stop. A voice would rise, in shock, out of control, and be stifled. It was too big, this thing. It needed this silence to be taken in, to be absorbed. Wise Eleazar. He began again. A statement rapped, like a command.

'Life is the calamity!' Absolute silence in the crowd.

'This is the teaching of our forefathers and those far wiser than we. Our souls come from freedom and in death return to that freedom. Our souls are *confined* in our mortal bodies and thus suffer, and know of misery and trouble. In death they are unfettered, cannot be slaves, cannot be tortured or maimed, cannot be violated, cannot be humiliated or torn to pieces by animals to amuse holiday crowds, cannot be scourged or crucified. To live is to be near to death, in *fear* of death. Yet that which gives us life is immortal. We, having been lent our souls by God, hand them back—and become *free*! After what we have all seen, my beloved friends, who can doubt the truth of our teachers, that *life* is the calamity?'

Now the crowd's silence had a different quality, impossible to define exactly. The imagery of the words was perhaps too difficult for some; unacceptable to others. But over everything, the words of Eleazar made *sense*. The big smith had spoken the truth when he said that in the past we'd killed six for one. We could fight to the last man, it was our way. But to the last woman? And once the women were slaughtered, what of the children? And the babies?

Eleazar's face was bloodless, and his eyes looked enormous. His voice took on a ring, a clarity that had tears in it.

'If only we had all died before seeing our beloved Jerusalem overrun by the enemy, our beautiful Temple burning and defiled. It was not to be—and our last stand is not to be, and our revenge is not to be. Our fate is sealed—and positive. But the way of it is in *our* hands. Let us choose death with honour, together, in the company of our families and friends. Death with honour—in freedom!'

The smith was the first to rise to his feet, and it seemed that in a moment all were standing; needing movement to break the tension, to begin the work.

'Burn only your belongings,' said Eleazar, 'leave the food stores and the water and the oil and wine. Leave the vegetable gardens and the fruit trees. Let the Romans see that we died among plenty, as free men, and thus remained free.'

Still they stood, and the smith, his head above the others, asked for them, 'How, Eleazar? How is it arranged? Tell us how it is to be.'

'Each father will give freedom to his children,' said Eleazar. 'Each husband to his wife. Men with neither wives nor children will then reward the husbands and fathers with their own freedom. They, and women alone, will be freed by the Ten and I, who will draw lots and follow in turn. The last one will free himself. May the Almighty give steadiness to your hands. Go and prepare.'

There was a slight pause before anyone moved, but soon the courtyard was empty. Soon the fires began. Sarah and I, 'without family and women alone', helped others pile dry twigs and oil-soaked rags in position, for this palace, of our last meeting, was to be burned. We worked in silence, each one with his own thoughts, courteous but silent. Time passed.

Then it was that Eleazar came to tell me that we and the five children were to live. We were to conceal ourselves on the steps cut in rock leading down into the great water cistern and wait for morning. I remembered his words and spoke them to Josephus for his History, with the same accuracy and truth with which I have recalled them for this, *my* chronicle. How could I not be accurate and truthful in the recollection of the last words and actions of my friends, of Eleazar?

When I stopped speaking the room was quiet. Outside the birds sang. The great table gleamed and shimmered. The scribes worked softly, the elder with a heavy-breathed concentration.

I had no sense of release, of sorrow, or of pain. I felt only a sort of numbness. I became aware of my hand still in Sarah's. Of a stiffness in my limbs. I did not know how much time had passed. I looked round into Sarah's face, which was worried and tense. On my breast the tearstain was larger. I turned my head. Jesse had not moved.

I was aware then of Josephus, whose face had light upon it, reflected upwards from the table. His face had an avid yet inward look, as though already composing his paragraphs. Aware of my look, his eyes changed.

'Thank you,' he said. 'That of the drawing of lots as an order of dying is a most remarkable happening. Remarkable.'

'And familiar!' snapped Sarah, and her eyes came back to my face. Her voice was loving: 'You are not finished, my treasure. There is more.'

My head throbbed and I had pain across the back of my shoulders and neck.

'Sarah dear,' I whispered, 'I don't feel—'

'For *me*, my dove. Get rid of it.'

'More?' enquired Josephus of Sarah. 'Perhaps *you* can add a detail or two.'

From Jesse: 'Help if you can, Sarah. Help Ruth. She is in great trouble of mind.'

Sarah spoke without removing her eyes from mine. 'All right, a detail. *I* collected the five orphans and then went back to the Western Palace courtyard for Ruth. She told me to go on ahead to the hiding place. She said she had made a promise to Eleazar to write it all down and she said . . .

'. . . How can I write of what I don't *see*!'

My voice rang in my head like a piercing bell. I could tell from Sarah's face that I had screamed aloud. How different from the first time I had said the words. Not to Sarah; that was the second time. To Eleazar, whose face had paled. From all over the plateau, over the roofs of the buildings around the empty courtyard came the crackle of flames. Not loud; a sibilant, secretive sound.

Eleazar had taken my hand, a rare gesture. 'Spare yourself this, my cousin,' he said, 'you know of death. It is an old friend.' He was going to say more, then his eyes narrowed to a look almost of pain as he looked past me at the arched entrance of the courtyard. I turned. It was a family of four. The parents no more than thirty, and two little girls. They saw Eleazar and approached. I drew to one side.

The man, whose name was Joel, said, 'We of the South

Wall dwellings want to be together, in the open, here. They are coming.'

They came through the arch singing. Nine families. They sang softly, a Zealot song:

> The Lord taught us what is right
> And taught us to fight
> Who better to fight for,
> Who better, who better,
> Than the Lord of Light—or Right!

They came forward and halted near Eleazar. Another group came through the arch, picking up the song.

> The Lord gave us the Law
> And gave us much more
> And taught us to fight
> For the Lord of Right,
> The Lord of Light,
> The Lord of Right,
> Stand up and fight!

The song, usually roared, was infinitely moving in its soft-sung murmured cadence. The second group halted, and their spokesman came to Eleazar, who had not moved.

'We of the Storehouse dwellings want to be with our friends. In the open. With our children we are forty-nine. We are all here. Others are coming.'

I went to the arch and through it and between the two gatehouses and out through the great entrance of the Palace. People passed me, in family groups, in pairs. I moved to a small rise a few yards away and stood.

From every side my friends were walking across the plateau to the Palace. The singing had stopped. There was no talk except for the occasional prattling voice of a child. No sound except that of walking people. The sound was unhurried, regular, rhythmic. The whole plateau, within the walls, was ringed with small fires, pitifully small, for we of Masada had few possessions to burn.

Soon the mountain-top was empty except for the Ten

making their quiet rounds. I went back to the courtyard, afraid to go in yet unable to stay outside.

The first impression was one of stillness. People were locked in embrace, silently. Husbands and wives held each other and their children as though never to let them go, exchanging kisses endlessly, with few words but many tears. Muscled fighters stood watching, wet-cheeked, many with shortsword already in hand. Others went from group to group to shake a hand, to leave a kiss, to say a word of last farewell. This movement of people then stopped, as did all sound. Heaven itself now seemed to listen and wait for Eleazar to speak.

His face was like an angel of compassion.

'Begin,' he said.

Oh Sicarii, whose stab and jab with the small razor-sharp knives had filled the land and the enemy with fear, how lovingly you stroked the white necks of children, how tenderly you dealt with your women. How carefully you concealed the blade, as of old, until the last second.

Now the voice was clanging in my head again. 'Why did there have to be so much blood!' Why did not God spare us the red flood. Oh, a miracle was needed here, Lord, to stop the blood. This was a moment of loving-kindness, Lord. Of the ending of lives in dignity and beauty. Among friends; helped and attended by friends. Full of trust, this moment, full of love.

The blood spoiled it, Lord. Why did you not stop the blood? It poured and welled and gushed and spurted until the very air stank with it. We slipped and slithered in it and could not escape it. We could not walk away, Lord, for the work had to be done. The fathers, blank-eyed, their duty finished, lay down in the blood of their families and put loving arms round the bodies and offered their own necks to those deputed for the work. These knelt to the work, then turned up their own chins for the work to go on. Oh God, how sudden is blood; how quick, how thick, how royal in its colour.

All the time the Ten walked among the thousand, making

sure the work was done well, the end quick and painless. So men knelt, and lay down, and did not rise again. The courtyard, now carpeted with bodies, had a strange order.

So tidily they lay, my friends.

So quiet it was. Only the whispering of the great torches in their iron holders on the walls of the courtyard. Only the Ten now moved about. Eleazar stood alone, to my right, his head bent. The Ten moved to the torches and took them down, going in a planned way to set fire to the outer parts of the Palace where we had piled wood for them. I watched them go and when I turned Eleazar was by my side.

'The Palace will burn,' he said, 'but not the buildings around the courtyard, and not—' He stopped, and made a gentle gesture across the field of bodies. We stood alone, his hand in mine. With many of the great torches gone from the walls, the sight was more merciful, and the moonlight turned the red to black, merging it with shadow, giving the eyes rest from the blood.

Our handclasp was sticky with blood, Lord, and often I feel it on my palm and between my fingers.

Soon the Ten returned, each one as he came through the arch hurling his torch in a flaming arc up on to a roof.

They came and stood before Eleazar, in line. He walked forward and clasped each man in his arms, and then came to me.

'Go, Ruth. There is nothing else to see. It is done. I am to be the last.'

'How will you do it?'

'Upon my own sword.'

I turned away, my mouth filled with gall. It was a thought impossible to accept; a picture in the mind beyond endurance.

His hand on my arm was strong, rough. 'Go, Ruth.'

I fought nausea, fought to find words. 'Wait, listen, ours are swords to cut, not to thrust. The edges are keen, not the points. The point is wide in angle, not like an arrow—how can you be sure?'

He stopped me. 'You have a practical mind, my cousin. I have shortened a javelin. Go!' His voice was harsh.

I left him and walked past the line of the Ten looking into each face. I could not speak. They stood straight, dirty with smoke and blood. Each nodded as I passed. I did not look back as I went through the arch of the courtyard and then out of the Great Gate. I turned right along the front of the Palace and right again, going now south along the plateau. The ring of fires, smaller now, still burned. There was no wind. I stopped and looked back. The Palace was beginning to burn in a dozen places. Our placing of the bundles of faggots had been directed by men expert in such things. It would ignite slowly, burning the whole night till the Romans came. It would burn least where my friends lay, yet ring them with clean flame.

I felt weak and heavy-limbed. I leaned against a low wall that was part of the forecourt of one of the small villas. I tried to pray, to say the Prayer for the Dead, to gather strength. I felt alone in the whole world. The moon was high. My clothes smelt of blood. There was a singing in my ears. Suddenly I heard, perhaps only in my mind, or heart, a cry—and I was running back to the Palace, back to the courtyard, back to Eleazar whom I was certain had called to me.

He was on his knees, bent over, with his head, turned on one cheek, on the chest of one of the Ten as though listening for a heartbeat. His body was propped up by the javelin shaft which had broken under his weight. His left hand was near his face, his right underneath him, still locked on the shaft.

As I halted, my heart thudding, the shaft slipped toward me and his body lowered itself onto its side, showing a gleam of metal as the unembedded javelin head caught the light. His head and shoulders did not move. I knelt in the blood and looked at his face. It was as white as the moonlight that lay on it.

He was alive.

His eyes opened tiredly, and he tried to speak, but the words turned into a grimace of agony and blood crept from his mouth. He tried again to speak, and again.

I put my head down, my cheek to his.

'I am here,' I said, 'I won't leave you.'

His voice came at last, whispering, like a tired child. 'The shaft slipped in the blood . . . It is badly done . . . Help me . . . Help me . . . The pain gets in the way . . . Help me . . . a Sicarii knife . . . find one . . . do as you saw others . . . Help me. . . .'

'Don't ask me, my darling, don't ask me. I will stay with you. I am here.'

He did not reply and I thought he had lost consciousness. I tried gently to turn him over and his eyes opened instantly and he screamed without sound, the blood welling anew.

I lay down by him in the dark evil puddles and put my head also on the broad chest of the dead man, who was still warm. I put my arm gently across Eleazar's shoulders and a great tremor shook him. His eyes, closed exhaustedly, opened again and looked into mine, so close. His mouth again shaped a scream but no sound came. He whispered but I did not hear and moved my head nearer, my ear to his mouth.

'A last command,' he breathed. 'Kill me. The pain gets between me and God. Kill me. Life is a . . . calamity.'

His eyes remained open, and as I drew back, held me, unblinkingly. Again he gave a silent scream of agony but his eyes did not leave mine. Time passed. As I crawled away to look for a knife his eyes followed me.

The voice of Josephus seemed to come from a long way off:

'It would seem best, I think, to avoid needless detail.'

'Be quiet, you fool!' snapped Sarah.

He was unruffled. 'Your friend seems upset,' he said to her, standing up. 'Please thank her for me.'

'Do you think she was talking to *you*?' Sarah said, holding me. In her arms it was warm, and safe. I slept.

JERUSALEM
July 14th, 1971

LONDON
April 8th, 1972